RAGE

by

DIANE TIBBITTS

This is a work of fiction. Names, characters, businesses, places, events, locations, and incidents are either the products of the author's imagination or used in a fictitious manner. However, various historical figures and locations used are employed as accurately as is practical.

Dear Reader,
There are references and terms used in this work that are objectionable and inappropriate in today's society. They are used with deliberation in this novel because of the time period and the historical context the author is attempting to recreate.

Dedication

This book is dedicated to Pamela Anderson and Clara Brown.
Their friendship and understanding gave me the courage to write it.

Gray and Hankins Families

Thomas Gray b.1847
Sarah Gray—first wife (deceased)
Caroline Gray—second wife, living in South Carolina
MaryAnn—third wife
Henry—son b.1900
Carl—son b.1902
Pansy—daughter b.1904
Mary—daughter b.1906
Bill—daughter b.1908
Letty—daughter b.1910

Louis Hankins b.1970
Eliza Hankins—first wife (deceased) b. 1880
Alyne Hankins—daughter b. 1897
Emma Hankins—daughter b. 1898
May Hankins—daughter b.1902

J.W. Collins—uncle to Alyne, Emma, and May Hankins
Irma Collins— wife of J.W and sister to Eliza Hankins
   Aunt to Alyne, Emma, and May Hankins

Henry Gray b.1900
Catherine Gray—first wife b.1902 (divorced)
Joseph Gray—son, b.1918
May Hankins Gray—second wife b. 1902
Anna Gray—daughter b.1923
Dwayne Gray—son b.1926

Lannery and Rouche Families

Ella Rouche b.1870
John Rouche b.1862 –husband (separated)
Kathryn Rouche—daughter b.1892
Gladys Rouche—daughter b.1894
Leonard Rouche—son b.1897 (deceased)
Allyn Rouche—son b.1907
Francis Lannery b.1867
Arthur—son b.1884
Arthur Lannery b.1884
Gladys Rouche Lannery—first wife b.1894
Kathy Lannery—daughter b.1912
Doreen Lannery—daughter b.1913
Bill Lannery—son b.1915
Joy Lannery—daughter b.1926

Simpson Family
Clem Simpson b.1886
Della Simpson—wife of Clem b.1888
Cora—daughter b.1909

RAGE

**Evil doesn't look evil.
It comes clothed in deceit, looking and acting normal, hiding
in plain sight, taking pleasure in the deception.**

1918

Henry

He was dead when I left him, his head laying in a pool of blood.

I wasn't sorry I killed him.

I didn't even know his name.

What I did know was I had to run, and I'd need help to get away clean. I also knew Catherine and I were finished.

She sat on the floor in the corner before I left, hiding her face, afraid I'd come after her. And I would have beat her face in, but I needed her to care for Joseph, our three-month old son. I couldn't go on the run with a baby.

"You get out of here. Go home, and keep your mouth shut," I said. "If you tell anyone, I'll come back for Joseph. You'll never see him again."

She nodded.

"Get going. I'll send money for you and the baby when I can. File for divorce tomorrow."

She covered herself with a corner of the sheet that had fallen to the floor while I'd beaten her lover to death and crossed the room to where her dress lay folded on a chair. I watched her get dressed, watched as she tried to gather up a shred of dignity before she left.

She straightened her shoulders as she walked out the door. She didn't look back.

I'd come home early from my night shift managing freight at the rail yard and discovered Catherine gone. Joseph was asleep in his crib. What kind of mother leaves her new baby like that? Catherine had been restless since the baby was born, primping, wanting to go out, repeatedly saying she was bored.

Someone told me women go a little loco after having a baby, but Catherine has nothing to complain about. I have a good job, a steady income. All I want is what any man wants: a meal on the table when I get home from work, a clean house, a little loving, and no nagging.

I'm a man any girl would be proud to have as a husband. I finished my college degree at Denver University, and I'm a good provider.

Loyalty isn't too much to ask in return for what I'm prepared to give.

I thought I knew where she'd gone when I came home to find her absent. A man had been hanging around the block, sometimes across the street, looking at our apartment like he was waiting for something or someone. Catherine was young, and she was a looker, I'd give her that. I'd followed the guy one evening, knew he lived two blocks down.

Sure enough. That's where she was, naked as a jaybird in that bastard's bed. Nothing to do but start over, I told myself. Other fish swimming in that sea.

He was taken by surprise, stunned by the first punch, and out with the second. I carried brass knuckles at the rail yard, and I hadn't held back. I doubt his mother could recognize him now.

I pulled his body out the door and over to the edge of the lot. It bordered on Cherry Creek, a wooded stream with a six-foot bank. I rolled the body down. It wouldn't be long until he started to smell in the midsummer heat. Someone would come looking, but I'd be long gone by then.

I went to my father's house, a few blocks over. I took off my shoes and started up the back stairs, careful to place my feet next to the wall. I didn't want a creaking step to give me away.

In spite of my efforts, I heard the faint sound of a door opening above me. The light went on, and my father was standing at the top of the stairs holding a shotgun pointed at my head.

My heart was racing. My hands automatically went above my head, and I said, "Don't shoot, it's me."

"Damn it, Henry." He lowered his gun. We were both still for a second, listening for the sounds of other people stirring.

My father has a supernatural ability to know what I'm up to, especially if I'm up to no good. There's a darkness in both of us that we share, though we've never spoken of it. He propped his shotgun against the wall and pointed down the stairs.

He followed me downstairs to the kitchen, stoked up the fire, put some water on to boil. His back was to me as he stood by the stove. I sat at the kitchen table, silent, waiting for him to speak first. When the coffee was ready, he brought two cups over to the table and sat down across from me.

I reached over for my cup and took a sip. The rage I'd felt earlier melted away with the familiar taste and heat of it, putting some solid ground back under me.

"What're you doing here?" he asked. "I can see you're all bruised up."

My hands were starting to swell. There were cuts where the brass knuckles dug into my fingers.

The pain was satisfying. It felt like a badge of honor. I'd taken action, and that felt good, felt right. I didn't see much use in lyin' to him. "I killed a man just now. Caught him screwing around with Catherine."

He didn't act surprised, just asked, "Where's she at?"

"She went home. I didn't hurt her. I told her I want a divorce and to keep her mouth shut. I need to get away."

"The man?"

"Rolled him down into Cherry Creek. I don't think anyone but Catherine knows what happened."

"You sure he's dead?"

"I'm sure."

I started tapping my fingers on the table, a nervous habit. My father gave me a look, and I quit.

"Texas is the place to go. A man on the run can still get lost there."

My father should know. He'd been on the run himself after the war. Texas was where his first wife and daughter had been killed in a massacre, before he settled here in Denver.

"You have a bad temper, Henry, and that's a fact. I'm going to give you the benefit of my hard-won wisdom and send you on your way."

He drained his cup and went to the stove to bring the coffee pot over. He poured another cup for himself.

I stared into my cup like it might have answers hidden in its murky dregs."I want to say goodbye to Mother."

"No. And leave Carl out of it. He doesn't need to know about your trouble. Go the rail yard before it gets light and hop a train for Texas." He motioned to the door. "I'll get you a sack of food. Don't go home."

He got up and put two slices of bread, a slice of ham, and a hunk of cheese into a paper sack, while I stood at the kitchen sink, washing my hands. When they were dry, he helped me wind some gauze strips around my fingers. He gave me an old jacket and a pair of work gloves and helped me pull those on.

I felt his hand on my shoulder as I opened the back door.

"I'll see that Catherine goes to Kansas to stay with her family. Joseph will be fine," he told me.

"Make sure she files for divorce before she goes." I didn't turn back. I heard the soft click of the door behind me as it closed.

The night was at its darkest point, an hour before the dawn.

May

I've run away.

No one will bother to come looking.

Aunt Irma will be on her knees when she hears I've gone, praying loudly for me to see the light before she has to embarrass herself by explaining my sudden departure to her friends. Our uncle, J. W., will be strutting around the house, predicting I'll be back in short order and slapping his leather strap against his leg, hoping to get his licks in when I come crawling back.

Too late.

I'm never coming back, crawling or otherwise.

I wouldn't have guessed I'd have this much courage two weeks ago. We were sitting at the table, eating a supper of cold ham and potato salad left over from lunch.

"Douglas asked me marry him this afternoon." I said it like it was nothing special.

"He shoulda asked me first," J.W.'s frown deepened as he pointed at the green bowl. "Where's his manners? Pass that potato salad."

J.W.'s irritation didn't worry me. He'll be glad to have me out of the house.

I was calm as I passed him the bowl. "I told him yes. He's buying me a ring next payday, and we're going down to the courthouse right after."

Aunt Irma looked relieved. An ardent Christian, her duty to us didn't extend to paying for a church wedding with a reception.

J.W. helped himself to what was left of the potato salad, the spoon making a grating sound as he scraped the bowl.

Aunt Irma pursed her lips and started shaking her head, as if to say no. "Douglas is too old for you. He's twenty-four. You're barely sixteen."

"There's ten years between you and Uncle J. W.," I reminded her.

"Look who knows it all," J.W. winked at my aunt like he's a good-humored man, which he certainly isn't. "More power to him, I say. Douglas has his work cut out marrying you." His tone started to have an edge to it.

I took note. He gets ugly when he starts pretending to be someone he's not. He knew I wasn't asking permission, and it galled him.

"Amen." Aunt Irma quickly swallowed the bite of food she had in her mouth. She'd try to placate him before his mood got worse. "You're a headstrong girl, May. You'd best remember what the Apostle Paul said, 'Wives submit to your husbands as to the Lord.'"

"Ditto," said J.W., pushing his chair away from the table. "Good dinner, Irma. I'll get a piece of that berry pie in a while." He went outside to smoke.

And that was the end of it.

They're finally rid of me, the last one left and the youngest of the three little girls they raised. Our mother, Eliza, died of exhaustion and a chronic pelvic infection that hadn't completely gone away after my birth.

I remember being happy, living with Mama and my sisters in the modest two-bedroom house close to the railyard in Quanah, Texas. Our father has the same job now as he did then, a railroader working for the Fort Worth and Denver Railway. It's a job requiring him to be away from home most all the time.

It was Alyne, my oldest sister, who went for the doctor when Mama fainted. I can still see her laying there on the green linoleum floor, spots of blood on her dress. It was Alyne who went to the offices of F.W. & D. to have them telegraph our father to come home.

When she got back from sending the telegram, she sat us down. "Come here, y'all." We knew something was bad wrong as soon as we saw her red eyes and face streaked with tears. We sat on the sofa with her between us.

She put her arms around Emma and me. "I want you to be brave now. I have to tell you something hard. Mama's gone."

Emma started sobbing. She ran into our bedroom and slammed the door shut.

"Gone?" I asked, confused. "When's Mama coming back?"

"She didn't make it." Alyne started stroking my hair. "She died at the hospital."

She and I huddled together, crying, until our next-door neighbor, Deb, came over with a covered dish. Word traveled fast among railroaders. Her husband worked at the yard. "You girls go and wash your faces. I'm here to stay with y'all until your daddy gets home." She started bustling around the kitchen.

Daddy came home a day later to make arrangements. After the funeral, he took us on the train to Hillsboro to stay with our Aunt Irma, our mother's sister.

"I'll send money every month for their care." Daddy was standing in our Aunt Irma's living room with his hat in his hand.

The three of us, Alyne, Emma, and me, stood lined up for inspection like dolls, wearing our best dresses—the same ones we'd worn to our mother's funeral.

"C'mon in," J. W. said, showing us into the living room. The grown-ups sat on the sofa, sipping the sweet tea that we knew our daddy hated. He was too polite to say so.

"I'll do my best to see they get a proper Christian upbringing," Aunt Irma said, looking over at us and smiling. "I'll have to quit my job in the cotton mill now, won't I?" She didn't look like she'd mind. "We prayed and prayed that God would bless us with a family. Isn't that right, J.W? God surely sent us these three girls to us as a blessing."

My father looked pained.

"Statues," Alyne hissed under her breath. We pretended to be frozen in place, expressionless.

"I didn't mean—," Aunt Irma stopped, remembering too late her sister's death and the circumstances of why we were there.

J.W. frowned. He gritted his teeth, then forced a smile. "You'll need to send enough money for Irma to quit her job."

"J.W. We're fam-i-ly," Aunt Irma's teeth looked gigantic as she grinned. "Can I get you girls some cookies and milk?"

"No, ma'am," Alyne answered, squeezing our hands, her signal for us to stay quiet.

"You see, J.W.? You see what good manners they have? Eliza's sweet, sweet girls." She wiped a tear from her eye.

J.W. ignored her. "We're comfortable, Louis, but we're plain folks. We just get by. Three more mouths to feed, that's a lot to ask. Girls, at that."

"You can count on me, Ray," Daddy assured him. "My girls need a mother. I'm grateful you're willing to take them in, for Eliza's sake. I'd surely hate for them to be left to board with strangers, them so young and all."

"Lord, no," Aunt Irma exclaimed. "They have family. You can't come back in a few years and take them away, though. That would just about break my heart."

"I wouldn't do that to you." Daddy stood up and shook hands with J.W.

It was settled.

Before he left, Daddy hugged each of us and brought in the small trunk that held our clothes and toys.

Aunt Irma quit her job, but it was mostly Alyne who took care of us. We three were put to work doing Aunt Irma's housework as soon as we unpacked. Alyne did the harder work of cleaning floors and laundry. Emma did the ironing, while I did the sweeping, dusting, and washed the dishes after supper. We were fed, clothed, and reminded of our debt of gratitude every day.

Aunt Irma took Alyne to town once a year to buy one new pair of shoes and two new everyday dresses. Ella and I wore Alyne's hand-me-downs, except for our church dresses. Aunt Irma took all of us to Newberry's department store every year before Christmas to buy each of us a dress to wear to church.

"Now, you all look pretty as a picture. Everyone can see what good care you get," she'd say.

Daddy sent money to J.W. like he promised, and he visited when he could. He stayed just long enough to see us and ask if everything was all right before he left again. We always told him we were fine, even though we weren't. We missed our mama. We missed being loved and laughing with her.

"We have to make the best of it," Alyne told Emma and me when we complained. "There isn't any other place for us to go. You don't want to end up an orphan, do you?" She looked at me. "They might adopt you out since you're the youngest, and we'd never see you again."

The thought of losing my sisters was enough to keep me in line. We dreamed of fun times we had before Mama died. And we dreamed of leaving. We talked of nothing else in the dark bedroom before we fell asleep, revisiting the past when we had a mother who loved us, and imagining a future with someone who wanted us.

Alyne showed us the way to that future when she got married at fifteen. "I'm getting out of here."

We watched her as she folded two dresses, a nightgown, and some underwear to put in her new suitcase. Her fiancé had given it to her. It was cheap and ugly, little more than cardboard, brown with black handles.

When she finished, she said, "I'm sick of those two parading us around in public like they're such good people. There's no love in this house."

We could hear Aunt Irma praying at the top of her lungs in the next room, spouting scripture about the ungratefulness of children and the damnation they would face in the afterlife.

Alyne slammed the suitcase shut and gave Emma and me a hug. "Y'all get out of here just as quick as you can. I'll write you my address when I get settled." She cocked her head toward the sound of praying. "Be sure to get the mail before that old biddy gets a hold of it."

Daddy came by on Emma's fourteenth birthday. Alyne was already married and living in Dallas, so it was just Emma and me. He took us out to lunch at Sally's Diner where we sat in a booth.

"Order anything you want. I want this to be a special occasion."

We thought he was talking about Emma's birthday.

He wasn't.

"I have a new wife." He said it like it was nothing, picking up a French fry. He swirled it in a pool of ketchup on his plate before putting it in his mouth.

"When can we come to live with you?" I asked eagerly. Emma kicked my foot under the table.

"What's her name?" Emma stared at Daddy like she knew what was coming.

Daddy looked down at his plate, then lifted his head to look each of us in the eye before he spoke. He took a deep breath.

"Well, here's the thing, girls. We're having a new baby, and my wife, Hannah—that's her name, Hannah—is young." He looked at Emma. "She's older than you, Emma, but not by much. She's not ready for a big family."

"Maybe she's not ready to get married to you then," I said, narrowing my eyes to give him a mean look.

"I promised your aunt that I wouldn't take you girls away," he continued, picking up his hamburger and taking a bite. Between chews, he said, "I'll keep sending money. You'll be provided for, just like always." He put his burger back on the plate and looked like he expected us to be pleased.

Emma and I looked at each other. We wouldn't be seeing him again.

Emma hired on with the phone company in Waco two years later. She moved into an apartment she shared with two other girls. I was thirteen, left alone to be badgered by incessant scripture and yoked to an unending round of housework.

It's no wonder I didn't know what to expect from a man when I got married to Douglas. Alyne and Emma told me about periods, but I didn't know enough to ask about sex. Aunt Irma never mentioned it. Alyne told me many years later she'd learned about sex from her girlfriends. She supposed I would do the same.

The night before I was getting married, Aunt Irma gave me a new nightgown made of fine white cotton with lace at the neckline. She laid it out on the bed. "This is for your wedding night. You should have something special to wear for your husband."

"It's beautiful." I fingered the lace, surprised at her generosity. I wasn't taking much into the marriage besides myself—no hope chest, no trousseau. Even though Daddy kept sending money, he wasn't sending as much since he had a new family, and my sisters were gone. Somehow there was never anything extra.

I had no idea that marriage included touching a man's thing. I'd never seen a naked man. I'd never seen a naked boy, not even a baby. I only knew boys were made different. I knew enough to know we'd sleep together in the same bed. To my mind, that seemed like a close enough relationship for a man and woman to have.

Aunt Irma only had this to say about relations with the opposite sex. "Hugs lead to kisses, and kisses lead to trouble," she'd tell us. "We don't want any trouble around here, do we, girls?"

"No, ma'am," we'd answer.

When Douglas put my hand on him in the cheap motel room he'd rented for our wedding night, and told me what else he wanted, I felt sick. I broke away from him, grabbed up my clothes, and ran into the bathroom. I locked the door. I dressed and climbed out the window while he was still trying to coax me into coming out.

"Come on, May," I could hear him saying through the door as I pulled my new nightgown over my head. "Come on now. It'll be okay. You'll see." I didn't see how.

I had one ten-dollar bill hidden under the insole of my shoe that Alyne had given me when I visited her for a week last summer.

"Keep this for emergencies," she told me. "Don't let J.W. know you have it."

I went straight to the train station and used that ten dollars to buy a ticket on the train that was just about to leave the station for Fort Worth.

I was on my way.

Arthur

You wouldn't think it to look at me. I'm a man of slight stature with a nose too big for my face, hair already beginning to thin on top. My speaking voice is deep, resonant, and masculine. I can easily make myself heard above a crowd. My singing voice is that of a true Irish tenor, my tone rich and sweet. I have perfect pitch.

"I'm Arthur Lannery. I've come to ask if I might call on Gladys." My deep voice helped me project a confidence I didn't feel when Gladys's mother, Ella Rouche, opened the door.

"Come in." She moved to the side of the entry, motioning for me to go into the parlor while she closed the door.

She excused herself for a few minutes before returning with a tray holding two cups of coffee and a small plate of cookies. She sat in a wing-backed chair across from the sofa where I was seated, looking me over. I knew I looked presentable, wearing my best suit, the gold chain of my pocketwatch barely showing.

"I've seen you at church, haven't I?" she asked, as she handed me a cup. "You're the one who sang at Barbara Kominski's wedding."

"Yes, that was me." I took a sip of the strong coffee. There was no sugar or milk on the tray. "I'm a regular in good standing at St. Francis. Father O'Reilly can vouch for that. As well as for my good character." I smiled at her.

She didn't smile back.

She held the plate of cookies out to me. "You have your own business, I hear."

She had checked up on me. That was promising.

"I own a supply business for the oil fields." I took a cookie. It still felt warm from the oven. "I started out selling pipe for drilling water wells right before the oil business took off. I was in a good position to switch to supplying oil fields." I paused for her to respond, but she was silent, so I went on talking. "I've bought up a few mineral rights here and there. My business takes me all over the state."

"Where're your people from?" she asked, not taking her eyes off mine.

"Allentown, Pennsylvania. My father's a mason. My brothers too."

"How long have you been here?"

"I came out in '07. I'm not cut out to lay bricks. I wanted to make my own way."

Ella settled back in her chair. "I respect a self-made man. I'm making my own way now, providing for Gladys and my son, Allyn."

"Yes, Ma'am. Word is you run the best boarding house in Okmulgee." I knew she'd come to Oklahoma from Ohio, bringing her three children with her and leaving her husband behind. Gladys's older sister, Kathryn, had married an oil man from Mississippi last year.

Ella opened the boarding house in Okmulgee a few months ago. She already had a reputation as an excellent cook among the wildcatters and roustabouts. The five rooms she rented out by the month were always full.

"You may as well know that Mr. Rouche will not be around. James comes from a wealthy family, but he's a no-account drunkard. His family has disowned him because of it. He is destitute and likely to stay that way." She took a deep breath. "There will be no divorce, but he'll never be welcome here."

"I understand." I understood only too well. Catholics who were unhappy in their marriage either stayed unhappy or separated and put distance between them. Catholics did not divorce.

"It pains me to bring it up, but you'd best know the family situation beforehand if you want to court Gladys. She has nothing to bring to a marriage but herself." Ella finished her coffee and put her cup down. "Gladys is young. Just seventeen. May I ask your age?"

"I'm twenty-seven. I have a sister, Agnes, who is about the same age as Gladys. My intentions are honorable, I assure you. I'm in a position to marry, and I'd like to start a family."

"Then it's up to Gladys." She stood up. The interview was at an end. "You have my permission to call on her."

Seven years later, Gladys and I sit on our front porch after our 'meatless Tuesday' supper, enjoying the warm evening air and watching our three children as they play in the front yard. Bill, our youngest, toddles after Doreen and Kathy, while they pretend to get away.

"Don't touch us, don't touch us," they squeal, dodging to stay just out of his reach. "Cooties, cooties."

Bill laughs in delight, running after them on his short legs, arms outstretched.

"Mother's coming for a visit," I tell Gladys.

"Tell her to come when the war's over. When the flu's not so bad."

"I would, but she's already on her way. She telephoned the office today while I was out in Grady County. Left a message that she's getting on the afternoon train. She'll be here tomorrow morning on the seven ten."

"Typical," Gladys remarks, reaching for a cigarette. "I'll have Della fix up the spare room in the morning."

I strike a match, reaching over to light her cigarette, and watch as Gladys takes the first puff. I put the matchbook, printed with my company name on its cover, back in my pocket. "While you're at it, tell Della to go shopping and get some of those cookies Mother likes."

"How long is Francis staying this time?" Gladys asks, flicking the ash of her cigarette off into an ashtray.

"I don't know. There was another ruckus at home. You know how it is." My father's temper hasn't mellowed with age, nor has his drinking. Quite the reverse. He's worse than ever. Mother often leaves Philadelphia to get away. Her criticism and dour outlook is a strain on Gladys, whose usual good humor disappears as soon as my mother is around.

We don't keep any spirits. A cold beer occasionally hits the spot, but hard liquor upsets my stomach. Gladys took to drinking whisky to get through my mother's last visit and didn't stop. When Gladys was tipsy at the office Christmas party and let James Elwood kiss her under the mistletoe, I insisted she stop drinking altogether, and she agreed. We're both teetotalers now.

"How about I fix us a sweet tea?" I ask, standing up. We use our meager sugar ration in a glass of sweet tea after supper.

Gladys nods as she stands up to look over the porch railing at the children, her cigarette finished. "Don't be so rough with him," she calls out. The girls have Bill down on the ground, tickling him.

"We're not rough," says Doreen. "Look. He's laughin'."

"You need to let him up. Now." Gladys's foot starts tapping, a sure sign that Doreen's backtalk is aggravating her.

I stop in the doorway to see where this is going. Doreen lets Bill get up, and Gladys sits down again as the kids resume their game of tag. I continue on to the kitchen, relieved that Doreen obeyed. For once.

"What do you say we build a little house out back for Mother?" I ask, coming back with two tall glasses of tea. "I know she's not the easiest person to be around."

"That's a good idea," she says, smiling. "Can it be finished by tomorrow?" She laughs and I laugh with her.

"I'll talk to Mr. Freize about it tomorrow. That's the best I can do."

The pains I've had in my stomach since getting the message about my mother's visit start to ease up.

"Have him start as soon as he can. Your ulcers always flare up when your mother comes." Gladys takes my hand and gives it a little squeeze just as the telephone rings. It's our line, two shorts. "I'll get it," she says. "You finish your tea."

"Oh no," I hear her say. "Are you sure?" There's a pause. "All right, I won't come." Another pause. "Can I send Della over with anything?"

I hear Gladys saying a prayer, hear her say goodbye. Then there's silence. Her face is wet with tears when she comes out a few minutes later. I see she has her rosary, usually sitting on her bedside table, wrapped in her fingers.

"That was Mother calling. Allyn has a high fever. He's in the hospital. She's going to stay with him tonight."

I take her in my arms, holding her close. "Is it—?" I whisper into her ear, not wanting the children to hear.

"The damn Spanish flu," she whispers back, pressing her face into my shoulder. She pulls away and says, "We must pray for him, Arthur. Mother says he can't breathe."

Praying and wearing a mask is all we can do as the flu pandemic sweeps through the world, killing tens of millions. Allyn's only eleven years old, a thin, gawky boy with asthma. Not strong. Not even wearing long pants yet.

We stand at the porch railing hand-in-hand, murmuring prayers of intercession and healing. Our hearts are filled with love and fear all mixed together as our children keep playing, so happy, so healthy.

I can't even imagine losing one of them.

The phone call telling us Allyn has died comes right before dawn.

Gladys

Things are hard.

Kathryn left right after the funeral yesterday to go back to Mississippi.

Arthur's mother, Francis, has been a trial since the minute she stepped off the train. I can't abide that woman. She's so selfish. She thinks of no one but herself. I must remind myself every day to pray for my enemies, both the ones in the overseas war and the one in my kitchen.

Mother complains that she has a constant headache. She's worrying herself sick that the rest of us will get the flu and die since Allyn passed.

We aren't mask shirkers like so many others. We take precautions. The children are young, so we can keep them home. The only place we go is to Mass, and there we are within a congregation of masked faces, thanks to Father O'Reilly. He insists upon it.

"We don't want to lose a single congregant," he announces every week from the pulpit. "Wear your masks. Here and everywhere. God helps those who help themselves."

Our Colored girl, Della, goes out to the grocery, but she wears her mask at all times. Arthur wears his when he leaves his office and goes out into the field. The wildcatters working on the wells and rigs where he delivers pipe are mostly transient, unmasked because of the danger of the cloth getting caught in the machinery. Some are just coming home from the war, looking for any kind of work. As soon as one gets sick, there's another waiting to take his place.

I send Della over after dinner to help Mother with cooking supper for the boarders. I put on a smile when Arthur comes home, even though it's all I can do to drag myself out of bed in the morning and get dressed.

I hope I'm not pregnant again. Perhaps it's the grief dragging me down.

"When's Allyn comin' back?" Doreen's shrill voice penetrates my thoughts.

Doreen asks me the same queston every day. Every day I tell her the same thing. "Allyn isn't coming back. The angels took him up to heaven."

"But when's he comin' back?" she whines. "When?"

I feel tension rising in my chest, a tight pressure around my heart.

"He's dead," Kathy says. "Dead and dead. Like that smelly raccoon we saw at the side of the road when we went to the lake."

"He's not. He's not a smelly raccoon," Doreen wails. "He's comin' back to play with us, isn't he, Mama?"

Bill starts crying in sympathy.

I feel my patience fraying at the edges. I wish there was some whisky in the house, just a nip to take the edge off.

"Go to your room, Doreen," I say. "Now. Don't come down until I tell you."

"He's not dead. He's comin' back." Doreen pulls at my skirt.

I swat her hand away.

"Now. Before I slap you." My hand's twitching. I feel guilty as soon as the words leave my mouth.

Doreen runs out of the room with Kathy right behind her as I pick Bill up to comfort him. He puts his head on my shoulder and quiets. I should be comforting Doreen, but for some reason she rubs me the wrong way. Has ever since she was born.

Maybe because she and Bill were nearly Irish twins. They were born so close together that she didn't get everything she needed before there was a new baby taking up my time and attention. Maybe it's because she reminds me so much of Francis. She has the same skin tone, the same hair color, the same grating tone in her voice.

"You have to get Francis out of here," I told Arthur when she arrived the day after Allyn died. "I can't stand her being here. Especially now."

"I will. I promise." He patted my hand. "Right after the funeral. I'll buy her a ticket home and tell her she can come again when the house in back is finished."

"Must she stay for the funeral?"

"I can't ask her to leave before. It wouldn't be right."

Francis scowled her way through most of this past week. She seemed incapable of understanding what any of us are going through, the pain we feel at losing our Allyn, a boy so young, so beloved. I left her with Della and the children while I spent as much time with my mother and sister as I could.

Arthur gave Francis a ticket for the train back to Philadelphia when we were having breakfast this morning.

"I'll be back at noon to take you to the station." He stopped to give his mother and the children each a kiss before he left for work.

"Go upstairs and get dressed," I tell the children. "Kathy, help Bill with his buttons, please." They run upstairs, happy to get and back to their toys.

Francis starts in as soon as they're out of earshot. I'm helping Della clear the table

"I know you don't want me here," she hisses at me. "You're going to burn in hell."

"Why, I don't know what you mean," I say, feeling a flood of anger flush through me. "I'm sure Arthur told you that we're building a house in back, so you'll be more comfortable when you come next time."

I heard Della, her back to us as she stood at the sink rinsing dishes, give a little snort.

"Because you don't want me in the big house," Francis snarls.

"Because you can't stand to stay in your own home," I snap. "Don't start up a fight with me, Francis. I'm in no mood. You won't win, and it will only hurt Arthur."

"Your true colors are finally showing, Gladys," she says, lifting her long nose into the air in a show of superiority. "Lucky for you I don't tell Arthur how you treat me when he's not around."

She turns away and stomps upstairs, slamming the door to the guest room.

I drop down onto a chair at the kitchen table where we eat breakfast, my energy already spent.

"You earned yourself another cup of coffee, Miss Gladys," says Della, coming over with a cup and the steaming coffee pot.

"You're right. Thank you, Della."

She pours the coffee. "Yes'm, and have one a'them rolls before I put 'em away. You gonna need to keep up your strength for what's to come."

What's coming is more life and death and everything in between.

I don't want to think about it.

I could use a drink. Something stronger than coffee.

Della

My Lord—Miz Lannery gettin' on my nerves, the way she disrespects Miss Gladys. I sure be glad to see that nasty ole backside o' hers goin' back where she belong.

I knowed Miss Gladys since I worked for her mama, Miz Ella, over at her first boardin' house in Tulsa. Miss Gladys, she never do nobody no harm if she can help it. She like a different person when Miz Lannery comes. We all on pins and needles when she's around.

Miz Lannery sure is a miserable woman. She don't never smile. She don't like this, she don't like that, and she don't mind lettin' you know it.

I's so surprised to hear Miss Gladys talkin' back to her like she did. Inside, I's sayin' good for her.

Mr. Arthur gonna get a'earful from his mama when he come back to take her to the station. And him buildin' that nice little house for her in the back. 'Course, that's mostly so's Miss Gladys don't have a breakdown, Miz Lannery comin' so often like she does. An' she don't just stay a week or two. Oh, no. She stay for months. I ' spect she won't never leave once that house gets built.

That little house gonna be all new and nice, a sight better than where me and Clem live. That ole shotgun house weren't nothin' to begin with, and it's 'bout fallin' down 'round our heads now. I'm not complainin'.

Clem and I like workin' for Mr. Arthur and Miss Gladys. They's fair, and they talk real nice to us and our young'uns. They give us a ham and a turkey at Christmas and a bonus besides.

"For the kids," Mr. Arthur says when he hands Clem the envelope.

Clem do all the outside work and repairs for Mr. Arthur. He works for Miz Ella over at the boardin' house, too. I do the cookin' and housework for Miss Gladys, shop for groceries, and do up the warshin' and ironin'. I tends to the childern when Miss Gladys ask me to—if she ain't feelin' good, if it's her turn to host the ladies for luncheon and mahjong.

"You go on home," Miss Gladys tells me after I got supper fixed, and all that's left for her to do is cook it. "Your girls'll be getting home from school about now, won't they?"

"Yes'm, they will. Thank you," I say, taking my apron off and hanging it on its hook by the back door off'n the kitchen. I'm not like some help, harborin' meanness in my heart while pretendin' to be nicey-nice on the outside. I know my place, I keep to it. That's how I was raised.

What I like best is tendin' to the Lannery childern. Miss Kathy is five, and she mostly does for herself now. She a pretty little girl, bossin' ever'one. She keep a good eye on the other two. My Lord, they cain't get away with a thing, but she be tattling to me or Miss Gladys 'bout it.

Mr. Bill still in diapers, but we workin' on it. He a mama's boy. He do love Miss Gladys. If he ain't with Miss Gladys, he tags after Miss Doreen somethin' awful, but she don't seem to mind.

Miss Doreen, now she's some different kind o' child. I try to give her somethin' extra—just here 'n there, you know, when Miss Kathy ain't lookin'. Miss Gladys tries not to show it, but she short with Miss Doreen. She pushes that child aside more'n her fair share.

I know Mr. Arthur sees Miss Gladys talkin' mean to Miss Doreen sometimes, makin' her go to her room for somethin' the other two get away with. I see him watchin' Miss Gladys when he home. If she starts raisin' her voice, he ready to step in and bring some peace back to the situation.

Mr. Bill come along too soon after Miss Doreen got born, that's what I think. It was barely over a year after Doreen was born that Mr. Bill came along. Him bein' a boy an' all—well, he just the apple of his mama's eye, and that's all there is to it.

Truth told, Miss Doreen has some real difficult spells. She a moody child, with a frown so fierce it like to pierce you. No joy inside that girl. She gonna be one a'those people who go through life wantin' what she ain't got.

"Your face gonna freeze up like that," I tell her one day when I'm rollin' out a pie crust. She and Miss Kathy sittin' close by on kitchen chairs, watchin' me work and hopin' to get some edges of leftover crust. "Then you ain't gonna catch no man."

"Huh." She pouts even harder. "Don't want no man no how. I'm gonna marry a prince."

"You cain't marry a prince 'cause you ain't no princess," says Miss Kathy.

"Am, too."

"Not."

"Am, too."

"Y'all stop arguin'. Here now, take a taste o' this," I say, handin' each of them a piece of pie dough trimmed off the edge of the pan. They pop the bits of dough in their mouth and put out their hands for more.

They too young to know they both live like princesses compared to the rest o' us. I don't hold it against 'em. Mr. Arthur come up from pullin' on his own bootstraps, and he don't forget it. He don't put on any airs, even though he getting' close to bein' rich.

Lots of white folks gettin' rich off oil 'round here. Negro folks're prosperin' right along with 'em.

We Negroes got a real nice section called Greenwood up in Tulsa . People call it the Negro Wall Street. There's money there—big houses with nice lawns, women wearin' fur coats, and men in suits walking 'round nice and big as you please.

When Miz Ella had her boardin' house there in Tulsa, I used to take the bus over to Greenwood ever' week to see my brother, Elwyn. He's three years younger than me, the only family I have now Mama and Daddy's passed.

I'm real proud of Elwyn. He works at the Stradford Hotel. Started out as a bellboy, but he so good lookin' and speaks so good, he got moved up to work at the desk. Mr. Stradford hisself give him the promotion.

"Mr. Stradford likes me," Elwyn said when he told me about it. "He says I have ambition." He laughed. "My looks don't hurt none neither. Lookee here." He pulled out a card with his name and picture on it. Stradford Employee: Elwyn Johnson.

I still go up to see how he's doin', but this past year I only been able to go once. I have to wait for a time when Mr. Arthur's goin' to Tulsa and Miss Gladys don't need me. I was able to go three Wednesdays ago.

"I'll be back in a couple of hours," Mr. Arthur said, stopping in front of the Stradford.

He didn't even have to get out. One of the bellboys came right up and opened the car door for me.

Elwyn was sittin' behind the counter in the lobby, checkin' people into their rooms. He smiled big when he seen me. "Sit over there a minute," he said, pointing to the sitting area in the lobby. "We'll have lunch as soon as I can get someone to cover for me."

I sat myself down on one of the chairs. It sure was nice, upholstered in gold brocade. Magazines were spread out on a coffee table in front of it. I thumbed through the June issue of Life magazine while I waited because I liked the cute cover. It has a picture of a little white girl sitting under a tree knittin' bandages for our soldiers overseas. Two white boys, one army and one navy, watch her from behind a brick wall.

Elwyn came over to me after ten minutes or so.

"You look right handsome," I told him. "Is that a new suit?"

"It is."

"Well, I got's somethin' for you." I pulled a little box out of my purse and handed it to him. "It's not much, just a little thing."

He opened the box. A gold lapel pin was inside, with the letters EJ engraved on the back.

"It's classy," he said, giving me a big smile. "Pin it on."

I pinned it on the left lapel of his suit and took a step away so I could see how it looked. "It looks fine. Just a little somethin'-somethin' to dress it up, not too flashy."

"I'll wear it every day. Come on, let's eat. The food here's the best in the city." He took my arm as we walked to the dining room. It was luxurious: crisp white tablecloths, mirrors on the walls, and a crystal chandelier. I was glad I wore my best hat and my purple Sunday dress. The way folks was dressed, you'd have thought they was goin' to church, but it was just a Wednesday like any other.

"You eat here ever' day?"

"I have to pay, but I get a good discount," he answered. We followed a hostess to our table, where a waiter seated us. "I get a box lunch in the middle of my shift for free, and it's real good, too. Sometimes I take it home and eat it for supper."

We looked at the ornate menus. "Order whatever you want," he said.

"What's this?" I asked the waiter, pointing to escargot.

"It's snails cooked in butter and garlic sauce, Ma'am."

Snails don't hold any appeal for me no matter what sauce they be cooked in. "I'll have the fried chicken."

"Can't go wrong with that," the waiter said, flashing a big smile at Elwyn.

That was the best fried chicken I ever did taste. Lord, it just melted in your mouth. When we were finished and we stood up to leave, Elwyn shook his leg. His pant leg'd got caught up on somethin'.

"What you got goin' on there?" I thought I knew and I didn't like it.

"It's just for protection," he said in a low tone, as he ushered me out into the lobby. "I work the night shift sometimes."

I zipped my lip, but it worries me, him carryin' a gun. White folks'd shoot him just for havin' it if he goes outside of Greenwood. A Negro man has to be careful 'bout stuff like that. There be lots of white folks scared of Negroes, even these days. We might think things be changin', then some l'il somethin' happen to set us back agin.

We got to remember to keep our place, or we got trouble. Mama and Daddy taught both of us that from the time we's born. They knew about that kinda trouble firsthand.

Mama was born a slave in Georgia. She got freed when she were six years old. Daddy born a slave, too. His daddy was a field hand who turned to sharecroppin' on the same plantation where he were born.

Mama and Daddy come to the Territory after Daddy refused to say Sir to a piece a'white trash who was botherin' Mama, saying dirty things 'bout her with my Daddy standin' right there. Auntie Cora come knockin' on their door after dark, dressed in black, all three hundred pounds o'her like nothin' but a shadow. Anyhow, that's how Mama tells it.

"Make tracks. The white folks is comin' up right behind me," Auntie said, handin' my mama a bag of food and three dollars. "Hyram heard Mr. Jerome talkin' 'bout a lynchin'. I reckon they got their minds set on it."

Mama and Daddy took off. They could see the torches comin' down the road. They was that close. For three days they hid out in a hollow tree on a little piece o' land in the middle of the Etowah River. Until a big storm come along. With the storm covering their tracks and keepin' the white folks indoors, they ran 'til they knew they'd crossed the state line.

Mama said she never been so scared. They made it out with their lives. Never went back. They kept on goin', doin' odd jobs and such, 'til they got to the Oklahoma Territory.

That were a long time ago.

Things's different now. We got places like Greenwood, and nice places like the Stradford Hotel.

Negroes is startin' to come up in the world.

We startin' to get a piece of the pie.

1920

May

"Lookin' for work?" I heard a voice ask as I was leaving the newspaper office. I turned to see a handsome man with twinkling blue eyes behind me. "I overheard you askin' for an application."

"Yes," I said.

"I don't mean to be forward, Miss—"

"I'm May. May Hankins." I answered.

He held out his hand. "I'm Henry Gray."

I could feel the warmth of his hand through my thin cotton glove when my fingers met his. His hand felt strong, his nails looked clean.

I withdrew my hand.

"Might I buy you a cup of coffee?" he asked. "I don't often see a woman as pretty as you around Muskogee."

I blushed, feeling the warmth spreading in my face and neck. I was unused to compliments. My appearance was attractive enough, and my sisters even told me I was pretty, but Aunt Irma had discouraged any sort of vanity.

It was four o'clock. I didn't have to meet Emma for another hour, but I hesitated. I'd stayed away from men since my disaster of a marriage had been annulled. It had been nearly four years since I'd entertained any thoughts of having a man in my life—years of working as a filing clerk and typist to support myself, living in a small apartment with three other girls. Maybe it was time to reconsider.

A man coming out of the newspaper office paused and touched his hat. "Mr. Gray."

Henry acknowledged him with a nod. "Mr. Walker." The man went on, and Henry said, "See? Everybody 'round here knows me. I work for the Midland Valley Railroad."

"My daddy's a railroad man." I tried to seem more disinterested than I felt as I looked at my watch. "I'm meeting my sister at five, so it will have to be some place close."

"Turner's Café is just down the street a couple of blocks. No Colored allowed." He put his arm out and I took it. "After that, if you permit me, I'll walk you to meet your sister."

Turner's had big windows in front, with a sign saying "Coffee, 5 cents." He steered us to a booth by the window.

"Two coffees, Connie," he told the waitress, a hefty blonde wearing a pink and white uniform.

"Comin' right up," she answered, giving me the once-over.

As she walked away, I said, "She likes you."

"Oh, she's married with three kiddos. I get my breakfast here most mornin's, that's all." He shifted his position, uncomfortable. He settled, fixing his eyes on me. "Tell me about yourself."

"My sister works over at Veterans Affairs. I thought I'd see if I can find work while I'm visiting her."

"Lots of young men coming home from the war who need help. Some of them're in pretty bad shape."

The waitress brought our coffees. He fixed his with cream, I put two teaspoons of sugar in mine, and we both stirred.

"Are your people from Muskogee?" I asked, curious about his family.

"Born and raised in Denver. My daddy went there from South Carolina after the Civil War. My mama's from South Carolina, too. How about you?"

"Born in Texas. I was brought up in Hillsboro."

He smiled at me. "You think you might like living in Muskogee?"

"I might. My sister likes it here, and she'd like it if I came to live with her."

He motioned to the buildings across the street. "There's a lot happenin' in the Three Rivers country. Muskogee's growing. Haskell put us on the map."

"I want a secretarial position. I like it. It's not hard work, and the hours are regular. I've been at my job in Fort Worth for nearly two years. I wouldn't mind a change." My heart started racing as I thought about changing my life, and I felt a sudden desire for him. I hoped he couldn't see my skin flushing.

"It's okay for a woman to work 'til she gets married. After that, her work's at home. Anyhow, that's the way I see it." He motioned to the waitress to refill his coffee.

"I suppose."

"That's the natural order. It's a man's job to provide for his wife and family." We heard church bells ringing the half hour. I'd have to leave soon to meet Emma.

"Are you a Christian, Henry? Have you been saved?" I could hear Aunt Irma's warnings about men in the back of my mind. The questions came out before I could stop them.

"I'm not a religious man," he answered. "Don't get me wrong, I was raised in church. It doesn't suit me, but I don't hold it against people if it suits them."

"I'm Southern Baptist. Emma's a member of First Baptist Church." I expected him to make a comment, but he didn't. His expression stayed the same. I lightened my tone. "I'm one of those look-the-other-way Baptists. I don't mind a drink when I'm out for the evening. I play cards, and I love to dance." I raised my finger. "I don't hold with gambling of any sort."

He laughed at my pretend scolding. "The guys at the yard sometimes get up a penny-ante game of poker. Nothin' big. I'm usually up two bits or so by the end of it."

I looked at my watch. "It's about time we were going. I don't want to keep Emma waiting."

True to his word, he walked me to the Veterans Affairs office where I introduced him to my sister.

"Will you ladies do me the honor of having a picnic with me after church on Sunday?"

"Why, yes," Emma said. "That would be right nice, wouldn't it, May?"

"I'll pick you up Sunday about noon," he said, looking at me.

Emma told him the address of her apartment as I reached into my purse for a scrap of paper. "I'll write it down for you."

He pointed to his head. "No need. I can remember it. Have a good evenin'."

I felt elated as we watched him walk away.

Emma and I were fixing supper the next evening when she said, "I'm just looking out for you, so don't get mad. I asked around about Henry. My friend, Clara, says her husband knows him. He says Henry mostly keeps to himself. He's an outdoor man. Hunts and fishes most of his days off."

Any other time I'd be annoyed with Emma for butting into my business, but I was eager to find out more. I kept chopping lettuce and tomatoes for a salad and didn't comment.

"He knows Henry from some meeting they go to every week. The word he used was 'solid.' Maybe I'll have a bit of a headache after church and have to take a rest." She flashed a grin at me.

"Maybe that's a good idea."

Henry was at the door right on time for our picnic, a Model T parked in the street.

"I borrowed a car from a friend. I thought we'd go to a spot you might like. It's by a creek, where it's shady and cool."

"I'm looking forward to it. My sister isn't coming, though. She has a headache."

"Nothin' serious, I hope." He looked like he was trying to hide a smile.

"Nothing a little rest won't cure."

The spot at the creek was only a ten-minute drive. Henry spread a blanket on the ground underneath a willow tree.

"Should I take the job?" I asked Henry, as we sat on a blanket sharing news of our week. We were eating a picnic lunch from Turner's—cucumber sandwiches, potato salad, and slices of chocolate cake. It felt like we were the only two people in the world. "I told Dr. Wilson I'd let her know before I catch the afternoon train." I'd already accepted the job, but I wanted Henry to think he had a hand in it.

"Come back to Muskogee. I want you close to me." He took my hand in his.

I held his eyes with mine. "Then I'll take it. Because you want me to."

He leaned forward and kissed me. I liked it. I kissed him back.

We kissed until we heard the sound of boys laughing and calling to each other. He pulled away. Now we could see three young Negro boys running along the other side of the creek,

Henry stood up. "Yall get on outta here," he yelled. "There's white people here."

The boys stopped and looked, then turned and ran back the way they came.

He sat back down on the blanket. "I can't abide uppity niggers. Got to keep 'em in line." He patted his waist and showed me that he had a pistol under his shirt, tucked into his belt. "You'll be safe as long as you're with me."

I liked the sound of that. It felt right, being with a man who wanted to protect me, but there hadn't been any danger. Not really.

"They're just boys. No harm there."

"Boys grow into men. They should know better." He frowned. "You're not one of those nigger lovers, are you?"

"Of course not. The Bible's against mixing races."

His frown disappeared, and I was happy to please this man who had such a strong sense of right and wrong. I didn't want to ruin our relationship bringing up things he'd find hard to accept.

Later, I talked to Emma about my feelings for Henry. "Should I tell him about my first marriage?" Emma and I were sitting at the kitchen table, drinking sweet tea and fanning ourselves. It felt like there was a storm brewing. Not a breath of air stirred in the heat.

"No," she said. "Why rock the boat? It wasn't consummated, and it's been annulled. That's just like it never happened."

"Never happened," I repeated, trying to convince myself by saying the words out loud.

She made a wry mouth, showing her distaste for the subject. "You know better now. Every wife has certain duties in the bedroom. The important thing is you're still unspoiled. That's all men care about."

I want Henry to think well of me. He's a forthright person, definite about his likes and dislikes, but maybe he has his own secrets. Neither of us talked about our past.

I want him to love me.

Any imperfections that might cause him to doubt that I'll make a good wife must stay hidden. I'll figure out what kind of woman he wants to marry and shed this old skin, become that person. I'll be born anew.

I don't tell him I was married once before, and I don't tell him about how my sisters and I were abandoned after our mother died. I don't tell him about my father's other family in Dallas, his new young wife, and their children the same age as his grandchildren.

I especially don't tell him how desperate I am to move away from Texas, a place with nothing but painful memories, shadows I haven't been able to outrun.

Henry

It was like I'd never been gone.

I sat at the kitchen table with my mama and my brother, Carl.

Thomas had been seventy-three years old, his standard response to the question how are you was the answer "still full of piss and vinegar." His death—so sudden—had come as a shock.

"He fell over like he was poleaxed. Just that quick." Mama snapped her fingers, then reached for her handkerchief. "He didn't suffer."

Her handkerchief was a wet ball. I took a clean handkerchief out of my pocket and handed it to her. "That's good to know," I said. "Probably for the best."

He wasn't the kind to go out suffering. He'd have found another way. I didn't need to say it.

We heard a knock at the front door, another covered dish coming our way. The kitchen counter was full of them. I heard my sister, Pansy, saying, "Thank you, Miz Sellers. Appreciate you thinkin' of us. I'll tell Mama you stopped by."

Pansy came into the kitchen, carrying the dish, covered with a towel. "Another batch of rolls. We're running out of room."

Mama turned to Carl. "Help carry some of this food to Grandaddy Alf's, so it don't go to waste. It's time they were leavin' anyway."

Daddy learned to be a wheelwright from Grandaddy Alf. He was ninety now, all bent over, walking with a cane. He and Grandma Ellen lived in a little house not far away where Mama could keep an eye on them.

Grandma started to protest.

Mama interrupted her. "No use fussin'. Y'all can come back in the morning. You're lookin' done in. Besides, Henry's here to see to things now."

Carl scowled. He'd done the lion's share of helping Mama, not me. His nose was still out of joint when he left with our grandparents, and I knew he'd be bending my ear later on about how he never gets the credit he deserves.

Thomas waited twenty-five years to remarry after Sarah and his baby girl were killed. We knew he had a second wife and family in

South Carolina that he went to see once or twice a year. He didn't talk about them much.

He'd taken Carl and me with him on the train once to meet his other wife, Caroline, and our eight half-brothers and sisters. They were a lot older than us, all grown up with their own families.

That was years ago. Daddy hadn't taken any of us with him since.

When Carl had picked me up at the station, he'd said, "I sent Caroline a telegram to tell her Daddy passed."

"Is she comin' for the funeral?" I asked.

"She sent her condolences and said she wasn't up to it. Her family will hold their own memorial service."

I figured Caroline didn't want the hassle of mourning our father and meeting his third wife for the first time. She was getting up in years. "Well, that's okay. Easier on Mama that way."

We were still half a mile from the house when Carl said, "The missionaries are bunking in your old room. You'll have to sleep on the floor in my room."

"I wish to hell Mama'd get rid of those missionaries."

"That'll never happen. She'll work herself to death first." He changed the subject. "Are you gonna see Joseph?"

"Catherine's livin' in Kansas. I doubt she even knows Daddy's gone. I'd rather not see her this trip if I can help it."

"Up to you, but she might find out anyway."

He was right. The Mormon community is a small one, tightly connected. It was likely someone would tell her, but I didn't expect her to show up at the funeral.

I didn't tell Carl that I'd met someone else. She's a woman named May, not five feet tall, who I want to get to know a whole lot better. I'm not the kind of man who likes to do for himself for long. I miss havin' a wife to do the cookin' and cleanin'. But I need a woman who's loyal and faithful, someone who'll let me go my own way and not make a fuss about it. May seemed like that kind of woman.

Three days later we buried Daddy. That was a hard, hard day.

"I saw Catherine sitting at the back of the church. Did you see her?" Carl asked when we were back at the house. It was just the two of us in the little kitchen. The girls were setting food out on the dining room table, expecting a crowd.

"I saw," I answered.

"And?" His curiosity was getting the better of him. Thomas wouldn't have told him anything about why she and I split up.

"And nothin'. I saw her leave just as we stood up to carry the coffin." It's like there's a radar between me and Catherine. Even now, I know whenever she's around.

She's the only one left who knows what happened that night, the only one who could hurt me with it. That thought's always in the back of my mind. I'd do somethin' about it if it weren't for Joseph. He needs someone to care for him, and I don't want to be saddled with a motherless baby. I figure it this way—if she's kept her mouth shut this long, she'll keep it shut. She wants the money I send her every month. She knows I'll take action to protect myself if she starts blabbin'.

Mother came in and asked us to greet people, and Carl dropped the subject. It was dark and most of the food was gone before the last of the mourners cleared out.

I joined Mama on the porch after everyone else had gone to bed. I found her sittin' out there in the old rockin' chair. "What do you want of your daddy's things? You want his shotgun?"

I took out a pack of Camel cigarettes, tapped one on the porch railing, and lit it with a match I'd taken from the kitchen. "I don't want nothin' of his."

I threw the the matchstick on the ground and leaned against the porch railing, so I could tap the ashes onto the grass. Mama didn't hold with smokin', but she wouldn't say anythin' about it tonight. "Give his shotgun to Carl or Bill. I'm fine just the way I am."

She looked away. "I'm gonna miss your daddy somethin' awful."

"Yeah, we all are." I didn't speak for a few minutes. "How you fixed for money?"

"There's a little bit put away, and I'll still get his pension from the railroad. They're real good that way."

"I can send you some extra," I offered, flickin' the butt of the cigarette onto the grass. "I don't need much."

"If I have need of it, I'll ask. That Bessie woman sent us a little money after she sold Granddaddy Jonathan's farm. Your daddy was real mad about it. Said he didn't want nothin' from her." I knew the history, had seen the expression of disgust on my father's face when I walked in on him saying "that nigger bitch" after he'd been on a trip to South Carolina.

"That was a sorry deal, her sellin' the farm like that."

"Your dad surely thought so. I socked the money away in a hidey hole upstairs behind my dresser. Just in case." She yawned. "I'm tired enough to lay down. You?"

"I'll be in directly."

After she was gone, I lit another cigarette. I felt my father's presence, just out of sight in the shadows, and the words of the Cherokee Death Song came to mind: For the son of Alknomook shall never complain.

Mama asked me to go through Daddy's papers with her the next day before I left on the evening train.

"Can I have this?" I asked, thumbing through the pages of a booklet titled "Ideals of the Ku Klux Klan."

"Oh, that's from those meetin's your dad went to," she said, looking over to see what I was holding. "I don't want it."

"I didn't know he joined up with the Klan."

"He started goin' after he saw that moving picture show, Birth of A Nation. There's a group has meetings every Tuesday and sometimes on weekends. Mostly at night." She emptied another drawer.

I started sorting bills into two piles, paid and unpaid. "He never mentioned the Klan to me."

"He didn't talk about it once he joined," she answered, rummaging through other papers. "Here it is. Take this one, too," she said, holding out another booklet. "It's for women."

She stood up, stretching her back. "I told him I'm sticking to the Word of the Prophets, and that's it. I don't hold with Klan views on Catholics—or organized labor, for that matter." She handed me a stack of old bills held together with a rubber band. "Conditions at the cotton mill—well, they're terrible."

I put the booklets in my bag. I'd already been approached by a man at work about joining him at a Klan meeting, but at the time I was getting' sent in and out of town. Now I work steady in the railroad yard every day.

I'll go to a meeting when I'm back in Muskogee. See what Daddy saw in it.

Arthur

"It's a gusher."

I saw it and heard the yells from the men at the drilling site as I got off my horse to survey the well. I was making my rounds, taking orders for pipe and fittings. The plume, going up in the air for over a hundred feet, looked like dirty water. Capping it would be no small feat, but it would pay out a big reward. Wells like this were coming in all over the Oklahoma.

The Lannery Oil Well Supply business is booming right along with Oklahoma's oil exploration. There's an increased demand for oil and gasoline. Henry Ford's Model T is going to be the transportation of the future. We'll all have one soon. I see nothing but good times ahead for my business.

I went to the Mayo Clinic in Rochester, Minnesota, last month. It's has the best doctors in the country. Poor digestion has plagued me for several years. My doctor sent me to have a complete workup.

The train trip took two days, but the service in the dining car was first rate. Rochester streets were full of motor cars, and I took one for hire from the train station to the boarding house where I was staying. It was run by Miz Rose, and she catered to folks receiving medical care. The food was fresh and well-cooked, and it's located only a block from the hospital, so I walked to and from my appointments.

Those doctors were thorough, I'll give them that. I had tests and consultation appointments every day. At the end of the week, they gave me a report to take to my doctor and told me I have ulcers. I'll be on a regimen of Milk of Magnesia every day for the rest of my life. They recommended that I take an afternoon rest when possible and avoid worry. That last one is a kicker—Gladys tells me all the time that I worry too much.

I've been thinking of buying one of those motor cars ever since I got home. It would make checking on the wells much easier, and our carriage house could be converted to a garage. I'm going to talk with Gladys about it one of these evenings when she's in a good mood.

Gladys was sitting at the dining room table reading the newspaper when I got home from work today. "Della took the children down to the park for some running around time," she said, looking up as I came in. "The Nineteenth Amendment is passed and signed. At last." She folded the newspaper, knowing it's my habit to read it after dinner. "It's high time women got the right to vote."

"You're turning into a suffragette. Next thing I know, you'll be out marching and carrying a sign."

"Every grown person should be allowed to vote. It's disgraceful it took so long. I wonder how long it'll take for Negroes to get the vote."

"Be careful who you talk to about that," I said, sitting down beside her. "People around here might take offense." I smiled and tried a lighter tone. "It could be bad for business if word gets around that my wife is spouting off radical political ideas."

"Oh, I don't talk about politics or religion with anyone but you. We should view all people as equal before God."

I pointed to the crucifix on the wall. "The Negroes don't want to be Catholics, all our Latin and Hail Mary's. They'd rather be clapping and singing gospel music in their own churches."

Her eyebrows raised. "You don't know that."

"I do know it. St. Francis is full of bigots."

She shook her head in disagreement. "Father O'Reilly won't stand for it. Not with the Klan trying to shut down our schools with anti-Catholic laws. The bombs, the burning crosses— there's even talk about St. Mary's changing its name to avoid trouble."

"Father O. knows when to turn a blind eye. Jerry Flanigan asked me and Glen Moore if we wanted to go to a Klan meeting. It was after church two Sundays ago, and Father was right there, not saying a word about it."

"What is Jerry thinking?"

"He's thinking if more Catholics join the Klan, they'll focus on the Negro problem and leave us alone."

"I hope you gave him what for."

"I told him I had a trip coming up, and Glen said he'd get back to him. Jerry knows we made excuses. He won't ask again." I stood up and started pacing, then stopped to put my hand on her shoulder. I felt the hand of worry starting to squeeze my gut.

"I'm telling you those Klan boyos are spoiling for a fight, and they don't care who gets hurt. You don't know who's in or out. Their wives sit at your table playing mahjong and bridge—they're right in the thick of it, though they'll never say a word."

"If you say so," she said.

"I do say so."

She went over to the mahogany buffet where she kept a pack of Lucky Strikes in one of the drawers. "I'm going to have a cigarette before Della brings the children home."

I stood in the doorway to the living room to block her from leaving. "Promise me you'll not talk about Negroes getting the vote. I don't want the children overhearing us and repeating what we say."

She gave me a quick hug and patted my stomach. "Don't get yourself upset. I promise to keep my opinions to myself from now on."

I moved aside, and she went out onto the porch to smoke. As I watched her go, I thought about how much I love her, love our children. I do my best to give us a good life, to protect us. We don't often disagree, but I must stand firm on this issue.

Her father wasn't much of a provider, but he didn't need to be. He comes from a wealthy family. Her grandfather made sure the family had what they needed to be respectable when they lived in Ohio. They never sank into poverty, never knew hunger.

My grandparents were immigrants. We lived in the working-class neighborhood of Allentown— stores with signs No Irish Need Apply, cartoons in the newspaper showing us as apes. I grew up with the ugly face of prejudice, know what it feels like to split one potato between six children when times are tough. I know how it feels to be ridiculed, hated, and attacked because people in my family have a foreign accent, have different beliefs, have too many kids and not enough money.

I remember the fear I felt every day when I walked to and from school, praying I wouldn't get a beating. I don't want my children to ever feel that kind of fear.

I wouldn't wish it on a dog.

1921

Henry

George Rhodes is my best friend. He's seven years older than I am and has a dry-cleanin' business in Muskogee. Weekends, he's usually at Tenkiller Lake where he built a one-room cabin with an outhouse, no runnin' water. I met him when I was camped at the lake doing some fishin' last summer. He strolled into my camp just as the sun was settin'.

"How 'bout a drink?" he asked, pullin' a flask out of a pocket of an old fishing vest he was wearing over a shirt that had seen better days.

"Sounds about right." I pointed to a log close by. He sat down and we had a pull. I'd had a good catch that day, so I fried up six crappies in lard and cornmeal over the campfire. We ate and sipped from the flask while we watched the moon rise over the lake.

"Ain't nothin' like bein' on the lake when the moon comes up," George said. "That's when you know God's in his heaven."

"That's about right."

"I have a boat," he told me. "Nothin' special, just a two-man deal, but you can catch a bass with it. We'll take it out next time you come. Give me a holler."

We met often to fish after that, either at the lake or off the bank of the Arkansas River where we'd fish for catfish. Those catfish're hard to kill, but fry 'em up and there's no better eatin'.

George reminded me of my father—even-tempered and practical, a self-made man. He knew the country. He'd grown up in the hills of southern Missouri, right over the state line. I missed the wild country of Colorado, and George showed me all the wild spots around Muskogee. Besides an automobile and a dinghy, he had a bird dog and a coon dog. We went chasin' coons in the summer. In the fall, we went bird huntin' on private land owned by George's cousin. We could go for hours without sayin' a word and feel all right about it.

George has a wife, Betsy, who takes good care of him and works the counter at the cleaners. She knows enough to make herself scarce while we have a few drinks and talk about man-things—our next huntin' and fishin' trip mostly. Sometimes politics and how the country's goin' to hell in a handbasket.

George nominated me for membership in the secret society he belongs to, the one my daddy'd been in. I knew from the first that those boys were on the right track. It's our Christian duty to keep the niggers, Jews, and Papists in line before they destroy our God-given white protestant way of life. I'm a regular attendee now.

We aren't afraid to back up the sheriff with vigilante justice, swift and sure. He's one of us.

We know what the people of Muskogee want—a court of the people, by the people, and for the people.

That's how I see it.

May

White satin and tulle drape every surface in the small living room, made smaller yet by a table Emma's put in the middle of it. There's hardly room to squeeze around the edges. It's the last day of May, and Emma's getting married to Harry Yates next month. She's busy making her wedding dress.

She's already given notice at her job here and told the landlord that I'll be taking over the apartment. Harry's a good man, a railroader. I guess we're doomed to marry men like our father. She'll be living in Hillsboro again. I'm just glad it isn't me going back to live there.

"Help me straighten this," she mumbles, her mouth full of pins.

I pull on the slippery satin, patting the wrinkles out while she pins the pattern.

"You'll look beautiful in this." I wish Henry would talk about an engagement. We've been seeing each other for a year, but he's made no move to formalize an agreement between us.

"It'll be you next," Emma says, through with the pinning and picking up a pair of dressmaking shears. "Keep it from sliding."

"Henry's taking his own sweet time."

"That's because he's divorced. He's gun-shy, that's all. He'll come around."

Maybe.

Henry told me of his previous marriage when we were on a walk in the park earlier this afternoon. We were holding hands, but when we passed a statue of a little boy beside a wading pool, Henry pulled his hand away.

"Let's sit. I have somethin' to tell you." He wiped a park bench with his handkerchief, and we sat.

He looked me in the eyes, and I held my breath, expecting him to ask if I'd marry him. I've practiced my answer a thousand times.

Instead, what he said was, "You should know I'm divorced. I was married, and I have a little boy, Joseph. He lives in Kansas with my ex-wife, Catherine."

I felt my heart sink, visions of my imaginary future fading away. Divorce carries the stigma of failure, along with attributions of wrongdoing or flaws in one's character. It isn't respectable.

"What happened?" I asked.

His expression changed. It got cold. Hard.

I saw for the first time the reservoir of anger he carried just under the surface of his calm exterior. I didn't know what to make of it.

"I found her with another man. I ended it."

I tried not to show how relieved I was that the blame for the divorce fell on her and not him.

"It's over now. The divorce is final." Before I could comment, he took a softer tone. "I go and see Joseph sometimes when I'm in Denver. It isn't too far for me to drive. I borrow my Mama's car." He paused and shifted his weight restlessly. "I'm tellin' you because I got a letter yesterday from Catherine. She got married again, a man I've never met by the name of Ed Glasser. Joseph has a new daddy." His right hand, the hand I'd held so recently in mine, was now a fist.

I tried to assure him by saying, "You'll always be his daddy. That never changes no matter what. I don't remember my mama, but my Aunt Irma could never take her place. Hard as she tried, me and my sisters kept pushing her away."

He unclenched his fingers. "Maybe when the boy gets older, I can have him stay here for part of the summer."

He took my hand in his, lacing our fingers together. We sat in silence for several minutes, my heart fluttering like it does when I'm too excited. He'd opened up and shared a part of his past, one darker and more complicated than my own. I felt there was a new closeness between us that didn't need words.

He let go of my hand and stood up, saying, "Let's move on."

I looked at his face. The anger had left him.

"We can stop by the drugstore and have ourselves a soda on our way back." He loved sodas. I pretended I like them, too, although a milkshake was my favorite.

"I'm gonna get chocolate. After that, I'll take you home. I have some business to attend to this evenin'."

"Business?"

"No women allowed kind of business."

"A lynching," I nodded my head. "I know about it. Everyone's talking about what happened in Tulsa."

"Nothing for you to concern yourself with. It'll get taken care of."

I decided to trust him with a piece of my shadowy past, a piece I knew he could relate to. "My uncle took all us girls to a lynching once. I was only six. I remember thinking it was the Fourth of July because of all the people there, like a big party. When they hung him, the crowd broke out in a cheer. My uncle put me on his shoulders so I could see, but I didn't know what was going on, not really. That Colored man looked like a big doll hanging up there. The worst part is they set his clothes on fire. I'll never forget the smell—like singed hair and roast meat mixed together. People were clapping like it was nothing bad."

I looked away. "I still have nightmares about it sometimes."

"Your uncle should've known better." Henry dropped my hand and put his arm around me. "A little girl shouldn't see those things."

I shuddered. I felt stuck in that memory. I was already trying to forget it again. "That's just how J.W. is. Ignorant."

I put my head on Henry's shoulder. He felt strong, like he could shield me from all the badness in the world.

Henry

I met George at the courthouse after I'd seen May home. I felt restless and unsettled after hearing May's story. That, combined with the news of Catherine getting married, of another man raising my son, awakened a suppressed rage I hadn't felt since the night I'd killed Catherine's lover.

Fire in my belly.

Ready for action.

Twenty automobiles were lined up on Main Street waiting to take off. The Tulsa Tribune had reported that a Negro teenager, a shoeshine boy named Dick Rowland, accosted a young white woman who operated an elevator in the Drexel building. Rowland had been arrested and was being kept in jail on the top floor of the courthouse. The call had gone out earlier to Klan members to meet up and caravan to Tulsa to set things straight.

"Over here, Henry," George yelled. "We're 'bout ready to get goin.'

I ran across the courthouse lawn and jumped into the passenger seat of his Model T. "I need to stop and get my pistol."

We made a stop at the rooming house. I came out with my pistol stuck in my belt, and my shotgun, too, plus a box of shells.

"Just in case." I tossed the box of shells under the seat.

There was a long line of cars in front of us when we turned onto the main road out of town.

"There's rag balls that Betsy rolled up and a can of turpentine in the back," George said. "Word from on high is for us to get Rowland, then burn Greenwood down. We'll teach those uppity sonsabitches a lesson they won't forget."

"Plenty of matches here." I shook the box of kitchen matches sitting on the seat between us. We laughed like boys, like we didn't have a care in the world, as we set off to a lynching.

A mob was already at the courthouse when we got there. Hundreds of white men had answered the call. A group of about eighty Coloreds showed up to help protect Rowland. It was a standoff between the whites and the Coloreds for a couple of hours, just shooting words back and forth.

As time passed, tempers flared. A couple of shots were fired.

All hell broke loose.

"The armory," I heard one man shout. "Get a gun and get a nigger." The mob started moving down the street.

George and I were already armed and ready for action. We got in the car and started off to Greenwood. We met with some resistance at the tracks on the border of Greenwood, but there were several carloads of men behind us and we got through the barriers.

We drove on to the main street, and George parked across from the Stradford Hotel. "This's as good a place as any," he said, setting the brake. "Ol' J.B. Stradford thinks it's the Ambassador Hotel for Coloreds. People parade around here all dressed up like the organ grinder's monkey."

The streets were nearly empty, the night dark, with only a waning crescent moon. We saw more headlights turning onto the street a few blocks down.

"Start soakin' these rag balls." George put them on the seat. He set a bucket and a can of turpentine on the sidewalk. I dumped the rag balls in the bucket, poured on the turpentine, and we stood around letting them soak for a few minutes.

There was the sound of breaking glass down the block where some white men were breaking windows. Some were throwing bricks, others had bats. A few were carrying armloads of goods out of the businesses and putting the goods into their automobiles.

"Now that's just wrong." George watched a white man carry a chair out of a furniture store two doors down from where we were standing. He loaded it in the back of his truck.

"That there gives all the rest of us a bad name," George said. "We're not thieves." He went over to the truck with his pistol out and had a word with the man. The chair got unloaded onto the sidewalk. The man drove away, his truck empty.

George came saunterin' back to the car. "White trash. Not one of ours." He picked a turpentine ball from the bucket and inspected it. It was soaked through. "This oughta do it."

We walked up and down the block lighting turpentine balls on fire, lobbing them into buildings, up onto the roofs. We heard the sound of an airplane, watched as flaming bottles and a few small bombs were dropped onto the roofs of the taller buildings. Some of our boys were pilots in the war, and they had a few tricks up their sleeves for situations like this. The black smoke about choked us as the fires took off burning, but we kept on until the bucket was empty.

We walked back to the car, joining a group of men who were rounding up Negroes staying at the Stradford. There were nearly a hundred of 'em, men and women, standin' together in a group on the street. Most had been awakened from sleep to be taken out here to wait and wonder what their fate would be. All had been searched for weapons. The plan was to march them, and any others we came across, over to the Convention Hall on Brady Street.

A young man in a suit broke away from the edge of the crowd and made a run for it.

"One's gettin' away," George said, pointing.

I had a clear shot, so I aimed my pistol and pulled the trigger. The man fell and lay in the street. There were a few screams from the women in the crowd, and some angry mutters from the Negro men, but none of them were armed.

"Get 'em out 'a here," George yelled.

Men started herding the crowd down the street, away from the body. George and I walked over to where the man lay on the ground, motionless, blood pooling around his head.

George looked down at the body. "Lucky shot. Right through the back of the head." He looked at me in admiration. "It ain't sportin' to shoot an unarmed man in the back," he chuckled, "but that's because he ran, so I won't hold it against you." He nudged the body with his foot, bent down, rolled him over to get a closer look.

The man was wearing a suit. There was a gold pin on the left lapel. George removed it. "Souvenir," he said, handing it to me. He took a leather wallet from the inside breast pocket of the suit jacket. He flipped the wallet open and took out a card, squinting in the dim light. "I can't rightly see this. Light a match so's I can get a better look."

I slipped the pin into my shirt pocket, lit a match, and held it up to light the front of the card.

"Elwyn Johnson. He must 'a worked at the hotel. It says Employee."

Not that it matters.

George took the match from me, set fire to the card, and dropped it onto the body. "Let's head back home before we choke to death on this smoke."

We felt tired, but victorious, as we got back on the road.

"What a night." George thumped his hand on the steering wheel. "Get that flask out. We earned ourselves a drink."

"Or two."

"Or more," he agreed. "I'll never forget this. You and I did some kind of good work tonight."

We rode in comfortable silence, passing the flask between us, watching the sky beginning to grow light as we made the hour-long drive back to Muskogee.

The next day the article in the Tulsa Tribune showed the pictures of the blackened rubble that had once been the prosperous Negro Wall Street, the neighborhood of Greenwood. Thirty-five square blocks with nothing left standing—no houses, no businesses, no churches, hospitals, or schools. Six thousand people with no place to go back to, eight hundred wounded, who knew how many dead.

I was proud to have been part of it.

Della

I woke up, feelin's of dread in the pit of my stomach and heaviness pullin' at my heart—bad, bad feelin's. I put on my house slippers and stopped one of the boys on the street who was on his way to deliver papers for the white folks. He let me take a peek at the front page. Then I knew why I got these bad feelin's.

I went back inside and got dressed quick so's I could get to the Lannery's house early. The newspaper and the milk's delivered first thing in the mornin'. Miss Gladys was still in her robe when I walked through the back door into the kitchen, carryin' the milk and the paper in with me. She know'd right away why I come early. She spread the newspaper out on the kitchen table so I could see it.

She pulled a chair out and gestured for me to sit down. "We heard about it on the radio last night. I've been praying for all your people."

"Thank you, ma'am. I shore 'preciate it." I sat down at the table like I never do when I'm workin'.

The front page of the Tulsa Tribune stared back at me, picture after picture of smokin' ruins, block after block of destruction. Greenwood burnt to the ground in less than twenty-four hours, takin' with it the dreams of our people to have good businesses, nice homes, a safe neighborhood to live in.

One picture showed white men marchin' our people through the streets to a holdin' center. I scanned the blurry faces, hopin' to see Elwyn's face in the crowd, but I didn't see him.

I picked up my apron, wiping tears away before they fell on the newsprint and made it run. The article said there were several holding centers throughout Tulsa. It said a Negro can't be released until a white person comes to vouch for his or her character.

Elwyn worked for a Negro business in a Negro community. Weren't nobody there in Tulsa to vouch for him.

"Paper says thirty-six people were killed," I said. "Hundreds more hurt."

Mr. Arthur come in just then, and he heard me say it.

"Don't believe everything you read in the Tribune," he said. "Their reporting started a lot of that mess. They slant the news to be what they want it to be."

Miss Gladys stood up. "I'm going up to get dressed. I'll get the children dressed in their play clothes. You fix Mr. Arthur some breakfast, Della."

I started rustlin' around the kitchen, gettin' out eggs and oatmeal.

Mr. Arthur sat down in the chair where I'd been sittin' and started reading the newspaper.

"What breakfast you want this mornin'?" I asked, openin' a cabinet and takin' out mixing bowls. "You want I should cook you some pancakes or scrambled eggs?"

"Cream of wheat with a little butter will do just fine." He didn't look up.

My arms felt like lead as I turned on the stove. Mr. Arthur let Miss Gladys get rid of the wood stove last year. He bought a Sentinel Automatic Cook Stove that uses gas and electricity. It sure is nice not havin' to chop wood and come early to make a fire. It took me some gettin' used to before my cookin' started to come out just right.

I kept goin' through the motions, feeling numb as I stirred cream of wheat into boiling water. I prepared pancake mix and heated up the syrup. I didn't need to ask what the children wanted. Saturday was always pancake day.

"Here you go." I set a bowl of cream of wheat, a pat of butter still melting in the center, in front of Mr. Arthur.

"A glass of milk, too, please," he said, still reading.

He do like his milk. Prob'ly 'cause it help settle his stomach. 'Bout the only time I hear him complainin' is when his stomach's upset.

He folded the paper up and put it aside when I set the glass of milk in front of him.

"I guess we'd best drive into Tulsa later on and see if we can't find your brother."

"That'd be real Christian of you, Mr. Arthur." My voice choked up with tryin' not to cry. "If it ain't too much trouble."

"No trouble. It's Saturday, and I wasn't planning to do much of anything. If we find him, he'll need someone to sign for his release."

Someone. A white person.

"Yessir, he will."

"The trick'll be finding him, but we'll try to figure that out when we get to Tulsa."

I felt like huggin' him, I was that grateful.

I felt like it, but that's not somethin' the help can ever do unless it's a young child you're tendin' to. We're close to the families we work for. We knows everything goin' on in the house—who's abusing who, who treats their elders nice, who's havin' an affair, who's neglectin' their children, who's behind on their bills, who's havin' troubles in the bedroom. We can't never let on we know those things.

My mama told me about that the first day I went out for hire. "You be the invisible eyes and ears, the fly on the wall that can't never tell nobody what you done seen and heard." She gave me the eye. "I mean, nobody. Not even me."

I was sixteen, and I'd quit school to go to work and help out. Mama wasn't happy that she needed me to hire out, but she'd done it herself when she was only thirteen. She walked with me as far as the laundry where she worked. "White folks might tell you you're family. Mark my words—you're not and never will be. It don't matter how long you're with 'em." She gave me a quick hug, careful not to leave a wrinkle in my uniform. "You're only the help, to be hired and fired. Don't talk back, and don't go puttin' anything in your pockets 'cept your hands."

We came to the laundry, and she gave me a nudge with her elbow, "You go on now. Don't never go oversteppin' your place, and you'll do fine."

"I'll be okay, Mama." I smiled at her like I wasn't feelin' scared. "Don't you worry 'bout me."

Mr. Arthur drove us into Tulsa after lunch, after I'd put the supper into the stove to keep it warm. Miss Gladys wouldn't have to lift a finger while we's gone.

"What do you say we stop by your place first? You can let Clem know we're going," he said.

"If it ain't too much trouble." I can tell Ruby, my next-door neighbor, where I'm goin' if Clem ain't home. Saturday's his day to visit his mama and do her yard.

The neighborhood where I live was deserted. It's generally bustling, what with Saturday bein' the day Colored's are allowed to go to town and be in the park. Not today. No children playin' in the street or the park, nobody out walkin' to town. Some men was out sittin' on their porches, keepin' a watchful eye.

"It's quiet," Mr. Arthur remarked, parking on the street in front of the house.

"We knows how to keep our heads down when troubles come."

"That you do. Not like us Irish. We stick our heads up higher and dare somebody to chop it off." He chuckled.

White folks can disrespect themselves and poke fun all they want, but we can't cross the line to join in with it.

I went inside and changed out of my uniform. I put on my purple Sunday dress and my best hat even though it was Saturday. Mr. Arthur didn't have his old clothes on. He had on his workin' suit and tie.

Clem and the girls were gone, pro'bly over to his mama's house. I went to the cookie jar and took out a one-dollar bill and four quarters. I put the money in my pocketbook, then headed over next door to tell my neighbor, Ruby, where I was off to. She answered my knock and came out on her stoop, closing the door behind her.

"I'd 'preciate it if you tell Clem I'm leavin' for Tulsa with Mr. Arthur. We gonna try findin' my brother, Elwyn. Mr. Arthur says he'll sign his release if'n we find him."

Ruby crossed her arms over her ample chest. "Hmmph," she said. "Better you should wait 'til tomorrow—better yet, day after. Let things cool down some." She leaned closer and lowered her voice. "Johnny heard tell it's real bad up there in Tulsa. Lots hurt. Lots dead."

"Mr. Arthur offered for today, so I'm goin' today. Elwyn can't get released without a white man signs for it," I told her.

"Well, I sees your mind's made up. I be prayin' for y'all." Ruby looked over at Mr. Arthur sittin' in the car, his fingers lightly drummin' on the steering wheel. "Don't you be lettin' go of your sense, just 'cause that man offer you a ride to Tulsa. He a white man like all the rest."

I knew what she meant. Mr. Arthur weren't like that. I'd never felt uneasy around him for a minute.

"I'll be fine. Just let Clem know."

"I will." She reached out and made the sign of the cross over my forehead.

Mr. Arthur made small talk on the drive into Tulsa. He was tryin' to make me feel better, but I's havin' a hard time keepin' up with it, the worry had such a hold of me.

"Your brother was working at the Stradford Hotel. That right?" he asked when we were getting close to the courthouse.

"Yessir, at the Stradford, workin' the desk. I don't rightly know if he was there last night, but prob'bly he was. Elwyn Johnson."

We parked across the street from the courthouse where armed white men were guarding the front doors and patrolling the grounds. A small crowd of white men stood milling around outside.

"Stay in the car. I'll see what I can find out." Mr. Arthur got out of the car, straightening his tie.

It's funny, he such a short man, but he have a certain swagger to him—not like he full of hisself, but like he know what's doin'.

One of the guards stepped out as soon as Mr. Arthur crossed the street, and they started talkin', Mr Arthur wavin' his hands like he do. I couldn't hear what they was sayin'. Pretty soon the guard went back, and Mr. Arthur started talkin' to some of the men in the crowd. The thing about Mr. Arthur is, he a big talker. He can talk to anybody like he know'd 'em all his life. Miss Gladys calls him Mr. Friendly.

He came back and got into the car. "They rounded people up and put 'em all over the damn place. There's a bunch from the Stradford over at the Brady Street Armory. We'll start looking there." He put the car in gear, and we started driving again.

I'd had enough of sittin' in the car. When we got to Brady Street, Mr. Arthur let me get out with him. The guards wouldn't let me go inside the armory building, so I stood a good ways off to one side of the door. Mr. Arthur, he went in alone.

The two white men at the door had their rifles at the ready. They were real tense, wound up tight. I could tell they didn't like me standin' outside with 'em. They kept a watchful eye, but they let me be. Probl'y cause I'se with a white man.

I could hear Mr. Arthur's big, deep voice calling out, "Elwyn. Elwyn Johnson. Your sister's here." Mr. Arthur was alone when he came back out, motionin' for me to follow him. He didn't say anything until we got to the car.

"Elwyn's not in there, but I talked to a couple of people who saw a man get shot in front of the hotel. They think it was him."

I felt myself freeze up inside. "Shot?"

"One of the men who worked at the hotel tried to make a run for it. He got shot down in the street."

I couldn't take it in. I leaned against the car, needin' some support to keep me on my feet.

"Most of the folks inside there," Mr. Arthur cocked his head toward the armory building, "are still in their pajamas or robes, rousted out of their rooms after they were in bed. The man who got shot was wearing a suit, like he was working." He put his hand on my shoulder. "A bellboy told me he heard the shot, saw him fall. He said it was Elwyn."

"Who'd do that?" My hands went up to cover my face, and I began sobbing. "Maybe he got took to a hospital. Maybe he just hurt."

I didn't want him to be dead. My mind told me one thing, and my heart told me to think somethin' else.

Mr. Arthur cleared his throat. "You get into the car," he said, opening the door for me. "I'll go over and see if those men know where the wounded were taken."

I sat in the car, feeling numb, my mind blank, while he went back across the street. With Greenwood gone, there wasn't a hospital in Tulsa that would treat Negroes.

We left the armory and drove to a park where a makeshift hospital tent left over from the war had been set up. Hundreds of Negroes were there, some wounded, some taking care of those who were.

People stood in a line outside the tent, waiting for a doctor. Others lay down or sat on the grass. Red Cross volunteers with armbands carried buckets of water and a ladle, giving out drinks and paper fans.

We walked around looking for Elwyn, asking people if they knew him or if they'd seen him.

No Elwyn.

"We've done what we can," Mr. Arthur said as we walked back to the car an hour later. "The only thing left is the morgue."

I felt weak, done in. Even my tears had dried up. "If'n you don't mind, I'd like to check it out before we go on home."

He swept his arm toward where Greenwood used to be. "Such a waste, this whole business. Now all these people, people who didn't do a thing wrong, have lost everything. Whether a person's black or white shouldn't matter, but it does. This world we live in—it can surely be cruel."

Worse than cruel.

Mr. Arthur went back to ask where the morgue was located. There was an empty place in my heart where Elwyn used to be. I knew he was dead.

Mr. Arthur came back and started the car. "No one seems to know where the bodies have been taken, but one man told me they're stacking them up at Oaklawn."

Oaklawn is over by Greenwood. As we drove past the entrance to the cemetery, we saw several men loading pine coffins onto a flatbed truck.

"Stay here. Let me see what I can find out," Mr. Arthur said.

He talked to one of the men for what seemed like a long time. A breeze came up, and it would have been welcome except for a strong odor of decay that came with it. When Mr. Arthur came back, he was holding his handkerchief up to his nose. He took it away when he got into the car and closed the door.

"There's over a hundred bodies stacked up further on in the cemetery. They're digging a trench, fixing to bury them all together in Potter's Field. They aren't letting anyone through." He wiped his neck with his handkerchief, then started the car. "I'm sorry, there isn't anything more we can do."

"I 'ppreciate you bringin' me."

My soul felt like lead, my body like wood. Only my tears were still working. I hung my head as the wet droplets fell, leaving dark purple splotches on my skirt. "Elwyn's gone. I can feel it."

He didn't say much during the ride back. There wasn't anything he could say to ease my sorrow and he knew it.

One thought kept runnin' through my mind, a thought I could never say out loud. If ever I find the man killed Elwyn, he won't live to see another day.

1922

Gladys

This baby can't come soon enough.

Arthur likes putting his hand on my belly to feel the baby kicking, but I must admit I was in hopes that three would be the end of it. God decided otherwise. The baby will be named after me if it's a girl, and after my father if it's a boy.

Francis has been here for three months, enjoying herself by making my life a misery. She prefers not be around the children since it's summer now. She stays in the back house or sits in the shade in the back yard in the afternoon, waiting for Arthur to get home so she can monopolize him for the evening.

The park is two blocks down the street. It has a large, shallow wading pool with a cement bottom in the middle of it, shaded by big oak trees. The playground is old, but the children love to swing and hang from the monkey bars.

We've hired Della's oldest daughter, Cora, to watch the children during the summer. She's thirteen, a tall, soft-spoken girl. She gets the children up and dressed, then takes them to the park after breakfast before it gets too hot. Today I'm going with them.

Bill is ready to play as soon as we get there.

"Let's play tag," he says.

"Hide-and-seek," says Doreen, and they're off to find hiding places.

I sit on a bench close to the water fountains, and Cora sits on another close by. Pretty soon the children come running up to get a drink.

"Look, here comes Amanda," says Kathy.

"And Amanda's cousin, Walter, from Kansas," says Doreen.

Kathy bumps Doreen with her shoulder, and Doreen bumps her back.

"You're sweet on him," Doreen teases.

I reach my hand out to stop Kathy from bumping Doreen a second time. "Y'all just have a good time while we're here."

The girls run to Cora, chattering away about Amanda and her cousin. Cora listens, then takes an orange out of the sack she brought. She peels it and gives them slices.

"Look, Mama," says Kathy. "Cora knows what we like."

"We love her," Doreen adds, taking another slice of orange.

"She's the best, all right." I wipe beads of perspiration from my forehead. The sun's getting higher in the sky, and my feet are beginning to swell.

"I'm going to walk on home now," I say.

"No, Mama, we want to stay," Kathy begs. "Please."

Cora says, "I can bring 'em home directly."

"All right. Y'all can stay with Cora and come home for lunch." I get awkwardly to my feet, walking home slowly. More of a waddle than a walk, I admit.

When they come running into the house, hot and thirsty, Cora gets glasses of water for each of them. Bill drinks his down in one long gulp, holding his glass out to her for more.

Smiling at the children, I say, "I'll watch them for a few minutes while you help Della with lunch. Y'all come into the living room. Tell me all about what you did after I left."

"Cora won't play with us," Kathy complains when we get to the living room. "She just sits on the bench and waits. Make her play with us, Mama."

I sit down in the upholstered armchair and put my feet up on the ottoman, the only comfortable place in the house for me these days.

"Yes, make her." Bill is jumping around. "Look, I'm a jumping bean."

"Cora can't play with you at the park, just like she couldn't sit on the bench with me. She has to sit on her own bench and drink from her own water fountain. The park's only for white people—except on Saturdays—then it's only for Colored."

"That's stupid," Doreen says. "Who made up that rule?"

"Stupid, stupid, stupid," Bill repeats.

Doreen has to be contrary no matter what. She says, "If that's true, where's the sign? There's no sign."

I count to ten, masking my irritation. "It's the law whether or not there's a sign. Cora can watch you, but she can't play with you at the park." As Arthur says, we live in a Jim Crow state and the children have to learn to be careful. "You don't want Cora to get in trouble, do you?"

"No, Mama." Kathy turns to her sister. "We like Cora, don't we, Doreen? You said you loved her when we were at the park."

Doreen looks sullen and doesn't answer.

Hoping to smooth things over, I say, "Cora can play with you while you're here at home. In the back yard, but not in the front yard, not when you're out in public."

"How about Cora takes us to the picture show?" Doreen asks, her expression brightening at the thought of going to a movie. "Robin Hood's playing."

"Robin Hood. Watch this." Bill jumps onto the first step of the stairs and off again, pretending to swish a sword through the air.

"Cora would have to sit in the balcony with the other Colored people. She wouldn't be able to see you from there, so no."

Doreen's face falls, and she purses her lips together. "Prissy Holter's got a white girl looking after her. She gets to go to the picture show 'most every week. Why can't you hire a white girl to look after us?"

"Lunch 'bout ready." Della's standing at the entrance of the living room.

"The children were just telling me how much we like Cora. I was telling them that I'm going to need her help with our new baby." I have an image of myself working endlessly to iron out wrinkles in a fabric woven out of strained relationships.

"Yes'm." Della turns to go back to the kitchen.

I watch her go, her shoulders slumped, her steps nearly as weary as mine. She hasn't been the same since her brother died.

"That's enough talk for now," I say, clapping my hands. "Kathy, go tell Grandma Francis that lunch is ready." Kathy makes a wry face, but she starts for the door without any backtalk. I point to Bill and Doreen. "You two go up and wash your hands and face. While you're at it, scrub the grass stain off those knees."

"It's rude to point, Mama," Doreen says.

I say a Hail Mary. Silently.

I left when August ushered in the first week of relentless heat—the dog days of summer. James Ray Lannery must have been waiting for her to leave because he was born two days later, a healthy boy with a loud cry.

The rest of the summer passed in a blur. We slept out on the screened sleeping porch where Jimmy woke everyone up at least twice a night. I'd pick Jimmy up and take him back to our bedroom to nurse him and rock him back to sleep.

A few nights I was so tired I fell asleep holding him, only to wake up later, dehydrated and drenched in sweat. Sometimes I'd wake up in the middle of the night to find Arthur's cot empty. I'd get up to find him standing at the crib watching Jimmy sleep.

School started after Labor Day. I don't have Cora to help me since she went back to school. Jimmy's an easy baby—good-natured, happy, with big, big smiles.

Arthur adores him. He walks Jimmy for hours when he's home.

"You're making it hard for the rest of us who have to get things done around here," I tease.

Arthur pinches Jimmy's fat cheek and grins. "You're a special one," he coos, bouncing Jimmy up and down.

Arthur gives his best imitation of a leer in my direction. "We have to get busy and have another one—maybe two—of these. Our Jimbo needs some brothers and sisters close to his own age."

"We'll see," I tell him.

The older children love their baby brother, too. I thought Bill might be jealous, but he's the one who pays the most attention to Jimmy, handing him rattles, talking to him, making up stories to tell him.

Kathy would rather read a book or play with her friends. "I don't want to be a mother when I grow up," she says, wrinkling her nose as she stands and watches me change a dirty diaper. "Too much smelly diapers."

"You'll change your mind when you're older," I tell her.

"Won't either," she says, holding her nose.

It's Saturday afternoon. Arthur went out to deliver some pipe and won't be home until supper, so I take Jimmy down to the back yard and spread a blanket on the ground for him in the shade of the oak tree.

"Give me those caps," I say, holding out my hand. "It's Jimmy's rest time."

Bill comes over to the blanket, and I remove the caps from the toy six shooter he got for his birthday. Jimmy's eyes start to get heavy.

I just want a half hour of quiet.

I sit on a lawn chair and open my new book, The Mysterious Affair at Styles. It's a mystery written by a woman author from Britain, Agatha Christie.

"Mama, I want to be the cowboy now. Tell Bill to be the Indian," Doreen whines, her face red from chasing Bill around the yard. She's wearing a feather headdress that Arthur brought home for them after one of his trips into western Oklahoma.

"You two work it out," I say, putting my finger up. "Shhh."

"Bill won't take turns." Doreen raises her voice even more. "Make him, Mama." She tugs on my arm, forcing me to close my book.

Now I've lost my place. I take a deep breath just as Jimmy's eyes spring open. He starts crying, and I brush Doreen's hand aside as she reaches out for Jimmy.

"You woke Jimmy up." I'm irritated. He won't go back to sleep now.

"I didn't do anything," she whines. "Billy won't take turns. I want to be the cowboy—

"Don't call me Billy," Bill yells.

"Billy, Billy, Billy." She makes a face at him.

My patience is at an end. "Go to your room. Right now. I don't want to hear it."

Bill's standing by the hedge at the edge of the lawn, looking smug that Doreen's getting in trouble. He thinks he's pulled a fast one on me.

"Your game is over, too, Bill," I tell him as I bend down to pick Jimmy up. "You should take turns with your sister. Now, grab this blanket and come inside"

The two of them follow me into the house, Bill dragging the corner of Jimmy's blanket behind him, Doreen pouting.

"You're going to trip on that lip of yours," I say. "Both of you go to your rooms and have some quiet time." Doreen pouts even more and stomps up the stairs two at a time, making as much noise as possible. She stops halfway up the staircase and turns to stick her tongue out at Bill, who's right behind her. She thinks I don't see her.

But I do.

I add it to the list.

May

I'm getting married tomorrow. I have a ring with three small diamonds, and a new blue suit, a hat to match, and new shoes. Emma's traveled here from Texas to be my Maid of Honor. She wanted us to be married in the Baptist church, but Henry wants a civil ceremony. His friend, George, is going to be his Best Man. We've arranged to have refreshments after.

I just want to get married. I don't care where or how.

Henry bought a house for us on North Sixteenth Street. It's dark red brick, has three bedrooms and a bath upstairs, and a large front porch with a pillar on each side. Not too big, but not too small.

He takes me to see it for the first time. He puts a key in the lock and opens the front door. "It's a good family home. We'll be happy here."

"Where's my house key?" I ask.

"You won't need one."

"I'll want to lock the door when I leave." I'm puzzled by his response.

"No need." He ushers me into the entry.

I'm not sure what he means—there's no need for me to leave, or there's no need to lock our doors—but I don't ask.

The entry is small, the only light coming from the three small windows across the top of the front door. The dining room is on the right, the living room on the left. There's a fireplace with built-in bookshelves on each side on the outer wall of the living room.

"Do you like it?"

"Yes, I do."

Henry wants me to like it. Being left out of the decision leaves me feeling unsettled. I push the feeling away before it ruins my mood.

I go to the red brick fireplace and run my hand over the walnut mantle, imagine it holding a vase and a wedding picture. "With some furniture, and a few touches here and there, it'll be nice."

"It's a lot for you to take care of." Henry gestures at the empty space. "I don't want you getting' any ideas about me hirin' help. I won't have any strangers comin' into my home and nosin' around."

"I can keep it up. It'd be good to have it cleaned before we move in, though."

The house isn't dirty, but it hasn't been lived in for a while. The floors need to be dusted and waxed, the windows washed, a few spider webs knocked down from the corners.

"I'll do that myself. Make a list, and I'll get it done before we move in. I'll take care of mowin' the yard, too."

We go into the kitchen. It's located at the back of the house, an average size. There's one small window over the sink.

"It's big enough for a breakfast table. The stove is fairly new," I say, looking in the oven. I straighten up and wave across the room. "That's just a cooler." It won't be easy to keep food fresh with only a cooler. "We could use a Frigidaire."

He frowns, leaning against the door jamb. "We're gonna have to make do with what we have. At least for a while. First off, we need a bed and some living room furniture."

I'm not willing to give up so easily. "I'll have to walk to the grocery every day without a Frigidaire, or you'll have to stop on your way home from work."

"You make a list, and I'll pick up what we need."

"How about we order delivery of milk and butter from Hiland Dairy?" I ask. "That way it'll be fresh."

"If it's a reasonable price."

That's as good as a yes, so I keep going.

I put my hands out like I'm holding a steering wheel. "I've always wanted to learn to drive. One of these days, we'll need to get a car. I could drive you to work, pick you up after, and get the shopping done myself."

He picks me up and swings me around, lifting me off the ground like I'm a child. "You have me to do the drivin' for you."

"Put me down," I squeal, throwing my arms around his neck.

He puts me down, but not before he kisses me. "We'll get a car when I say so. Don't go gettin' any ideas about drivin'. I'll be the one doing the thinkin' and the drivin' for both of us."

I remember what he'd told me about his first wife and realize he doesn't want me to learn to drive. He wants to know where I am—at home, waiting for him to take me places. That could get old.

Maybe he'll change his mind after we're married.

Isn't that what married people do? Try to make each other happy?

Arthur

Only three weeks ago I was on top of the world. Three weeks ago, I was riding the train back home from Washington, D.C. I'd been in high spirits then. I thought I had it made.

The Okmulgee Daily Democrat had a picture and article about our trip on the front page the day before we left. There's a lot of drilling going on in our area, a lot of pride in how Okmulgee is growing.

"Look." I'd spread the newspaper out to show Gladys. "There's a picture of our group." I was standing in the front row, listed as one of the men chosen to represent oil interests in Okmulgee. "Politics is everything. The whole country's going to prosper when people in charge want to listen to men in business."

"Surely politics isn't everything," she said. "There's faith."

"After faith," I said, humoring her.

She isn't Irish. Irish cut their teeth on tales proving that all the important events in history are about who's in power—politics. It makes the difference between liberty and oppression, justice and inequity, even life and death.

Our group traveled in two special train cars. The railroad made sure we got the royal treatment all the way there and back. We held spirited discussions about the future of the oil business, the state of Oklahoma, and the politics of the country. We're an optimistic bunch of men selected by the Governor to represent Oklahoma. I was proud to be one of them.

"This was a great day, a terrific day for all of us and the oil business," I told the other men in the club car as the train left the station to take us back home. Our delegation of thirty businessmen talked in person that morning to Herbert Hoover, the Secretary of Commerce. "Hoover knows oil and gas are the future of America. We're going to increase production and surpass all other energy combined by the end of the decade."

"To Oklahoma," Barnaby Lewis said, raising a glass of beer.

We all raised our glasses and cheered. "To Oklahoma."

All was well when I got home. Gladys always manages to keep the household running, even with three lively children and a baby. Everyone was happy to see me, and I just couldn't get enough of little Jimmy.

"Dada, Dada" he screamed when he saw me, holding out both his chubby arms. I picked him up and swung him high. He squealed with joy. I'll never forget that moment.

I brought little gifts: a china replica of the White House for Kathy, a necklace with a cherry blossom pressed between tiny glass plates for Doreen, and a framed picture of the Capital building for Bill. I gave a wooden trolley car to Jimmy, painted green and black, which he promptly put in his mouth.

"We're so happy you're home," Gladys said, taking Jimmy from my arms. "We always miss you so."

"Oh, but you should have been there. It's grand. Our nation's capital is really something. I wish you could see it."

"Perhaps we can plan a visit for all of us when Jimmy's older. You could show us the sights."

Two nights later, our world turned upside down.

"Wake up." Gladys put her hand on my shoulder and gave me a shake. "You have to call the doctor. He's burning up."

She was holding Jimmy, and he was coughing and struggling to breathe, his head resting on her shoulder.

"What's wrong?" Doreen asked. She looked like a wraith standing in the hall way in her white nightgown.

"Jimmy's sick. Go back to bed," Gladys told her. For once, Doreen did what she was told.

I put my dressing gown on, called the doctor, got dressed, and went outside to wait.

"Arthur, come quick." Gladys sounded frantic.

I ran back upstairs. Jimmy was in his crib convulsing, then he lay still, not breathing. I tried to revive him by rubbing his arms and legs. I started giving him the breath of life. There was no response from his limp body. He was gone.

I ran to open the bedroom window to set his spirit on its way to heaven while Gladys sat on the bed in shock.

The doctor arrived ten minutes later.

"Diphtheria," he said, putting his stethoscope away after he had examined Jimmy. "The fever and convulsions stopped his heart." He put his hand on my shoulder. "I'm so sorry. There's nothing you could have done. It happens sometimes."

It happens sometimes.

A terrible answer. No answer at all.

My mind doesn't stop. It won't quiet down, it keeps asking why. Why Jimmy? Why now? Why us?

I keep asking myself if the wooden trolley car I brought him from Washington might have been infected, or if the other children gave the disease to him. They all played with the trolley car. None of them are sick. A part of me understands that even if someone gave me an answer, I couldn't accept it.

My heart is broken now, missing him, missing a part of me. I can't face another day without him.

Gladys sits on the bed beside me, rubbing my back. "Arthur, please get up and get dressed. Your business needs you, and you need to get back into a routine. We need you."

I hear her praying for me, she begs me to say the rosary. I can't. Father O'Reilly came yesterday, but I've lost my way, lost my faith. His words held no comfort.

God has forsaken me.

It's my mother, Francis, who came for the funeral and hasn't returned home yet, who finally comes in and drags me out of bed.

"Arthur Hugh Lannery. Get up this instant." I hear her voice as I lay motionless on the bed. "Enough of this. You'll have a breakdown if you keep it up."

She grabs onto my arm and yanks it hard. I don't move. The weight of grief on my heart feels so heavy I may never get out of bed again.

"Della," I hear Mother yelling down the stairs. "Bring a bucket."

The next thing I know I'm doused with cold water. The shock breaks something loose in me, and the force of my anger drives me to my feet, wet and shaking, my legs unsteady and weak from several days of not eating. "Get the hell out of here."

Mother is unphased. "Get dressed." She's hanging a shirt and a pair of pants on the door of the chifforobe. "And no nonsense. I'll be back if you aren't down in five minutes flat."

I'm wishing the funeral had been mine as I button my shirt.

1926

Henry

I can't do nothin' to make her happy.

May promised me that having her father come and live with us would make her happy. Louis was only in his fifties, but he'd had a hard life. His second wife left him for a younger man, took the kids with her when she went. Then they all died in a house fire while her new husband was drinkin' himself silly down at the Tracks Saloon.

He wasn't the same man after he found that out. He couldn't work, so he swallowed his pride and asked May if he could live with us.

May was excited about it. "He wasn't much of a father to me when I was growing up. Maybe we can make up for lost time."

In spite of his failings as a father, he turned out to be a good grandfather. The one joy in his life was our baby, Anna. He loved holdin' her, walkin' her around.

"I'm taking this baby girl for ice cream," he'd say. He'd carry Anna the five blocks to the ice cream parlor where he'd buy her a one-scoop bowl. He'd sit with her on his lap, feed her with a spoon while she held her rosebud mouth open, eager for the next taste.

"Strawberry's your favorite," he'd tell her. "We've tried all the flavors, haven't we, baby doll?"

When she was old enough to walk, Anna would follow Louis around the house wherever he went. He died in the spring when May was pregnant with the boy. May hasn't been the same since that day, like some part of her got broken that can't be fixed.

She whines and complains like nobody but her ever had a baby. I'm gettin' so I can't stand the sight of her. She wants more help, she needs me at home, why do I have to go to another meetin'. The naggin' never ends.

"Having Dwayne split me wide open," she says, refusing to get out of bed. "It hurts so bad. I'm so tired. I can't move." She groans and closes her eyes.

I send for Dr. Linda Wilson, though I don't like her much. May used to work in her office and she insists on going to Dr. Linda, the only woman doctor in town. Women doctors—don't know what the world's comin' to.

The doctor made things even worse. Just like I knew she would. I stood in the back of the bedroom, refusing to leave during the examination.

"It's a heart problem," Dr. Linda told us, putting her stethoscope back in her bag. "One of the valves isn't working right. Having two babies so close together made it worse. That's why you're so tired."

I'm not likin' this. I called the doctor to encourage May to get up and get goin', not give her more excuses to lay in bed. Anna's not quite two years old, still in diapers, into everything.

"She has two babies to take care of," I say. "I have work to go to."

Dr. Linda doesn't miss a beat as she responds, "You'll need to hire someone to come in, Mr. Gray—a wet nurse and someone who can help with the housework and the baby. May isn't going to have her strength back for quite some time."

I follow her out into the hallway and shut the bedroom door so May can't hear us. "Will May get better?"

"May's condition may get worse if she doesn't have the rest she needs to recover. I can give you the name of a wet nurse."

"Colored?"

"Yes, Colored."

Her face is impassive. She's a bold one. She knows who I am, what I stand for.

"No, ma'am. I won't have any Colored nursin' my son."

"Suit yourself. You'll need more bottles. Boil the milk before you give it to the baby, and make sure it's only lukewarm before feeding." She stops at the front door to give me a stern look as I show her out. "The birth was hard on May. Call me right away if she has a fever. Childbed fever can be fatal."

No one seems to understand that I'm the one who's alone here. I'm the one who needs help.

My mother died last year, worn out from a lifetime of takin' care of missionaries and kids, just as Letty, my youngest sister, finished eighth grade. Mary and Bill work at the cotton mill, Carl's gone who knows where. Don't expect I'll ever see him again. Pansy married a man in the army corps and went to live in Milwaukee with his family. Bill will be gone once Letty graduates, but for now he and Mary will take care of her until she's out of school. They can't leave Denver to come to Muskogee and help me out.

There's no one for me to turn to.
I'm stuck with a sick wife, a two-year old, and a newborn.
Whoop-de-damn-do.

Gladys

This time I didn't take any chances.

I went to the hospital instead of having my usual home birth because the baby we had after Jimmy died was stillborn. We named her Mary. She has a nice little stone in the cemetery beside Jimmy with just her name on it.

Our new baby daughter was born a week ago, and we named her Joy. She's perfect.

Arthur seemed determined to have another baby after Jimmy died, even though we both understand there isn't a replacement for him and never will be. Arthur insisted on getting rid of Jimmy's crib. We bought a bassinette before Mary was born that's never been used. It will be Joy's now.

My intuition tells me that Joy will be our last child. I was afraid Arthur wouldn't be able to love her after all the grief we've been through, but he's just as taken with her as he was with Jimmy. He's been passing out cigars all over town.

It eases my heart to see him so happy again.

"Joy looks like me, doesn't she, Mama?" asks Doreen, leaning over the bassinette and fingering the lace on the edge of the baby blanket.

"The two of you could be twins. She has our dark hair."

Doreen looks pleased. Today she's in a good mood, all too rare these past months.

"What's Kathy doing?" I ask.

"She's listening to the radio in the living room. She wants to listen for her favorite song, Baby Face." Doreen hums the chorus of the song softly as she watches Joy.

I silently thank Arthur for finding something to occupy Kathy while I try to rest. I wish Doreen would find somewhere else to be, but I don't want to upset her by suggesting that she leave.

Bill runs in and buffs Doreen on the arm. "C'mon, let's go outside and play ball."

"I want to stay here. Mama says Joy and I could be twins, we look so much alike."

"Aw, she's okay, but babies are boring." He looks into the bassinette for a brief moment. "C'mon," he pleads. "It's nice out. Let's play ball." He starts for the door.

"Go ahead. I'll have Della call you when Joy wakes up. I'll let you give her a bottle," I tell Doreen.

"Okay." Doreen is halfway to the door when she turns around, frowning, and says, "Don't forget."

"I won't. I promise." I close my eyes, grateful to have a few minutes of quiet. Joy's going to grow up surrounded by love and affection. She'll never be alone.

A letter came from my father, written on a piece of cheap note paper. His handwriting was hard to read, barely more than a wiggly scrawl. He must have been having tremors when he wrote it.

Dear Gladys,
I hope this finds you well. I'm living in New York. I have a room in a boarding house. My health is so bad I'm not able to work. If you can spare some money for your poor old father, I would appreciate it. Don't tell Ella. She wouldn't understand.
Love, Father

Arthur and I talked about it. He's always so generous about helping family, even though I'm reluctant to support my father. I'll tell Mother about it once the deed is done. I know she thinks it's a waste to give him anything.

We're sending money for his room and board to the woman running the boarding house. Any money we send to him directly will go to the nearest tavern.

Dear Father,
I was surprised to hear from you after such a long time. I'm sorry to hear you aren't feeling well. You might consider getting help for your drinking. Even at this late date it might do you some good. I'm sending money to the boarding house to give you a few more months in your room. Please take better care of yourself,

Your loving daughter,
Gladys

My father didn't write again. His landlady called me to tell me he had died. There was no money for his funeral. Arthur and I made arrangements for a simple casket and burial with the funeral home she recommended. It was a sad end for the once-promising life he destroyed drink by drink.

He was born with a silver spoon in his mouth. He ended up with nothing but ashes.

1933

Arthur

I waited until this evening to tell Gladys just how bad things are.

"You look lovely tonight," I tell her. "Is that a new dress?"

"Thank you. I bought this the other day at the sale at Bloom's. They're going out of business."

Like so many other businesses. Including mine.

"We need to have a talk." I put my Coke down on the table between us.

We were settled into our chairs in the living room after supper, having a Coca Cola nightcap. Kathy was out on a date, Bill and Doreen went to see a movie, and Joy was asleep.

"What's bothering you? Is it that young man Kathy's dating? I know he's a little wild—."

Walter's father was a Methodist minister, strict and rigid in his beliefs. It appeared that Walter Jr. was doing everything in his power to practice the opposite of what his father preached.

"No, not that. I'll just come out and say it. The business is going under. Oil dropped to twenty-two cents a barrel yesterday, and it'll go lower. We overproduced in Oklahoma, then East Texas struck oil. The market's glutted." I get up from my chair and start to pace. "No one's drilling any more wells."

"Can't you sell supplies for water wells like you did before?"

"There's no money. The depression is taking us all down." I'm unable to contain my anxiety any longer. I blurt out, "I'm going to lose the business. We're going to have to sell the house."

She looks shocked. "It's that bad?"

"I hate telling you this. I don't know if anyone will even have the money to buy the house when we put it up for sale." My stomach tightens. I'm not going to sleep well tonight. "We're on the brink of losing everything—everything we've worked for."

Gladys is silent for a few moments. She says, "We can go to Mother's if it comes to that."

I know that's not going to be a solution. "Ella may need to live with us before this is over. She's worried, too. She lost two boarders last week. Two more, and she won't have anyone left."

Gladys always wants to see the best in things. It's a good quality, but I'm a realist. I know that the next few years are going to bring a big change. It won't be for the better. We aren't in as bad a fix as the farmers who are fleeing with all their goods stuffed in the beds of their pickup trucks, but it's bad enough.

I look her square in the eyes. "It's bad, very bad, and it's going to get worse. The bank in Norman failed yesterday. Others will follow." I sit down again. "I've been asked to take a job in Muskogee with the Works Progress Administration."

"The WPA? Is our situation really that bad?" Going to work for the WPA was taking charity, an admission of financial ruin and defeat.

"Our savings are nearly gone. I can't keep a roof over our heads much longer without any money coming in. The governor has been contacting a few men to take administrative positions in the WPA. It won't be what we're used to, but it pays enough for us to live on."

"Enough to keep Bill in college?"

"Maybe we can tighten our belts enough to help him through this next year until he graduates. I don't know."

Gladys goes to the window overlooking our front yard where she stands looking out. "What will you be doing in Muskogee? Do we really have to move?"

"I'd be managing supplies for construction of public buildings and improving the roads and sidewalks—a desk job. Muskogee is where the administrative offices are for that program."

Gladys doesn't speak for a minute. "If this is what you think is best, then we'll do it."

"I'll let the governor know tomorrow."

"When—?" her voice trails off.

"He wants me there in two weeks, as soon as I can get the business closed down. You can get the house ready to sell."

"I'll have to let Della know right away. I worry about her finding another job." She comes back to the sofa and picks up her Coke before sitting down.

"We won't be able to afford help," I warn. "We're going to have to economize."

I don't want her to know yet just how much we'll have to give up. We've gotten used to having luxuries the past several years. We've had Della and Clem to do the heavy work, Cora to help with the children during the summer months. I took the family to Colorado for a tour of the Rocky Mountains for our summer vacation two years ago. Usually, we spend two weeks out of every summer at a nearby lake resort with some of our friends. We won't be able to afford any of those things now.

I'm fifty years old. I might be too old to start another business and make a go of it by the time the depression ends.

"I can manage." Gladys pats my hand. "You've worked so hard to provide a good life for us. I know we'll get through this. You find us a small house in Muskogee. It's only another five weeks until Doreen's graduation, so I want to stay here until then."

"Della can stay long enough to help you get things packed up."

Kathy comes running into the living room, her boyfriend Walter right behind her. "Look," she squeals, waving her left hand in front of us. "Walter asked me to marry him, and I said yes." A diamond ring sparkled on her ring finger. "There's a pretty wedding band to go with it. Walter got just the ring I wanted. Isn't it beautiful?"

Walter's a good-looking young man, a sharp dresser. Gladys and I think he's too stuck on himself, always combing his hair with his pocket comb. Vain.

His job at Montgomery Ward depends mostly on commissions. He's born to be a salesman. He could sell shoes to a shoemaker, he's that charming. I should know—I have a bit of the blarney myself.

"With your permission, Mr. Lannery, I'd like to marry Kathy," Walter says, smiling. "I have a good sales job at Montgomery Ward. I can take care of her."

"I have my job at the warehouse," Kathy adds. "Until we have kids, of course." She turns her head to gaze into Walter's eyes. "I want a dozen."

Kathy finished a short training program to be a bookkeeper after she graduated from high school. We want all our girls to be trained to do some kind of work, to have something to fall back on. You never know what life's going to throw at you.

Gladys and I look at each other.

"You know we're Catholic," I say, stepping up to the duty of talking about religion. "We don't expect you to become Catholic, Walter, but we do want you to baptize your children as Catholics and raise them in the Catholic church."

Kathy says, "Don't say I didn't warn you."

She sits on the sofa beside her mother and pats the empty cushion on the other side of her.

"Okay by me," Walter says, plopping down beside Kathy. "Kathy told me you'd want that. My father soured me on the Protestants anyway." He takes Kathy's hand and squeezes it.

"Will it be a problem for your parents?" Gladys asks.

"Don't worry about them." Walter frowns, letting go of Kathy's hand and putting his arm around her to pull her in close. "They'll have to get used to the idea."

"We're going to the courthouse tomorrow to get the license. No big wedding for us. We don't want to wait," Kathy says. "I'm moving into Walter's apartment right after the ceremony."

So much the better.

Gladys and I had a small formal wedding, only forty people. Our ceremony was at St. Francis, performed by the priest. Gladys wore her sister Kathryn's long wedding dress with the ten-foot train. I wore my tuxedo. Ella had tables set up in her big dining room with white tablecloths, fresh flowers, and real silver dinnerware. I paid for all of it, plus the catered meal. It had been a considerable expense even back then.

We can't afford to do any of that for Kathy. Walter can't either. People aren't having many big to-do's in these times.

"I'll tell Della to bake a nice cake, and you can come here," Gladys offers. "I can check with Father, he might be able—"

"No," Kathy interrupts. "Just a civil ceremony. You'll come, though, won't you?"

"Of course," I say. "We'll all be there."

Ahuh, ahuh, ahuh! Ahuh, ahuh. We hear coughing sounds coming from upstairs. Gladys is already on her feet. "Excuse me. It sounds like Joy needs help."

Joy's been sick for the past year since she had her tonsils out.

The doctor says she has asthma, that the removal of her tonsils probably caused it."That happens sometimes when the immune system doesn't have the tonsils catching all the irritants. We tried to solve one problem, but another one cropped up," he told us.

I'd heard those words before from doctors—it happens sometimes. Doctors. I don't trust 'em any more than I can fly. They use that excuse for every damn thing that goes wrong.

Joy coughs the worst at night. We have to make a tent over the bathtub and run the hot water. Steam can help her breathe if she has a really bad spell.

"I'll be going," Walter says, standing up. He and Kathy go to the door, where Walter takes Kathy in his arms and kisses her in a way that makes me feel uncomfortable. After all, I'm her father. I'm sitting right here.

"I'm going up," Kathy says as soon as she waves Walter goodbye. "I'll see if Mama needs some help."

I hear water running in the upstairs bathroom. Joy is still coughing.

Bill and Doreen come in, laughing and talking. She and Bill have always been close. He takes her out with him whenever he comes home from college.

"Daddy, you should take Mother to see King Kong," Doreen says, sitting beside me on the arm of my chair. "It's a real adventure."

"It's wild all right. Best picture of the year. Fay Wray is a bombshell." Bill makes a curvy motion with his hands.

Kathy hears them and comes running down the stairs to tell them her news. "Look." She holds out her left hand to show off her ring. "I'm getting married."

Doreen oohs and aahs over the ring. Bill grabs Kathy and waltzes her around the living room, singing Let's All Sing Like the Birdies Sing.

"Married, huh?" he teases when he stops singing. "Who's the unlucky man?"

"Walter, of course." Kathy answers, pulling away and laughing. "You're both invited to the courthouse to witness the ceremony three days from now." She pretends to look at her watch. "Thursday. Cake afterward, compliments of Della."

"I'll give you something borrowed," Doreen offers. "Maybe my new hat?"

"Maybe," Kathy replies. "Come up later and help me pick out what to wear. I'm thinking my blue suit with a corsage of white baby roses."

"I'll kiss the bride." Bill makes kissing noises. "Hey, I'm hungry. Fix us some sandwiches, Dorie."

"Come and help." Doreen grabs his hand and pulls him toward the kitchen. "Want one, Daddy?"

"I don't need it." I say, patting my substantial waistline.

"Ice cream, then?" she asks, knowing I have a weakness for it.

"No, I'm going up to bed."

I leave them as they're on their way into the kitchen, thinking I'll let them enjoy a few more days of being carefree. News about our troubles and the move to Muskogee can wait.

Doreen

I have to get out of here before they sell the house.

I'm going to enroll in the St. Francis nursing school in Tulsa as soon as I graduate. Mary Jean Parmenter is enrolling, too. She isn't a close friend of mine, but at least she's someone I know. Maybe we can be roommates. All the nursing students have to live in the dormitory.

I'm going to make lots of friends. And make all my own decisions without Mama looking over my shoulder. I'll feel much better then.

I feel so depressed and nervous. Once I get away from Mama, I'll be fine. She's never liked me, never treated me like the others. Daddy loves me—he calls me his dark angel—but he still goes along with Mama whenever she's mad at me.

Bill's the only person in this family who truly loves me. He stands by me no matter what.

I can't wait to graduate. I want to go to nursing school, and wear a white uniform with a cute nurses' cap. I'll marry a handsome man who adores me, has a good job, and likes to dance.

I'm not moving to Muskogee. No way, no how.

May

I smell the scent of the other woman on Henry's clothes when he comes home from going to meetings. Meetings, my foot.

There was a red lipstick smear on the front of his shirt last night. I never wear red.

"What's this?" I asked, holding up the shirt he'd been wearing.

"What's what?"

"This's is someone else's lipstick."

He looked away. "It's nothin'," he said, buttoning his pajama top.

"Nothing good, that's for sure." I threw the shirt on the floor. "Who is she? Tell me."

"Don't make a big deal out of this, May. Let it go."

That's his answer for everything. Don't make a big deal. Let it go. Forget it. He wants me to move along like nothing happened. Like I'm blind and stupid.

I've tried doing that. It doesn't work. I feel resentment building up until I'm exploding with a thousand things. I let go then take back, forget then remember, move forward until it happens again. It's no way to live.

I'd already had a run-in earlier in the day with some men who were working on the sewer line. I'd sent Dwayne outside to play, and when I checked on him, he was standing at the edge of the ditch the men were digging.

"Look, Mama," he said, pointing to the ditch. "They're putting in new pipe."

A little while later, here comes Dwayne, carrying a thin stick about a foot long. Five baby snakes, black with green stripes, were draped over the stick. Sally Miller yelled as soon as she saw the snakes, startling Dwayne. He dropped the stick, and snakes went slithering in all directions.

What a commotion. Eight ladies shrieking, some jumping onto their chairs or running outside, others making for the kitchen. Dwayne knew he was in trouble. He headed out the front door. We could hear the men outside, laughing their heads off.

Needless to say, our card game was over.

"You gather up every one of those snakes," I told Dwayne, holding him by the arm and bringing him back in the house. "Take them outside and kill them."

Anna was standing outside looking through the screen door to see what was going on with the ladies. "I'll get the shovel and we can chop their heads off," she told Dwayne, taking his hand. "You get a shoebox to put 'em in after we catch 'em."

"I'm sorry," I said to my friends as they were leaving. "I'll see you next week."

Cynthia Riggs stopped before she went out the door to say, "You better do something about that boy. He's a terror."

Dwayne isn't a terror. He's quiet for a boy his age, a little bit shy, smart in school. He remembers everything. He just needs some attention from his father.

Henry doesn't spend much time with him. Any time Dwayne spends with Henry is on Henry's terms—being seen and not heard, going hunting, or going to the lake to fish with George.

Henry spends Saturdays on the golf course. He tried to take Dwayne golfing, but had to bring him home when Dwayne had an asthma attack. After that, Henry acted like he was disappointed in him, and Dwayne felt it.

The swimming incident was my fault for suggesting it to Henry. I thought it would be something Dwayne could do that wouldn't give him asthma.

"He can't go to a public pool," Henry said. "Not with the polio the way it is. I could take him out to Tenkiller, teach him myself."

Henry took Dwayne out to the lake. He and George had a few drinks before they got around the boy. The three of them got in George's boat and went out to where the water was deep.

"Just throw him in. He'll either swim or drown." That's what George said right before Henry threw Dwayne into the water with no instruction at all.

He nearly did drown. By the time Henry dragged him out, he'd gone under several times. Dwayne told me what happened after I woke him up from a nightmare.

"I never want to go to the lake again, Mama" he said, throwing his arms around my neck. "Don't let me drown."

Henry will make him go if he thinks Dwayne is scared of the water. Henry can be mean that way. The only one he's nice to is Anna.

"You don't have to go to the lake with your daddy. I'll tell him I need you here." I bent down and whispered in his ear, "Now that's our little secret. No need for your daddy to know anything about it." He nodded and went back to sleep.

I'd been really angry with Dwayne about the snakes.

"You get out there and cut me a switch," I told him, pointing at the door. Weekly card club was my only recreation, those women were my only friends.

"The men outside told me to," Dwayne whined.

"This'll teach you not to listen to nonsense from every Tom, Dick, and Harry. Now git. Anna, you get a switch, too. You knew what was going on and didn't tell me."

Anna came in with a few thin switches.

"Ow, that hurts," she cried as I switched her legs.

Dwayne came in carrying a thick tree branch as big around as my arm that was so long and heavy, he could barely carry it.

"Oh, my Lord," I said, and then broke down laughing so hard that I didn't switch his legs at all, just sent him to his room without supper.

Anna might've sneaked something up to him later, I don't know. I went to bed with one of my sick headaches.

I didn't bother to tell Henry about what happened with the snakes.

He got the surprise of his life when he got up the next morning. "Aaaah. What the hell." He threw his slipper against the wall and a snake flew out, slithering quickly under the bed.

I put my hands over my mouth, but I couldn't help shaking with laugher. The kids came running in to see what was going on, and we all three started laughing our heads off. Henry just stood there.

"Nothing funny about findin' a snake in your shoe," he grumbled, bending down to look under the bed. "Get on the other side, Dwayne, and scoot under so I can catch it if it comes my way." Dwayne scooted under, but the snake was too fast and too small. It went behind the dresser.

We vacated the room, except for Henry, who was finally able to trap the snake under an empty shoe box he got out of his closet. He took the snake outside and killed it.

We ate breakfast like it was a normal morning, only occasionally breaking into giggles. When Henry entered the room, he sat down in front of his bowl of cereal and plate of toast, saying, "I don't see how that snake got in the house. You two kids know anythin' about that?"

"No, Daddy," Anna said.

"No, Daddy," Dwayne said.

"All that work on the sewer line must've stirred up a nest," I said. "Maybe you need to go under the house and check to see if there are any openings."

Henry grunted and started to eat. "I'll look into it this weekend. God, I hate goin' under the house."Anna

"He's pullin' us over," I heard Daddy say to Sam. "Act natural."

Daddy turned around to look at us as soon as he stopped the car. "Don't you kids say a word. Put that blanket over you. Close your eyes and pretend to be asleep."

Sam Butler was the man riding in the front seat with Daddy. They work together. They make us go with them when they want to buy whiskey over in Missouri. Daddy says they have to go over the state line because Oklahoma's dry.

I'm not sure what that means, but they sure come home with a lot of whiskey. They put cases of it on the floor of the back seat. We rest our feet on them, and carry a blanket to cover it up in case we get stopped.

Mama doesn't like us going, "You and Sam have no business drinking in the car when the kids are with you."

"We don't have nothin' to drink 'til we're back home. The kids'll be fine They have to go." Daddy reached out to tousle Dwayne's hair. "They're the reason we won't get caught if we're stopped."

The cop who came up to the window asked to see Daddy's driver's license. I could hear the rustle of cloth as Daddy got his wallet out of his pocket. The cop shined his flashlight through the window into the back seat where Dwayne and I pretended we were sleeping.

The cop turned his flashlight off. "Where you goin', Mr. Gray?" he asked.

"Just takin' the kids back home from visitin' their grandma," he answered.

"Can I take a look in your trunk?"

"Sure, go ahead."

I opened my eyes as Daddy got out of the car. I could hear his steps as he went around to the back and opened the trunk.

"All right, you can be on your way. Have a nice evening."

We heard the trunk snap closed. Once we were on the road again, I sat up and leaned over the front seat.

"Why'd that cop stop us?" I asked.

"Never you mind about that."

Dwayne piped up. "They was lookin' for hootch. Right, Daddy?"

Sam gave a little snort, like he was trying not to laugh.

"Just forget this ever happened. I don't want you tellin' your Mama anythin' about it, y'hear?" Daddy sounded serious. "Close your eyes and go to sleep for real."

We heard. We knew when not to ask questions, when to forget things like they never happened. Like we never talk about how much Daddy drinks. He drinks a lot. I've never seen him drunk except one time. And we never talk about how he talks mean to Mama, even though it hurts our hearts to hear it.

We love our Mama. She's good to us, but she doesn't go many places, just to church on Sunday. Daddy won't go to church with us. He says he had enough of that nonsense growing up.

"I'm not strong like you are," Mama tells me. "I have a weak heart. It runs in my family, but you don't need to worry. The doctor says your heart is perfectly fine."

I rub Mama's legs most every day when I come home from school. I don't mind. Her legs hurt her, especially on days when she's been on her feet more than usual, like when she has her card club.

If she has a headache, she has to lie down in her bedroom with the curtains closed. Sometimes the pain is so bad, she throws up. Daddy gives her a shot when it gets that bad.

Daddy showed me how to give Mama a shot the other afternoon when Mama was having one of her bad headaches. He keeps morphine and a syringe in his bedside table.

"Come with me. Now that you're ten, I want to show you how to do this for your mama," he said. He motioned for me to follow him into the bedroom, where she was sitting on the side of the bed. He took the leather case and the vial of morphine out of the drawer. He took the needle and the syringe out of the case, flushed them with alcohol.

"See, you put these together." He showed me how to screw the needle onto the syringe. "Push the plunger down, put it in the top of the vial, and draw the medicine up to this line here." He demonstrated, then pointed to the line on the syringe with a number one beside it. He got a cotton ball and put alcohol on it.

"Take your mama's arm, wipe it with the alcohol, draw up a little bitty bit of blood to be sure there isn't an air bubble, then give her the shot." He watched me as I did it to be sure I could remember all the steps.

"Don't you think she's too young for this?" Mama asked him as she lay back, putting her head on the pillow and closing her eyes.

"I'm not always here when you need a shot," he answered.

That's for sure. He's gone most evenings and sometimes on the weekends. He has union meetings, he's a Mason, and he has other meetings, too. When he's in a good mood, he jokes around with us. I wish he was home more—except when he's making Mama cry. When he's like that I'd just as soon he stayed gone.

He patted me on the head. "Anna's a smart girl. She can do it."

"I can give you the shot, Mama. It doesn't bother me. I pretend I'm a real nurse." I felt proud that Daddy thinks I'm so capable.

"That's right, baby." Daddy showed me how to rinse the needle and syringe again and put them back in the case all clean for the next time. It was easy.

He closed the case, putting it, along with the vial, back in the drawer. "Now, you need to tell me if we're runnin' out of medicine. I'll get more from the drugstore when it starts to get low."

"I will, Daddy."

After she's had a shot, Mama stays in the twilight sleep for several hours. She doesn't seem to mind.

I don't blame her.

Daddy isn't very sweet to her. He treats Dwayne better than he treats our mama, but he's the sweetest to me. I guess you'd say I'm a daddy's girl.

1937

Henry

It's an early July mornin', already hot. There's been record heat this summer with no end in sight.

I'm gettin' dressed to go to work when I hear a knock on the door. Two policemen I know are standin' there, Brett Stills and Jordie Myer.

"Mr. Gray," says Brett. "Mind if we come in?"

"What's this about?" I ask. I know both these men from the meetin's I attend, but I don't like people comin' to my house. May isn't even dressed yet.

"Do you have a son, Dwayne, who delivers the Daily News?" Jordie asks.

"I do," I say.

May comes out from the kitchen where she's fixin' breakfast, still in her robe, wipin' her hands on a dishtowel. "What's wrong?" she asks.

"I'm sorry to tell you that Dwayne was hit and run over by a milk truck while he was delivering papers."

May leans against the wall, holding her hands over her chest, the towel dropping to the floor. "Oh, my God! Is he dead?"

"No, ma'am. He's at the hospital. We can take you over there."

"I'll take my own car," I say, turning to look at May. "Get dressed."

"Oh, my poor baby," May moans.

I reach out to take her arm, afraid she might be going to faint. She pulls away and starts running for the stairs, saying. "Don't leave without me."

Once she's gone, I ask, "How bad is it?"

"Don't rightly know. Both legs are broken. I don't think the driver of the truck saw him until it was too late," Jordie says, shuffling his feet.

"Was the driver Colored?"

"Yessir, he was."

Jordie looks uncomfortable. He knows where this is going.

"I want his name." I open the door wider. "C'mon inside, I want to write it down."

They come inside, carefully wiping their feet on the mat. We go to the living room and they sit on the edge of the sofa while I look for a pencil. I find one that May left on a table beside the chair where she likes to do crossword puzzles.

"What's his name?"

"Well, now—Mr. Gray, we don't want any trouble." Brett looks down at his feet. "That driver, he's a family man. He's been workin' for the dairy for a long time. It was just an accident, same as anybody could have in the early mornin'. It was still half dark. Hard to see a boy on a bicycle."

"I respect that. I don't aim to make any trouble for y'all." They know who I am. What I stand for.

Brett adds, "The driver, he was real torn up about it. He did the right thing, calling it in. He could'a took off and left your boy there, but he didn't. He went to the closest pay phone and called for an ambulance."

I'm not impressed. "Well, I reckon Dwayne saw the truck that run over him. He'd tell who it was. Anyway, there won't be any trouble for you fellas. I'm gonna want to thank the man who did this."

Brett and Jordie look at each other, then Jordie says, "His name's Aloysius Poole. That's Poole with an e. He goes by Allie."

"Thank you," I say, making a note of it. "Now, if you don't mind, I'll finish getting' dressed, and my wife and I'll be on our way to the hospital."

Brett touches his hat. "We'll keep y'all our prayers."

We never saw a more pitiful sight than our ten-year-old boy, pale as a ghost, lyin' there on the gurney in the emergency room.

"He needs some surgery to set the bones right," the doctor told us. "He'll be all okay, but he's had a terrible shock. He's under sedation now for the pain. We need you to sign the consent so we can get him fixed up."

I signed the consent form and we waited to hear.

He was in a heavy cast from his chest to his feet when they rolled him out of the surgical unit.

"Oh, my God." May looked almost as white as Dwayne did.

"He's going to be at least eight weeks in that cast. That's going to be mighty uncomfortable for the boy in this heat," the doctor told us.

"You don't need to worry," I said. "We'll take good care of him."

"He's a lucky boy. No internal injuries that we know of, but two broken legs are bad enough. He'll need to be here in the hospital for several days before he can go home. He'll be in a lot of pain. After the cast is off, he'll have to do some exercises to get his legs working again."

I reached out and shook the doctor's hand. "We just want to get him home."

"I'll give you some pills for him to take, and you need to give them to him, especially at night, so he can sleep." He handed me a prescription. "You can get this filled before you bring him home."

"Will do."

May nodded.

I'll have to keep track of those pills. May likes to take more pain pills than she should. I wouldn't put it above her to sneak into his room and get a few extra for herself.

It's going to be one hell of a summer.

Aloysius Poole

There's nothin' special 'bout me.

I'm just an ordinary workin' man, never done nothin' bad to nobody. Been married twenty-nine years this September to my wife, Maisie. Have four kids and three grandkids.

Been drivin' and deliverin' milk for thirty years for the Hiland Dairy. Never missed a day of work. Never had an accident 'til that boy rode his bike in front of me a few weeks ago.

Guess none of that matters now.

My time has come.

I got struck dead tonight.

This ain't how my life's s'posed to end, lyin' helpless like a rag doll in the bottom of a ditch, all broke up.

Wish someone saw how that car swerved right into me, runnin' me down while I was walkin' home. But it was drizzlin' a little, nearly dark. No one was around to see.

How that car was waitin' for me to come along.

How it come up behind me so fast I couldn't get out of the way.

How I got throwed up in the air, then fell so hard, landin' in the rocky ditch with my back broke.

How a white man knelt beside me. Somethin' inside me knew his heart was bad, knew I was in trouble. I made my peace with God.

He tol' me his name before he made sure I took my last breath.

"I'm Henry Gray. That was my boy you run down the other day." He picked up a rock and raised it above his head. "Vengeance is mine. This here—this here's justice."

Anna

I spend as much time as I can upstairs, reading to Dwayne and playing Parcheesi with him. He likes the Hardy Boys, so Mama lets me go to the library by myself to check the books out. I've read The Tower Treasure, The House on the Cliff, and The Secret of the Old Mill since Dwayne got home from the hospital.

I hate sitting up there in his room, it's so hot. As hard as it is for me, I know it's ten times harder for Dwayne. He really suffers. They say this summer is the hottest one on record.

Dwayne can't hardly move himself with that big cast. We prop him up with a stack of pillows so he can swallow. The doctor says he'll have to stay in it for another six weeks.

I don't know how he stands it. His room has a funky smell, no matter how many times Mama comes up to give him a sponge bath. The doctor gave Mama some pills to give him at night that help with the pain and make him sleep.

"I hate these pills. They make me sick to my stomach and give me nightmares," he says.

He was crying yesterday. I know he hates it when he breaks down and cries. I don't see why boys have to pretend to be tough when they're hurt. Mama says it's just part of their nature.

My best friend, Nancy, went to the library with me this morning. She lives four houses away, and she's an only child who gets whatever she wants. My daddy likes her, even though he thinks she's a little bit spoiled. He says she comes from a good family. Her daddy goes to meetings with my daddy sometimes.

"Hey," I say, coming up to the edge of our front yard after leaving Nancy off at her house. "I'm back."

It's Saturday, and Daddy's outside oiling the lawnmower. His shirt's already showing big sweat rings under his armpits and down the middle of his back.

"Nancy and I are going to live next door to each other when we grow up." I want to put off going into the house as long as I can. "We're gonna marry brothers, maybe twins, and we're each gonna have three children and a white poodle dog."

"You two have it all it planned out, don't ya?" He reaches out to spin the wheels of the mower, making sure they're smooth.

"Yessir, we do."

"I approve." He wipes the sweat running down his forehead with a big bandanna handkerchief he takes from his back pocket. "Especially the bit about the white poodle dog. Now, go on in and help your mother." He turns the mower upright, and swipes at his neck again. "It's a scorcher today. Way too hot for girls to be outside."

It's just like Daddy to think girls can't handle heat as well as boys. It's a lot hotter upstairs in that stuffy little bedroom of Dwayne's. I force myself to think about reading the next Hardy Boys mystery, the one I checked out this morning, number four, The Missing Chums.

"Yessir. I'll take the newspaper in." The Muskogee Daily News is on the porch step. I pick it up and glance at the headline, Body Found by Old Mill Road. I stop in the living room and sit on the sofa to read the article. This might be a good mystery for Dwayne and I to puzzle over. But it's only about some old Colored man named Poole who was hit by a car last night. No sense wasting our time on that. The police don't even investigate what happens to the Coloreds. At least, that's what Daddy says.

Mama fixed egg salad sandwiches for our lunch while I was gone, the kind cut in half with the crusts trimmed off. I grab one and eat it standing up over the sink. It's messy, but it tastes good. Mama puts some sweet pickle relish in it with a little bit of celery for the crunch. If Mama was in here, she'd give me what for, eating over the sink, but she's gone back to her room. I'm in a hurry to get Dwayne's lunch up to him.

There's a bowl of saltine crackers and milk sitting on a tray. I grab a napkin and take it upstairs to Dwayne. I don't like crackers and milk, but he thinks it's great. He wants to eat it every day, sometimes twice a day. Mama says it's okay because he needs the extra calcium to help his bones knit back together.

I look out the one window in his bedroom while he's eating. "Hey, there's a girl playing with a dog in the back yard across from us. Looks like we might have some new neighbors."

The girl is about Dwayne's age, and she's skinny, dark-haired, and wearing a blue and white checkered sundress.

"Maybe something happened to Miz Callahan," I say. "What do you think?"

"Who the heck cares?" Dwayne swivels his arm out toward me, his hand holding the empty bowl.

"I'm gonna ask Mama what happened to Miz Callahan." I take the bowl from him so I can take it back downstairs. Mama's real particular about not leaving dirty dishes around the house. "Maybe she died. Maybe we have a mystery to solve in our own backyard. You and I could solve it—like the Hardy Boys."

"Huh, not likely. Miz Callahan was old, that's all." He frowns and squirms, trying to boost himself into a more comfortable position.

He's cranky today, not that I blame him. It must be a hundred degrees in here. I can feel my dress starting to stick to my back. Beads of sweat are forming under my hair.

"I'm turning the fan on," I say, flipping the switch to the high position.

Mama insisted that Daddy buy an electric fan to circulate the air in Dwayne's room after he got hurt. I overheard her and Daddy having an argument about it.

"I don't see the need for it," Daddy was saying.

"No, because it's not you who's sitting up there all day long. It's hotter than hell up there, and unless that boy gets some air, he won't be able to sleep at night," Mama told him.

I think it was Mama saying hell that changed Daddy's mind. The next day when he came home from work, he had a new fan with him. He took it right up to Dwayne's room.

"This is just to use at night," he said, plugging it in and turning it on. "To cool things off so you can sleep better. It has two speeds, but you keep it on low."

Daddy hates it when the electricity bill comes every month. He's always on us to turn off the lights, arguing with Mama about how much it costs. Mama says he's cheap that way. I know she right. It's the depression, but Daddy's kept a permanent job at the railroad. We've never gone without.

"Oh, that air feels so good," I say, putting my face up to the fan. "Here, I'll turn it so it blows on you."

Dwayne settles back on his pillow and closes his eyes as the moving air hits him.

"You know, that girl over there's about your age. She's cute, too. Maybe she'll be a new friend for you to play with when you're feeling better."

"I won't be playin' with any stupid girls." He scootches his shoulders around in the bed, trying to find a more comfortable position.

"She has a dog—it's a boxer, and he likes to play fetch. You're always asking for a dog." I could hear the girl calling, "Tuffy. Here, Tuffy."

"You hear that? Dog's name is Tuffy."

"Maybe I'll go over and play with Tuffy when I'm back on my feet." He's trying to move his shoulders back and forth. "Will you scratch my back?"

I keep the bowl in my left hand, and he leans forward. I give his back a scratch or two with my right hand. "You ought to make friends with that girl before you go asking to play with her dog."

"Hmph", he grunts. "If that girl don't quit runnin' Tuffy around in this heat, she won't have a dog."

I start for the bedroom door. "I'm taking your bowl downstairs. Need anything?"

"Come right back up here and read to me," Dwayne says.

Like he's in charge of me.

Boys.

What they know about girls would fit on the head of a pin.

Henry

The sheriff called the house on Saturday mornin' and asked if I'd come down to the station.

"What's this about?" I knew what it was about. I'd been expectin' the call.

"It's about the man who was drivin' the truck that hit your boy. He's dead."

"Okay, I'll come down directly." I hung up the phone, thinkin' about what I was goin' to say. It would be a pro forma interrogation. I'd say as little as possible.

"The sheriff's askin' me to come down and help him out with a few things," I told May, gettin' my jacket from the front closet. "I'll be back in an hour or so."

"What things?" she asked. She was suspicious, thought I might be slippin' over to see one of my lady friends.

"Nothin' for you to concern yourself about," I said, my usual answer to her when she's prying into my affairs.

Sheriff Coleman offered me a cigarette from an open pack after I'd seated myself in one of the straight-backed wooden chairs in his office.

"I don't smoke." I didn't tell him that's the only good thing I took away from my Mormon upbringing.

"Mind if I do?" He waited for my answer.

"No sir, go right ahead."

The sheriff struck a match and lit a cigarette. "I'd like to know where you were last Wednesday night."

"At a union meetin'." I hate unions, don't believe in 'em, but I attended the meetings without fail. Railroad workers had a closed shop. I wanted to know what the union reps were up to, how they were spending the dues they took out of my paycheck.

He parked his cigarette on the ashtray full of butts that sat on his desk. He wrote my name and 'union meeting' on the yellow legal pad in front of him.

"Can anybody vouch for that?" he asked.

"Only the twenty or so other men who were there."

The door opened. Deputy Stills stuck his head in, saw me sittin' there, and pulled his head out. He shut the door.

The sheriff looked annoyed at the interruption.

"Do you recall what time you left?" he continued.

"Usual time, 'bout nine o'clock. After, I went on home."

His eyes narrowed slightly. "Deputy Stills and Deputy Myer say you wanted the name of the driver when they told you about your boy getting hit."

I wasn't going to deny the obvious. "I did. Wanted to know who it was run my boy down."

"Well, Mr. Poole ran into some bad luck. He died last Wednesday night. Got run down in the road not far from his house."

I kept my face blank. "I saw the article in the newspaper. Too bad. Nothin' to do with me."

The sheriff shifted his considerable bulk in the uncomfortable wooden chair provided by the county. "His people are making a ruckus. They think he might've run into more than bad luck. So, I got to ask if maybe you run your car into Mr. Poole and killed him, maybe for revenge, to pay him back for your boy's suffering."

"No sir, I did not. I don't deny that I was mad when I first got told Dwayne was hurt, but he's healin' up okay. You know my wife, May. She's in Bible study group with your wife. Well, she convinced me to forgive and forget."

"Mr. Gray, in all due respect, that sounds like a load of bull to me." The Sheriff leaned back in his chair. It let out a loud squeak, and he frowned at the noise, saying "I'm gonna have to get some WD-40 on that spring."

I stayed silent.

The sheriff squashed his cigarette out.

I figured that was my cue to stand up. "Sheriff, if you're through askin' questions, I have things to do." I put out my hand. He shook it.

The interview wouldn't amount to a hill of beans. I knew it, and he knew it. We belong to the same group of white men who decide these things for the betterment of the community.

He'll rest easy now, tell the Poole family he's done his duty.

I'll put out his signs on my lawn like usual come election time, get contributions for his campaign, and tell all the men at the railroad to vote for him.

After that, we'll be square. A favor for a favor.

Joy

It's real lonely here in Muskogee. School was out by the time Mama and I moved, so I haven't made any friends. I see an older girl helping her mama hang out clothes sometimes from my bedroom window. Our backyards are divided by a fence.

Mama says I should go out to meet her. I just look down and shake my head. I shouldn't be so shy, but I can't help it.

Last week, Mama told me that I'll be starting fourth grade at the public school, not at the Catholic school.

"We can't afford to send you to Catholic school this year. Your daddy feels bad about it, so I don't want you making a fuss," she said.

"I don't mind. The nuns are mean. I'm a'scared of them, especially Sister Clarice."

"Now, Joy, that's no way to talk." Mama was trying not to smile, I could tell.

"It's true, Mama. Sister Clarice raps you on the knuckles if your skirt doesn't touch the floor when you kneel. Mary Louise Finnegan goes to public school, and she says the teachers there are nicer. Plus, she gets to wear cute clothes."

I'm looking forward to public school, to not having to wear uniforms, not having to follow in the footsteps of Doreen and Bill. Sister Clarice has it in for me because she thinks I might turn out to be a tramp like Doreen, which I won't, and because she thinks I should be as smart as Bill, which I'm not.

Our whole household has changed since we moved to Muskogee. Kathy married Walter, and she's still living in Okmulgee in a tiny apartment above the feed store. It isn't very nice, but she says they'll get a better one soon.

Doreen was going to nursing school at St. Francis in Tulsa, but now she's home again. Bill started going to the University of Tulsa, studying business. Unless Bill comes home for a day on the weekend, I don't have any fun.

Doreen acts like she barely knows I exist ever since she came home. She stays in her room most of the time, and when she does come out, she doesn't hardly talk. She barely eats anything. Sometimes she comes to supper and pushes food around on her plate. Sometimes Mama takes a tray up to her room.

Yesterday I knocked on Doreen's bedroom door. She always keeps it closed.

"What?" she yelled.

"Want to play Monopoly?"

"No, go away."

"Scrabble, then?"

"No. Go play with Tuffy."

"He's a dog, for heaven's sake."

I stood outside the door a minute longer, just to see if she'd change her mind. She didn't.

I've given up on trying to get her to do anything with me.

I'm not supposed to know she had a breakdown, like I don't have ears. It doesn't surprise me, the way she's always carried on—woe is me—her and her unhappy life.

Too bad, so sad. That's what she used to say to me when I felt bad about something.

Now that she's home, we're all on pins and needles waiting for her to have one of her fits. She's miserable, then she gets into a snit, then she's downright mean. When she gets like that Mama goes to her bedroom. Daddy tells Doreen to go to her room and rest. We're all upset for a few hours until the air clears. Doreen's okay for a day, maybe two, then it happens all over again.

Having all this turmoil makes me nervous. I had a real bad asthma attack last night, and they had to call the doctor to come.

Mama came in this morning with more bad news. "The doctor says you can't go to school this year. He doesn't want you getting a cold from the other children."

I'm sitting up in bed, and she tucks the sheet around my chest. "A cold or cough could make your asthma worse. We have to try and prevent these attacks. He wants you to use a nebulizer every day." She stroked my hair.

I want to go to school, but I'm so tired from having asthma every day. "All right, Mama. Will I miss a grade?"

"No," she says, sitting on the bed beside me. "I'll get your schoolwork. You and I can do it together. When you're back in school next year you'll be with your class again."

I'm so relieved that tears run down my face. Moving to Muskogee and leaving my friends hasn't been easy. I don't want to be known as the dummy from Okmulgee who had to stay behind a grade.

"There, now, don't cry," Mama says, wiping my face with her hankie, then giving me a hug. "It's going to set off an attack. You're going to get well and be just fine."

My room in the new house is small, with only one window, and it's up so high I can't look out of it.

It's going to be a long year.

Arthur

Doreen swallowed pills and when that didn't work, she cut one of her wrists with a razor. Her friends at the dormitory found her bleeding in the bathtub.

"Just let me die," she'd groaned after they pulled her out.

The dormitory matron from St. Francis called us to let us know what happened. "You'll have to come and get her. She can't come back until she's finished treatment and is released by a psychiatrist."

Gladys cried nearly all the way to Tulsa. She blames herself for Doreen's problems.

"Is It my fault she's like this? They say these problems are caused by bad mothers," she asked.

"You did your best," I answered. "The other kids are fine. Doreen reminds me of my father. She's always been hard to handle."

The emergency room doctor had stitched Doreen's wrist and pumped her stomach by the time we drove to Tulsa. "She's still sedated from the pills she took. Those will be wearing off in about three hours, so I'd get her over to Vinita as soon as you can," he told us. "Here are some notes to give to the doctor when you get there."

Shocked at how thin and pale she looked, we loaded her into the back seat of the car. She sat sulking and refusing to speak during the two-hour drive to the sanitorium at Vinita.

Doreen was taken into the psychiatrist's office as soon as we arrived. We waited in the foyer for an hour before he came out and ushered us into his office. Doreen sat on a sofa while we took two chairs.

"I've reviewed the notes, and talked to Doreen. She's having a manic episode. It's not uncommon in young women and men who are away from home for the first time and under stress. She needs rest and medication in a safe place until she doesn't feel like hurting herself."

Doreen stood up and started pacing as the doctor talked. A male orderly was standing in front of the office door leading into the hallway. He was a burly man who reminded me of a bouncer—only his job was to keep people in, not to throw them out.

"These people hate me." Doreen waved her hand in our direction. "Just let me go back to St. Francis, and I'll be good." She walked over to his desk and whispered, "They want me in Hell. They're demons. They won't let me sleep."

"You need to stay here for a little while. Your parents are bringing you for treatment out of concern. It's for your own protection." He wrote something down on the notepad in front of him.

"I said I'll be good, I'll be really, really, good," Doreen repeated in a little girl voice.

"We want you to get well." The psychiatrist motioned to the orderly, who came closer.

Doreen spun around and put her right arm out, pointing to Gladys. "You don't know what she is. She's wicked, she's a witch. She put a curse on me the day I was born." Doreen lunged for Gladys, but I stood up to block her while the orderly grabbed both of Doreen's arms. He sat her down on the sofa and kept hold of her by her shoulders.

The doctor pulled a syringe out of his desk drawer. He administered the shot while the orderly held her still, Doreen screaming, "I hate you. I hate you."

The shot took effect almost immediately. As Doreen's eyes went glassy, the orderly supported her, keeping her upright while the doctor called for a wheelchair. "Take her to Ward A and get her settled, please."

We watched as she was rolled out of the office. The doctor checked his pocket watch, then sat down behind his desk.

"Her condition has to stabilize before you can have her live at home safely. She's young, and that's in her favor. She should be well enough to be home in a few months, possibly sooner. She's still seventeen?"

"Nearly eighteen," I told him.

"You can commit her since she's a minor. It's be much easier that way. Once she's eighteen, we'll have to go through a judge. I think she'll be improved enough to go home by then. I'll have the paperwork ready for you to sign before you leave."

"What will we need to bring for her?" Gladys asked. "We didn't have time to get any of her things."

"She'll be monitored closely for a week or two, and the staff will provide her with what she needs. As soon as her condition improves, she'll be transferred to a different ward, one that isn't so restricted. At that point, you can bring some of her clothing and toiletries.

"Will she be able to go back to school?" I asked.

"Probably." He tapped his fingers on the file in front of him. "Nursing programs are tough on young women. They're worked too hard, and they don't get enough sleep. She may be able to return to her studies once she's rested." The doctor stood up. "We encourage visitation, but not for at least two weeks. It takes that long for the medication to begin working." He opened the door to the hallway to show us out. "The front desk can give you all the information you need."

Our hearts were breaking as we drove away. Gladys had papers in her purse explaining the rules at the hospital and visiting times.

I thought about my father on the drive home. Doreen's mood swings and resentments remind me of him, though he's never been diagnosed. He drowns his moodiness in alcohol. His anger flares out at home, at the people who love him most, same as Doreen.

Gladys didn't want to bring Doreen home after two months, but the doctor said it wasn't good to have such a young girl in an institution like Vinita for very long. She can go back to St. Francis, but she has to wait until the next term begins and that won't be for another month.

"I'm okay now, Daddy," Doreen says on the drive back to Muskogee. "Please let me go back to school."

"Just relax. You're going back there soon enough. You need more rest. The doctor said you still need to take it easy."

Doreen seems compliant enough on the surface, but her mood is brittle and unhappy. Gladys and I walk on eggshells when we're around her. We're afraid her mood swings will break through the thin layer of self-control she's been able to gain. She has to keep taking her medication every day. We definitely see a difference when she tries to skip it.

Joy's gotten so quiet since Doreen is back. She's afraid of Doreen's tantrums, of saying something that might set her off.

"It's hard to see Doreen moping around the house all day. She's bored, but it's beneath her to lift a finger to help with cooking or housework." Gladys sits at her dressing table, brushing her long dark hair. I kiss the nape of her neck and nuzzle her. She smiles at me in the mirror.

"You're getting some gray hairs, my dear," I say, touching her hair.

She laughs and says, "You're going bald. I'll just use a little hair dye, but there's no hope for you."

"We're getting old, no question about it."

She goes over to sit on the side of our bed. "This last year's been enough to give anyone gray hair. I hope Doreen's classmates won't shut her out when she returns to St. Francis. She's so sensitive."

"Surely, they have some compassion for those who are ill. But, you're right—girls this age—it's going to be a rough go until Doreen proves herself." I begin changing into my pajamas, carefully removing my coat and vest, hanging them up. "It might be worse for her to stay here. All her old friends are married or gone."

"Let's see if she'd like to live at Mother's boarding house. She gets along with her, and she'd have some privacy there. She wouldn't have to live in the dormitory, plus the house is close enough for her to walk to the hospital. Or she could take the bus."

Doreen won't agree to any suggestion coming from Gladys. "I'll ask her," I say. "We can afford to pay your mother something for room and board."

"Mother won't take it. She's already talked to me. She loves Doreen."

Doreen's always been the apple of Ella's eye, and she's the only one who can reason with her.

"We have to talk with Bill before she goes back to Tulsa," Gladys adds, getting under the covers. "I don't want Bill trying to take care of Doreen while he's still in school. I don't want her calling him at all hours of the night, either."

"I'll tell him." I settle into bed beside her and turn off the light.

We've had to put limits on Doreen's telephone usage while she's been living with us. She ran up a long-distance bill of over forty dollars in one month from calling Bill late at night. She wants to talk to him for hours. When I threatened to take the phone out, she agreed to call Bill once a week for ten minutes. Even that is an extravagance, what with all of her doctor bills and the cost of her medication.

I love her dearly, but she can't stay here much longer.

It isn't good for any of us.

May

Anna and I went upstairs last night with a stack of clean sheets to change Dwayne's bed. We have a whole routine worked out. I lift his legs just enough to slide the bottom of his sheet off and over to one side, then Anna slips the clean sheet on the bottom. We do the same on the top, and the job is done

After we finished, I leaned over to kiss Dwayne on the forehead. He was burning up.

"Why didn't you tell me you felt bad?" I asked him, putting my hand to his cheek to feel the fever.

"I always feel bad," he groaned. "My throat's killin' me."

"How long have you had a sore throat?"

"Yesterday," he mumbled.

"Open up." I looked into his mouth to see white spots on his fiery red tonsils.

"You should've told me. I'm going to get a thermometer and take your temperature."

Dwayne's temperature was 104.5.

"Oh, my Lord." I shook the thermometer. "That can't be right." It was the same the second time. I called Dr. Linda. She can't get over to the house until evening.

I got a basin of cold water and a washrag. I kept sponging Dwayne's skin, trying to bring the fever down, and turned on the fan. His temperature hadn't gone down any by the time Henry got home from work.

"You know I don't like you callin' the doctor. I don't believe in all that quackery."

"Yes, I know," I turned so I could look him in the eye. "You don't believe in dentists, either, but your son with two broken legs is burning up with fever. He needs a doctor. You don't want him to die, do you?"

Henry looked shocked. I stood my ground, staring him down.

I don't talk back to him as much as I should. I've been fooling myself into believing he'd change once we were married, once he was a father, once he felt secure. I've come to the realization that this is who he is, who he always will be. There's something missing in him, and I can't fix it.

"Go on back and take care of Dwayne. I'll run down to the chicken joint and get us some supper." Henry left.

The doctor came later. It didn't take her long to make a diagnosis. "He's got rheumatic fever. I've given him a shot of penicillin to get the infection cleared up. I'll leave a prescription for pills. You can pick those up at the drugstore in the morning. I'll be back tomorrow to check on him."

"He'll be all right, won't he?" I asked.

"He'll recover. This kind of infection can damage the heart, so it's good you called. We'll have to wait and see if there's any lasting damage."

Henry looked worried when he heard that. "Come back as much as you need to. We want him to get well."

"The good news is that he'll be able to get out of those casts in another few days. He's going to be weak. He'll need a lot of rest for the next few months. No paper route, and no school until he's stronger."

I showed her to the door. "Thank you for coming. We'll see you tomorrow."

After she left, Henry said, "I'll go sit with Dwayne. You've had a hard day."

He was feeling guilty about the fuss he'd made earlier.

I went into the bedroom and lay down on the bed, tired to the bone. Anna knocked lightly. She came in and sat down beside me.

"Is Dwayne going to be all right?" she asked. "He's mostly just annoying, but I love him all the same."

"He'll be okay. He needs some medicine and a lot of rest."

"That's good news, isn't it, Mama?"

"Yes, that's good. He'll be fine." I reached out and patted her hand. "Your daddy's going to stay with him tonight. You go on to bed."

She leaned over and kissed me on the cheek. "I'll see you in the morning, Mama."

I closed my eyes after she left the room and thought about the heart condition that runs in our family—my mother, my sisters, and myself all have it. I prayed for Dwayne's heart to be spared, prayed for him to get well, to grow up strong.

I fell asleep dreaming of wild stallions running free across the Texas plains.

Henry

I had all my teeth pulled and got dentures. I don't believe in dentists. If your teeth give you trouble, then have them out and be done with it.

"Your teeth are in pretty good shape. There's one that'll need to be pulled, but a few fillings should fix up the rest," the dentist told me.

I'm thirty-eight years old, and it's the one and only time I've ever been to a dentist. I don't intend to make a habit of it.

"Nossir," I told him. "Just pull 'em out and get me some false teeth."

The dentist shook his head, but he didn't argue with me, just commenced to pullin'. I can tell you that for the next week my mouth was full of pain and swellin' that I wouldn't care to repeat. I got my new teeth yesterday, and I'm just gettin' used to them.

I was rinsin' my mouth out with salt water this mornin' when I heard the phone ring. When I came out of the bathroom, Anna was hangin' up the phone, tears streaming down her face. She ran to me, and said, "Nancy's parents were killed in a car accident in Oklahoma City last night."

I hugged her close to me. "That's terrible, baby."

"She has only the one aunt who lives in Georgia, her Aunt Susan. She's on her way." Anna sobbed. "Daddy, we won't be able to graduate together if Nancy has to move."

"She can live with us if her aunt will let her," I said. I didn't even have to think about it. Anna and Nancy are best friends. Nancy's been in and out of our house since she was little-bitty.

"Will you tell her? Will you go over there with me? She'll know it's okay if you tell her."

"Yes, I'll go with you, and we can tell her." One of the things I like about Nancy is that she respects her elders. I went upstairs to tell May. She was still in bed with one of her migraines.

"Oh, that poor girl," she said, groggy from the medication she'd taken.

"I'm going to offer for Nancy to stay with us and finish school here."

"That's nice," she murmered, turning over. "Pull the curtains closed, will you? The light's killing me. Tell them I'll send over some supper later."

I pulled the curtains closed on my way out.

Anna and I walked down the street to Nancy's house where several cars were parked outside. A white-haired woman I didn't know answered the door.

"I'm Henry Gray, and this is my daughter, Anna. We've come to offer our condolences."

"C'mon in. I'm Sally Atkins, from their church. I was staying here with Nancy while her parents were gone. I'll stay until Nancy's aunt comes." She showed us into the living room.

"Do you know what happened?" I asked her after we were seated on the sofa.

"A head-on collision. So sad. They were on their way home." A pot of coffee, some empty cups, and a plate of store-bought cookies was sitting on the coffee table. "Please, help yourselves. I'll tell Nancy you're here."

She came back in a minute. "Nancy will be right out."

I poured myself a cup of coffee. "Miz Gray said to tell you she'll send over some supper later on."

"That's mighty kind of her. Tell her we sure appreciate it."

Anna ran to hug Nancy as she entered the living room, her face red and swollen from crying. "Daddy says you can come to live with us. Only if you want to."

"You don't have to decide now," I told her. "Take some time to think about it. We thought you might want to finish high school here in Muskogee. Just know that the offer's open."

Anna took Nancy's hand. "I'm so, so sorry. Let's go back to your room. I'll stay with you if you want me to."

She leaned her head on Anna's shoulder. "Okay. I can't stop crying. I want to lay down."

I finished the last of my coffee just as the doorbell rang. "Looks like more people are comin'. I'll make my exit."

"I'll come home later, Daddy."

I watched the two girls go down the hallway with their arms around each other's waists.

Sally showed me out. "It's very generous of you to offer a home to Nancy."

"I meant what I said. She's like one of our own." Offering to take a teenage girl into our family is a commitment I'd never consider if we didn't know Nancy so well.

Nancy's Aunt Susan arrived the next day. She agreed that Nancy could live with us during the school year and spend the summer months in Georgia. We moved Nancy's bed and dresser into Anna's room. It's a tight fit with the two girls in there together, but they don't seem to mind.

After the funeral, Nancy's family home was sold. The money was put into a trust for her to have when she turns eighteen.

"Thank you, Daddy," Anna told me. "I've always wanted to have a sister."

I hugged her. I wonder sometimes if I love her so much because she reminds me of my mother.

1940

Bill

The phone's ringing again. I turn over and squint at the clock.

It's two forty-five a.m.

I know it's Doreen calling. This is the fifth time in the past two hours.

I wish she'd stop. I know she's nervous about getting her cap at a ceremony for the graduating nurses tomorrow.

I have things to be nervous about myself. I have a big interview at Sinclair Oil. I need to be sharp.

All of us are going to the capping ceremony. Kathy's even coming, and she's as big as a house. Her baby's due in another month. Who would have guessed that the girl who was never going to be a mother would be so excited?

Daddy said he was thinking of starting the Oil Supply Company again. "The price of oil is going up. I could make a go of it."

"You should wait," I told him. "We might be going to war. The situation in Europe is very unsettled."

"The President said he won't send our young men to war."

I don't trust his words will last. "He may not have a choice. Wait another year and see what happens."

Some of my buddies are already talking about which branch of the service they're going to join. I think the Army Air Corps would be the place for me, although I hope it doesn't come to that.

I put on my best suit—my only suit—attend the capping ceremony, and catch the bus going downtown for my interview. My shoes are freshly shined, my hair newly cut. It's important to make a good first impression.

Sinclair Oil is a big company. Harry Sinclair's a legend among oil men. His company grew even during the depression. I interview with Mr. Conger. He has an impressive corner office with windows looking over half of Tulsa.

"Do you play golf, Bill?" he asks toward the end of the interview.

"No sir, I haven't had the pleasure." I've been scraping by since Daddy lost the business, working two part-time jobs to stay in college.

"Well, you'll have to learn. I think you'll be a good addition to our team here at Sinclair." He stands up, signaling that the interview is over. "Does two weeks give you enough time to get ready to come to work for us?"

"Two weeks is fine," I say. "Thank you, sir."

We shake hands, and he says, "I'm having a barbeque on Saturday afternoon with a few people from your department. Let me give you the address. It'll be a good introduction for you if you aren't busy." He writes his address down on a piece of note paper from his desk.

"I look forward to it."

"Give some thought to brushing up on your golf game. Big oil deals are made on the golf course."

I decide to buy a set of used golf clubs with my first paycheck.

Doreen

At last.

It only took three years of hell and a nervous breakdown to get my nurses' cap and a real job on the post-surgery floor at St. Francis. I'm looking for an apartment close to the hospital. And a husband.

It's too bad I don't like nursing. It gives me a paycheck, but it's not a calling for me like it is for some of the other girls. I swear, some of the other nurses have lost their sense of smell. The mess and the smells—ugh—I never get used to them.

As soon as I have some experience, I'm going to try and get a job in a doctor's office. Giving shots and taking blood pressures wouldn't be too hard.

If I had my druthers, I'd rather be a songwriter. Mama says it's no way to make a living, but I've sold two songs already. Of course, it didn't pay much since I'm just starting out, but it's something to do in my spare time while I look for a husband.

I just sent a new song to Lew Wells, the big music producer. I'm hoping he'll like it and buy it from me. It has an upbeat, catchy tune, and I titled it "Don't Sit Under the Apple Tree." It's about how I feel when I'm dating someone I like, wanting to be exclusive, you know?

That phrase, always a bridesmaid, never a bride? That's me. I've been to seven weddings in the past three months. Seven. Lots of the graduating nurses were already engaged, their weddings planned. I don't even have a steady boyfriend.

My friends keep introducing me to men, but either the guy doesn't like me, or I don't like him. I want a man with real prospects. Someone who has a job that pays enough for me to stop working as a nurse and spend time writing songs. It seems like all the men who date nurses are men who want a woman bringing home the paycheck.

Like my roommate, Margie.

I eyed her new coat with envy as she hung it up after coming in from her date with Tom, her fiancé. Her coat's the latest style, a dark forest green.

"I'm gonna have to borrow that coat one of these days," I tell her. "I'd look amazing in it."

Margie shrugged. "Guess what Tom said tonight." She looked unhappy.

Cindy, our other roommate, rolled her eyes at me. "What now?"

"He says I should keep working after we're married." She took a stance like Tom and imitated his voice. "Women. All women want is for men to take care of them from the cradle to the grave."

"Dump him. I examined my toenails to be sure the red polish was evenly painted. Satisfied, I screwed the applicator cap back on. "With an attitude like that, he doesn't deserve you. Plus, he hasn't kept a job more than a few months since you've known him."

Margie plopped herself down on the sofa. "Well, that's not his fault. He's had a run of bad luck."

I should have kept my mouth shut. She's defending him, like usual.

"Men see a nurse, and all they can think is 'here's someone who'll take care of me.' That's why I've sworn off men." Cindy grinned. "Until I catch a doctor, that is.' She walked over to the little bar we have set up on a tea table by the window. "Who wants a glass of sherry?"

I raised my hand.

Margie yawned. "I'm going to bed. I have early shift in the morning."

I don't want to marry a doctor. They're wrapped up in their work until all hours, and they're always surrounded by pretty, young nurses who are just waiting to tempt them out of their marriages.

I want someone who'll spend time with me, someone who likes to dance and romance. I want a husband who knows how to have fun, someone who adores me and wants to spend the rest of his life with me and only me.

And a man who wants children. I do love babies.

May

It was Henry's idea to take all of us to Milwaukee for a summer trip. Why Milwaukee? You can bet it wasn't because I'm dying to go there.

It's because Henry does whatever Henry wants, and he wants to visit his sister, Pansy. We've never met her or any of her family. She's married to a man named Joe, who works at the Schlitz brewery. They have three children, two boys and a girl about Anna's age. I only know this because she sends a Christmas card every year, sometimes enclosing a photograph of them. Henry calls her once a year on her birthday.

"I can get us tickets on the train for practically nothin'," Henry announced at breakfast. "You'll like your Aunt Pansy, and it's time you meet your cousins."

The lack of enthusiasm with which we all greeted this announcement would have caused some men to rethink the trip, but not Henry.

"Okay, Daddy." Anna was the first to respond, her tone flat. Nancy was with her aunt for the summer, and Anna wanted to be with her friends.

"That's my girl. Uncle Joe'll probably give us a tour of one of the biggest breweries in the country." He looked at me. "Better get the suitcases ready."

"You don't even like beer," I remarked.

He ignored me.

I got the suitcases packed, and we arrived yesterday, tired from riding the train such a long way. Joe and Pansy picked us up at the station.

We drove up to their house, a two-story home. It sat in row of similar homes built so close together they're almost joined together on the sides. It isn't far from Joe's work. The air has what Pansy describes as 'brewery smell.'

"You get used to the smell," Pansy told us, seeing Dwayne wrinkle his nose as we got out of the car. "We don't even notice it anymore, do we, Joe?"

"Not much." Joe grinned. "I'm around it all the time, and it pays my way, so to me it smells like money."

"I'll take you downtown to Gimbels Department Store," Pansy told us as we were walking into the house. "It's got all the latest fashions."

They had two boys, Roy, who's Dwayne's age, Simon, age nine, and Irene, who's Anna's age. Pansy let the boys sleep out on the screened porch, Anna was in Irene's room with her, and Henry and I slept in the boys' bedroom. We were comfortable enough. The kids were having fun getting to know each other.

I woke up with a migraine two days later. It was on the day we'd planned to go to Gimbels.

"I had to take one of my headache pills," I told Pansy at breakfast. "I won't be able to go anywhere today."

"Why don't the young people go by themselves? They can take the bus. It stops right by Gimbels, and Irene's taken it dozens of times," suggested Pansy. "Simon can stay here with me and ride his bike."

"Please, Daddy?" Anna pleaded. "Roy and Dwayne want to go, too."

"All right. If the boys are going. "It's rare for Henry to permit Anna to have an unsupervised outing.

I was pleased. Anna needs to have more independence. She'll be graduating in just a couple of years. She'll be leaving us.

She says she wants to go to nursing school to train to be a surgical nurse. Where she got that idea, I don't know. Henry won't hear of it. He says it's a dirty job and he didn't raise her to do that kind of work. He also thinks nurses are floozies. Not sure where he got that idea. Maybe it's because they bathe men.

Henry's a cheapskate about most things, but not when it comes to Anna. He'll deny Dwayne, but he usually gives Anna whatever she asks for. She's disappointed that he won't pay for nursing school, though she tries not to show it.

She knows there's nothing I can do to change his mind. I don't encourage her in thinking he'll come around just to make her happy.

I know better. Not a chance. Once his mind is made up, he never gives in.

Anna

We never made it to Gimbels.

We were all in good spirits when we left, laughing and horsing around, excited to have money to spend. We've had a good time here so far. Uncle Joe took us to a Milwaukee Brewers baseball game last night, and we had a real good time, even though the Brewers lost to the Brooklyn Dodgers.

I was so excited to be going to shop and pick things out for myself. Daddy still insists on going with me whenever I want to buy clothes. Last year when I wanted a white pleated skirt and red sweater vest like all the other girls, he took me right downtown and let me get what I wanted.

I never ask Mama anything. She doesn't have a say.

We caught the bus at the bus stop two blocks from the house. I sat with Irene, and Dwayne sat with Roy across the aisle from us. Everything was fine until the bus got close to the downtown area. It stopped in a Negro area of town, and three Negro men got on. Two of them took a seat in front of where Dwayne and Roy were sitting.

"Y'all get goin' to the back of the bus." Dwayne told them. He was acting big in front of our cousins.

The Negro men looked startled. They didn't get up to move.

"You hear me, boy?" Dwayne asked, leaning forward. "Get on back now. You can't be sittin' up here with white people."

"Hey, now," the bus driver said. He looked upset. He pulled the bus over to the curb, getting up to stand in the aisle in front of Dwayne's seat.

"You need to settle down. Those folks got a right to ride, same as you."

Dwayne stood up to challenge him. "The hell they do. Those niggers belong in the back."

The bus driver pointed to the exit tibdoor closest to us at the side rear of the bus. ""Off. You and whoever's with you need to get off this bus right now."

"Gladly," Dwayne said. As we all got up and started down the aisle toward the rear door, he muttered, "You nigger-lovin' asshole."

"What'd you say?" The bus driver took a step forward to follow us.

Dwayne stopped and looked back. "Nothin'." He balled his right hand into a fist.

"Sorry for the trouble," Roy said. He stood between the bus driver and Dwayne, not letting Dwayne go around him. "He's just visiting."

"He can go right back where he came from." The bus driver stood his ground. He wasn't going to back down. "We don't have that kind of talk here in Milwaukee."

I've never been so embarrassed in all my life.

Irene took charge as the bus pulled away, leaving the four of us stranded. "Let's find a pay phone." She clenched her teeth. "Mama can come and get us."

We walked three blocks to a gas station that had a telephone booth on the sidewalk in front of it.

"Who has a dime?" Irene asked. She looked right at Dwayne, who was still spoiling for a fight. He narrowed his eyes and was about to say something rude.

I held out a dime. "I do."

Irene deposited the dime and dialed Aunt Pansy. "Mama, you need to come and get us. Dwayne got rude on the bus. We got thrown off."

There was a pause. I guess Aunt Pansy was asking what happened.

Irene looked like she was about to cry, but she didn't. "Yeah, well, what happened is Dwayne told some Negroes to move to the back of the bus, but he didn't say Negroes. He used the bad word, and the bus driver stopped the bus. He threw us off. We're on Wisconsin Avenue and Sixth Street at the Standard filling station."

Another pause.

"Okay, we'll stay here." She hung up the phone. "Mama's coming for us."

We hung around the phone booth while Dwayne went over to a cigarette machine out in front of the station and bought a pack of Camels. He asked the filling station attendant for a light, and the man gave him a half-used pack of matches that said Standard Oil on the cover.

When Dwayne and Roy lit up, Irene and I moved twenty feet away to get out of the smoke. I hate the way my clothes smell after I've been in cigarette smoke.

"We don't talk that way here in Milwaukee. We don't use the word 'nigger.' It's rude." Irene talked like she was schooling me on etiquette.

"Whites aren't being rude to Coloreds when they're just asking them to do what they should be doing in the first place," I told her. "Where we come from, we don't sit with Coloreds, we don't eat with Coloreds. We use different bathrooms and different water fountains. Don't you know they have diseases?"

"That's nonsense. People are just people, no matter what color their skin is. We don't believe in segregation. It's barbaric."

"I didn't see any Colored people living in your neighborhood. If you come down to visit us there in Muskogee, you'll see why Dwayne said what he did. Our busses have signs telling Colored's they can only sit at the back of the bus."

"When in Rome," Irene retorted. "Dwayne was ignorant. He should have been taught better."

She's right—Dwayne's a scrappy boy with a short fuse, always spoiling for a fight. I broke up a fight between him and another boy on the last day of school. Collette came running up and told me Dwayne was outside fighting behind the building. I ran out and yelled, "Stop it. Right now."

To my surprise, Dwayne stopped and walked away, but not before the other boy had a split lip. Dwayne couldn't, or wouldn't, tell me what started it. I think he was ashamed of himself.

I didn't want Irene thinking she was superior to us, so I ignored her remark about Dwayne. "Our folks don't believe in intermingling of the races. That's in the Bible, and that's how it's supposed to be."

I felt my skin flushing pink over my shoulders and neck as I parroted what I'd been taught. Good thing Daddy wasn't with us. He had names I didn't want to repeat for people who thought like her.

Irene waved her arm over her head as she saw a blue Buick turn the corner. "Thank God. Here's Mama."

Irene sat in the front seat and told Aunt Pansy what happened on the ride back to the house. Dwayne kept his mouth shut. He'd never admit that he was as disappointed as the rest of us that we didn't get to go to Gimbel's.

Daddy was waiting for us, and he was mad. Dwayne's behavior embarrassed him, even though Daddy would have done the same thing. Dwayne was sent to the porch and told he couldn't have supper. That made Mama mad. She went upstairs and didn't come down to eat.

I thought it could have gone a lot worse. It was lucky for Dwayne that Daddy didn't beat him silly in front of our relatives.

Conversation at suppertime was strained, confined to 'pass the potatos' and other small talk about the weather and the news of the day.

"C'mon, Henry, let's go down to the tavern and get a beer." Uncle Joe pushed his chair back from the table. He and Daddy left.

Irene and I did the supper dishes while Aunt Pansy turn on the radio. She listened to a program about what was happening in Europe.

I sneaked a roll with some butter out to Dwayne after Aunt Pansy went to bed. "You got off easy, you know." I held the roll out and sat down next to him. "If we'd been at home, you'd have gotten the belt."

"I hate it here. Damn Yankee brats," he muttered, his mouth full of roll.

"Things are different here," I told him. "We shouldn't take it out on our cousins."

I went back inside and talked Roy and Irene into playing a game of Monopoly. We played until Roy won, then we all went to bed.

Daddy woke us up at dawn the next morning. "Get your stuff packed. We're goin' home."

1941

Gladys

We're settled in Muskogee now. I've convinced Arthur not to move back to Okmulgee until Joy finishes high school. We have friends at church, and May Gray invited me to join her card group. Each week we meet at the home of a different member who provides a light lunch and beverages. I'm writing down recipes for things to serve when it's my turn to host the group.

Marie Palowski said her husband told her that Mr. Gray's a high-up member of the Ku Klux Klan. I don't know that I believe it. Arthur says it's probably true.

I haven't met him, but May seems nice. If she goes along with Klan beliefs, she keeps it to herself. She knows we're Catholic, and I've never heard her say a word against our religion or any other. I don't think it matters to her.

Kathy showed up last weekend to show us their new baby girl, then asked if they could move in for a while. They're having a hard time of it.

"Walter lost his job last week. I've been looking for work, but I couldn't find anything while I was pregnant. We can't afford to pay the rent this month."

"You can live with us until you get on your feet," Arthur told her. "I'll move my desk out of the back bedroom, and you can put your bed in there."

"Things are going to be tight," I warned. The stress and strain of four more people in our small house is going to be a problem: the additional expenses, the cooking, the laundry, two babies in diapers, Kathy's bossiness, Walter's drinking. Arthur's stomach starts acting up and he's irritable all the time they're living with us, although he'd never tell Kathy she can't come.

"We can make do until Walter gets another job."

"Joy's up in the night if she has asthma. The babies will have to be in with you." I reached for my silver cigarette case with the engraved letters GL on the top, a recent anniversary gift from Arthur. I lit a cigarette, needing something to distract me. The nicotine rush pushed my irritation away. I exhaled, resisting the urge to give Kathy a piece of my mind.

Joy

Mama says not to let Kathy boss me around, but I can't make her stop. I'm glad to be back at school with so many people in the house. Every day after school I go to my room and say I have homework. It isn't really a lie, but it doesn't take me long to finish it. After that, I lay on my bed and listen to the radio.

While I listen to the song Stardust, I think about Johnny Cates and pretend he asks me to go to the school dance. It's on Friday night in two weeks. Johnny has a locker right next to mine. He's always friendly when we're changing classes. He and his two older brothers have a wild reputation around town. My friends think I'm a goody-two-shoes, but I like a boy with some spunk.

I go downstairs where Mama is in the living room reading Death on the Nile. Kathy has taken the kids to the park, and the house is quiet.

I sit on the arm on the chair and say, "I don't have a dress to wear if someone asks me to the dance."

"Do you want to go downtown and look at dresses?" Mama asks, putting her book aside.

"Okay," I answer. Anything to get away from the house.

She puts on her hat, and we walk the eight blocks to downtown. We window shop at Lanier's, where there isn't anything cute, then go on to Mary's Sophisticates.

"I like that one. The navy one, with the white piping."

"Let's go in and take a look," Mama says.

We go inside. Mama nods to the cashier behind the counter, takes the dress off the rack, and holds it up to me. She looks the dress over inside and out, then puts it back on the rack.

"I'm not sure about this one," she says. We leave the store.

"I'll go to the fabric store and buy what I need tomorrow," she tells me.

She's going to sew me a dress just like that one.

"How are you able to copy a dress like that just by looking?" I ask her the next afternoon, watching her lay the fabric out on our dining room table.

"My grandfather was a tailor back in Germany, and the story is that he made clothes for the King. I guess I got a talent for it," she says, busily pinning a pattern she'd made out of newspaper.

It wasn't an attribute I inherited. I can barely sew a straight seam, much less make a dress from looking at one.

For the next hour I felt relaxed. It felt like it did before Kathy showed up, just Mama and I working on a project together. I don't like to say it, but I think I'm Mama's favorite—of the girls, that is. Bill's everyone's favorite because he's the only boy, plus he's really successful at everything he does.

Even though I try to stay out of sight and out of Kathy's way, I can't always stay out of earshot. Like the other night, when Walter called Kathy to tell her he'd lost another job and wouldn't be coming to get her and the kids anytime soon. I could hear her crying when she got off the phone. "I don't understand it," she wailed.

Daddy was upset that Kathy was upset. He's losing his patience with the situation.

"Walter drinks too much," I heard him tell her. "He misses work and gets himself fired. There's not much mystery to it."

"He's doing his best." Kathy's tears dried up as she turned her anger on Daddy to defend Walter. "I'm not divorcing him, if that's what you want. I love him. Walter may not be Catholic, but I am."

"No one's asking you to get a divorce. We just want what's best for you and the kids," I heard Mama say.

Kathy's voice sounded hard when she answered. "If you don't want us here, just say so."

"You're always welcome here," Daddy told her. "But it hurts our hearts to see you and the kids with nowhere else to go, no home of your own. And Walter avoiding the situation."

"He's trying, he really is." She ran to her room and slammed the door.

I could hear her crying.

Grandma Ella left her husband, and she didn't get divorced, so I guess Kathy could do that, but Mama says Kathy won't ever leave Walter. Mama says when the two of them are up, they're up, and when they're down, they come to our house. I guess that's one way to be married, but it sure wouldn't suit me.

I met that boy who lives in the house back of ours. His name is Dwayne. He's real cute with his black hair and blue eyes. He's also a smart aleck. Mama told me I should ask him to come over to visit, so I did, even though I didn't want to.

"Would you like to come over and play?" I asked, trying not to sound as unenthusiastic as I felt.

"Okay." He climbed over the back fence instead of walking around the block like any normal person.

"I'm not much for playin' with girls, but I sure do like your dog." He scratched Tuffy behind the ears. "I'm good with dogs. See? He likes me better'n you."

He played with Tuffy, ignoring me, until Mama called out that it was suppertime.

I crossed my arms. "You have to go home now. My mama's calling me to come in."

He didn't say a word, just went to the back fence and jumped over it, like a show-off.

I don't like boys who won't play with girls. I won't ask him to come over ever again.

Dwayne

I'm at Aunt Letty's in Colorado for the summer, workin' on her farm.

I got in some trouble in Muskogee. Well, not really in Muskogee, in a little town close to the Missouri border. The Stateline bar's run by an old boy who'll serve us even though we're underage.

My buddy, Hank, quit school when he was sixteen to go to work at his dad's car repair shop. He's eighteen now, a big guy, two hundred thirty pounds and six feet tall. He has an old jalopy, and he takes me and two other boys over there to get drunk every Saturday night. We four Muskogee boys have been known to get into a few fights—just a few. I'm the smallest one, but I'm tough.

I was lying to my folks about where I was going until the four of us got charged with underage drinking and disturbing the peace. The charges could have been worse, except the old man knows some of those policemen.

"I'm takin' you out to Colorado for the summer," he told me, giving me a glance that dared me to defy him, which I was smart enough not to do. "You're goin' to do some real work. It ought to straighten you up some."

Aunt Letty picked us up at the Union station in Denver and drove us to the farm in the truck. I sat between her and the old man. It was a one-hour drive north to where they lived. Greeley was the closest town. The Rocky Mountains were snow-capped and majestic to the west, the land flat to the east.

Aunt Letty filled us in while she drove. "Our place is only four hundred acres. That's a small place for these parts. We mainly raise alfalfa." She honked at a cow that was too close to the side of the road. It didn't move, and she swerved around it.

"Must be tough to make ends meet these days," the old man said. "Oklahoma's not recoverin' very fast."

"Nobody has much money. Raymond cuts and bales hay for some of our neighbors over the summer. I sell eggs and grow a big garden. We make out okay." She slowed down at a road crossing. "I've got plenty of work for you, Dwayne. I told your dad when he called that we can use another hand for the summer."

"I'm ready to work." Not really, but the old man schooled me all the way from Oklahoma about what to say when I got here, to show gratitude to be gettin' this opportunity to stay out of trouble.

"My great-aunt Maggie is living here with us, so there's no profanity allowed and no smoking in the house."

Yes, ma'am." Great. Another old person who'll probably be buttin' into our business.

"I know you've been raising hell there in Muskogee with your friends," she went on. "You should know there's not much chance of that here. We're quite a'ways from town, and there's nothing to do but work and sleep. In the evening we listen to the radio or play some cards. We go to bed early. We get up before dawn."

The old man tapped the side of my head with his ring. Hard.

"Yes, ma'am." I rubbed my head. I was going to have a bump.

"You'll stay with our boy, Robert, out in the bunkhouse. We make a trip into Greeley once a week on Saturday morning to buy groceries and get any supplies we need."

"Yes, ma'am." I was quick about answering, not wanting another tap from the old man. "What grade is Robert in?"

"He'll be a freshman, same as you. I expect you boys'll have a lot in common."

I wasn't so sure about that.

We drove down a long dirt road to the small farmhouse, painted pale green with white trim. Robert was friendly. He took my bag and showed me to the bunkhouse, which was a rectangular frame building in back of the barn.

Robert set my bag on one of the beds. "We sleep out here and have meals in the house."

"This's cool," I said, looking around. The room was large, with two small windows, one at each end. There were four bunks. Scrappy quilts covered each bed. There was a black pot-bellied stove in the middle. "The folks won't know what we're up to out here."

"The shelves and closet are built in." Robert opened one of a series of small doors on one side of the room. "I cleared off this section for you."

"I didn't bring much. Just my clothes and a few books."

"Books, huh? I'm not much of a reader."

"I read most every day," I told him. "I can't go to sleep without readin'."

"You'll have to ask Mama for a lantern then. Once the sun goes down, there's no light in here. We get up at dawn anyways."

Evidently Uncle Raymond hadn't taken the trouble to wire the bunkhouse for electricity. Great. Early to bed and early to rise. I didn't think I'd be getting' wealthy or wise from this summer, but you never know.

The bunkhouse was comfortable enough. There was a sink with running water, an outhouse. When I asked her about it, Aunt Letty let me take a lantern.

We went to town on Saturday mornin', just like she said. The old man bought me a new pair of overalls and a work shirt. When we got back, Aunt Letty showed me how to kill a chicken by choppin' off its head. Blood spurted everywhere, and it ran around the bare dirt of the farmyard without a head far longer than I would've believed possible.

"Fried chicken still your favorite?" she asked the old man as he watched the scene from the back door.

"Yes, ma'am. Still is."

"I'll fix it for supper," she said.

"We should do something fun on your last night here," Uncle Raymond told the old man after we'd eaten. "Let's go into Denver to that new nightclub and have a few drinks."

"I'd like that." I've never seen the old man turn down a chance to drink.

"Me, too," Aunt Letty chimed in. "I'll just comb my hair."

She turned to Maggie, who was already back in her chair in the living room, half-asleep. She was ninety-seven and only woke up long enough to come to the table. "Maggie, can you keep an eye on the young'uns?"

"Yes, I'll be right here." Maggie opened her eyes as she spoke, then closed them again.

Robert and I were left to do the supper dishes and clean up the kitchen. It didn't take long.

"What say we take the truck out for a ride?" I was restless, missing my friends, pacing back and forth after we got back to the bunkhouse.

Robert looked scared. "I don't know. If my folks find out, we'll be in trouble."

"First, let's have a drink out of that bottle of hootch your dad keeps under the stairs."

Robert grinned. "Guess that wouldn't hurt. Let's go get it."

We went back to the house and opened a door under the stairs in the main house where the liquor was kept. "There's whisky and there's rum," he said.

"Whisky's my drink."

He took out two half-full bottles of liquor. I got two glasses and two coca-colas from the refrigerator in the kitchen.

I took whisky straight. He took rum with coke.

"This's my first drink," Robert said. He held out his empty glass. "It's not half bad."

"Who's countin'?" I poured each of us another one. After the third, I figured he'd had enough to be feelin' more adventurous, and I said, "C'mon, let's go for a ride. We'll be back before your folks get home. They'll never know."

"Okay." Robert grinned, staggering a little as he went to get the keys to the truck off their hook by the back door.

Neither of us had a driver's license, but we'd both been driving on back roads since we were old enough to reach the pedals.

"Let me drive."

Robert tossed me the keys.

The truck was old, the once-green paint scratched and beat up from years of farm work. Inside, it smelled like hay, wet wool, and the crusts of old sandwiches.

"We better push it," Robert said. "Aunt Maggie might hear it start up."

I didn't think it was likely. Aunt Maggie hadn't stirred when we were in the house. She was hard of hearin'. I guess that's why her snorin' doesn't wake her up. She was honkin' to beat the band.

All the same, we pushed the truck until we got close to the road, him behind the tailgate and me from the driver's side with the door open.

"Woohoo," I yelled. "Get in."

I started the engine and pulled out onto the road. We rode around the country roads. When we passed a large farmhouse with the lights on, Robert pointed. "That's where the Miller sisters live."

"Are they pretty?"

"Pretty, yesh. Wild. Plush, they're twins." He was slurring his words. The rum was hittin' him hard.

We finished off the bottles about a mile down the road from the Miller place. I felt free, like there wasn't nothin' I couldn't do.

"Oops." Robert threw the empty bottle out of his window. "Dad's gonna notice the bottles're gone."

"Who cares?" I crowed. "Let's see how fast this old tub will go." I revved the engine and got up to forty before we hit a deep rut in the road and careened into a ditch. We came to a sudden stop as the front fender hit against the ditch bank. The truck was leanin' to the passenger side, that door blocked.

"Are you okay?"

Robert nodded, wiping some blood from his forehead where he'd hit the window frame, then said, "I'm going to be sick." He vomited out the open window.

"How far from home do you reckon we are?" I asked when he slumped back in his seat, panting and wiping his mouth on his shirt sleeve.

"Maybe three miles."

"We better start walkin'. You'll have to scoot over here to get out." I opened my door and got out, then gave Robert a hand.

As soon as we climbed up the bank and were on the road, he sat down with his head in his hands. "The whole world's shpinning," he moaned. He tilted his head up to look at me. "You wrecked the truck. We're in deep shit."

I knelt down beside him. "I'll take the blame. Just sit still a minute or two."

We started walkin'. It was so dark out there, darker than I'd ever seen it. We were only about a mile from the farm when we saw two headlights coming down the road. A car slowed. It stopped as it came up beside us.

"Get in." Uncle Raymond said. He was driving with Aunt Letty in the passenger seat.

"We came home and saw the truck was gone," Aunt Letty told us after we got in, turning around to look at the two of us in the back seat. "You've worried us to death. You smell like whisky and puke, just in case you think we don't know you've been up to." She paused. "But you're not hurt, and I thank the good Lord for that. We're all going to church in the morning. Hangover or not. Don't even think about sleeping in. You're going to church with me in the morning."

The old man didn't say much when we got to the house. He was standin' outside smoking a cigarette, waiting for us. I couldn't read his face.

"Anybody hurt?" he asked.

"Nossir," I answered. "The truck's stuck in a ditch, though."

"We'll talk about it in the mornin'. I'm goin' to bed."

I was sure Uncle Raymond and Aunt Letty would change their minds about keeping me after that, but they didn't.

The old man left early the next mornin' to go back home. "I expect you to do a better job of takin' care of yourself." He got into the car. "You behave in church for your Aunt Letty."

The old man had never stepped foot into a church that I knew of. He didn't mind when Mama took us, but he never had a good word to say about how he was raised Mormon. Aunt Letty was still Mormon, though, and all of us went to church every week with her all summer unless there was farm work to get done.

"Yessir, I will."

"I'll be back to get you before school starts."

Aunt Letty started the car. She stuck her head out the window. "I'll be back to take you boys to the eleven o'clock service. Get on your Sunday best."

We rode on the tractor with Uncle Raymond to pull the truck out of the ditch. One of us would have to drive the truck back to the farm.

Once the truck was on the road again, Uncle Raymond stooped down and inspected its underside. "No real harm done. Another dent or two. I'm gonna take you boys out driving once a week." He looked up and grinned. "You need the practice."

"I'm sorry, Uncle Raymond. It was my fault."

"Yeah, I know it was." He took his hat off and wiped beads of sweat off his forehead. "Just so's you boys know, all the booze's gone, and I won't be getting any more. I'll let you have a beer after a hot day's work, but don't go asking for nothing else—and don't go telling Letty about the beer."

That was the end of it.

It turned out to be the best summer I ever had. I had different interests than Robert, but the two of us worked well together. We got along and learned to stay out of each other's way. I met the Miller sisters and kissed them both. I got tan, learned to drive a truck and a tractor, bucked bales, and grew two inches taller.

I stayed sober the whole summer. I didn't start any fights.

I was well on my way to being a man when I went home again.

Bill

We declared war on Japan. Now Hitler's declared war on us. I'm going home to tell the folks I enlisted in the Army Air Corps. They'll try to talk me out of it, but it's already done.

It's something of a madhouse there when I arrive. Walter and Kathy are in the living room having a loud squabble, two fussy babies chiming in. Mama and Daddy are sitting out on the front porch trying to ignore it all. Joy must be up in her room.

"Hi, Mama, don't get up." I lean down to kiss her.

"You're lookin' pretty good for an old man," I say to Daddy.

"Can't complain." Pointing in back of him to the ruckus going on in the living room, he says, "You can hear why we're out here. We spend a lot of time sitting on the porch nowadays."

"Lord help us when winter comes." Mama points to the shelf against the back wall of the porch. "We'll have to keep blankets out here so we don't freeze to death." She grimaces at the thought. "Can I get you something to drink?"

"No, but I'll stay for lunch. I've just come for the afternoon." I sit down on the glider. "I want you to know I joined the Army Air Corps. I'll be a flight officer, and they're going to train me to be a pilot."

Daddy hates the idea of flying. "Fly a plane? At least if you're in the infantry, you have your feet on the ground. You'll never get me up in one of those deathtraps."

Mama is more complimentary. "We're proud of you, son."

"I'll be leaving for Chicago in two weeks for some kind of special accelerated training," I tell them. "They're putting the Oklahoma bunch in a hotel downtown."

"All the way to Chicago—who'd have thunk it? Better watch yourself in the big city." Mama reaches for a cigarette. I flip my lighter open and light it for her. "Does Doreen know?" she asks.

"Not yet. I thought it might be best to wait. You know how she is."

We all know how she is—the incessant telephone calls, the accusations that no one cares about her, the hysterical fits of temper.

"Yes, that's probably best," Daddy says. "Although if she finds out we know and she doesn't, that might not set too well with her. Better tell her soon."

Mama taps her cigarette out in the ashtray on the side table. "Hard to tell with Doreen. She blows hot and cold. I'd better go tell Della to set another place for lunch."

"I'll go in and tell Della." I get to my feet. "She's like one of the family."

Walter and Kathy are nowhere to be seen when I go in. They must have taken the babies to their bedroom to put them down for a nap. Della's setting places at the dining room table. She stops when she sees me.

"Hey, Della, I'm going to be a soldier for real. What do you think about that?"

"Mr. Bill, don't you go gettin' yourself shot up."

"I'm going to be a pilot. Fly those big airplanes you see on the newsreels."

"Well, I'll be. That's somethin' fine. We'll all be prayin' you come back safe. Sit yourself down here." She points to a chair at the side of the table. "I'se just about ready to call folks for lunch."

"I hope it's your chicken salad." I pull the chair out and sit.

"It's tuna salad with a side of half a pear. It's real good."

I know it will be. Everything Della makes is good. She brought me a cold glass of sweet tea before she called the others to the table.

Lunch is a lively affair, mainly focused on my news and the talk of war. Oklahoma's gearing up to contribute to the war effort. The mild climate makes year-round training possible. Airfields are already beginning to training pilots. Manufacturing plants are securing defense contracts to make bombers and munitions.

"There's talk of women going to work in the plants," Mama remarks. "There won't be enough men left to keep factories going unless women fill the jobs."

Joy leaves the table, coming back with the camera I'd given her for her birthday. "I want to take a picture of you with the Brownie."

I stand up against the dining room wall. She snaps two photos of me alone, then Mama and Daddy get up to stand beside me in the third one.

"I'm out of film, but I want one of you in your uniform before you leave."

"Okay. I'll come back wearing my uniform, and you can take another one," I assure her. I look at Walter. "What about you, Walter? You joining up?"

Walter and Kathy look at each other.

"I'll wait to be drafted. Kathy's not too happy about it. You know, with the babies and all—"

"I get to have an opinion." Kathy didn't bother to mask her irritation. "If you enlist, at least we'd have some money coming in."

Walter tries to placate her. "Honey, there's gonna be a lot of work soon. I'm sure to get a job in sales with all these plants startin' up." Walter walks away from the table, Kathy following him. And the arguing is on again.

I decide to make my escape.

When I get back to Tulsa, I stop by Doreen's. It's only four in the afternoon when I park outside her apartment complex. I hope she hasn't started drinking yet. She's harder to deal with when she's had a few drinks.

Her apartment is on the second floor, number 1B. Music's coming from inside as I walk up to the door and knock.

"C'mon in," I hear Doreen yell.

I open the door and see five people, including Doreen, in the living room. The coffee table is littered with glasses, liquor bottles, and ashtrays. It looks like they've already been drinking a while.

Doreen gets up, running to give me a hug. "Hey, everybody. This's my best friend, my brother, Bill."

"Hey, Bill, I'm Jerry," says a tall man with sandy hair. He points to the man sitting next to him. "And this fine man is Allen. We live next door."

"I'm Trixie." A petite woman with bleached blonde hair and a bare midriff gives me a wave. "I live downstairs. 1A."

"And I'm Trixie's roommate, Wanda. Nice to meet you, Bill. Pour yourself a drink and join the party." Wanda waves at the bottles.

I don't see any clean glasses.

"I'm Doreen." Doreen laughs too loud as she pours herself another drink.

The most popular song in the country starts playing on the radio, "Don't Sit Under the Apple Tree."

"That's my song." Doreen gulps her drink, then says, "I sent it to that lousy producer, and he stole it from me. Now look. They're playing it every hour."

Wanda shakes her head and reaches for a cigarette. "Sorry, honey. That's real tough."

It's obvious from their reactions that Doreen's told them about this many times before. I'm not sure if I believe her story. I know she writes songs, and she's sent some of them off, but she also makes things up.

"I just stopped by for a minute to tell you my latest. I joined the Army Air Corps."

Doreen raises her glass. "To Bill, Billy, Bill—my little soldier boy."

"To Bill, Billy, Bill," everyone says in unison. They clink their glasses together.

I get a clean glass from the kitchen and have one drink with them to be sociable before I leave. On the way home, I stop at Lou's for a burger and fries.

It isn't until two a.m. that Doreen starts calling.

Anna

I was walking on air last week after the formal coming out dance Daddy gave for me at the country club. Everyone who was anyone was there. All of my friends, and everyone from church, and a bunch of people I didn't know—they must be Daddy's golfing friends.

Mama made a special effort to look nice. She bought a new dress and went to have her hair done. Dwayne whistled a wolf whistle when she came downstairs, and she smiled. She's beautiful when she fixes herself up. Daddy doesn't take her out very often, and I thought she might be nervous, but she wasn't. She had a good time.

"Your dress is aces. You look amazing." Nancy admired the formal she'd helped me pick out, a baby blue tulle with thin straps and a big skirt. I love the way the tulle is so light and airy. It looked like I was floating when I danced.

Daddy bought matching corsages of white baby roses for Mama and me. He and Dwayne both wore suits with a single white carnation boutonniere.

"May I have the honor of the first dance?" Daddy asked when the orchestra started playing.

"Of course. Thank you, Daddy. This is so wonderful," I told him as he waltzed me around the ballroom.

He looked pleased, and he was nice to Mama all the rest of the evening.

I danced with nearly everyone that night. We had the best time. My friends had such a good time that no one was even jealous or said anything mean-spirited afterward.

Then this happened. I honestly don't know what came over Daddy, telling Lyle Cormack and Billy Butler they couldn't take me out. I was in my bedroom when I heard the doorbell ring.

"May we take Anna out for ice cream?" I heard Lyle say. He's a Senior this year, and so dreamy. I've been hinting around to him that I'd like to go out sometime.

"Who's drivin'?" Daddy asked.

"I have my parents' car," Billy said. "I'm the one driving."

"Then she can't go."

Daddy shut the door in their faces. He is so rude.

I couldn't believe my ears.

I'll probably never see them at my door again.

Dwayne

What a night.

The doorbell rang after supper. It's the first week of April and the evenings are longer and warmer, shirt-sleeve weather. I answered the door, and there was Nancy's boyfriend, Lewis, standing with his hat in his hand, asking to see the old man.

I don't think the old man even knew that Nancy had a steady, but she's been sneakin' around with Lewis for months. He's five or six years older than she is, and if the old man knew he'd put the kibosh on it right away.

So, Lewis comes in and sits down, all quiet and polite-like, wearing his army uniform. He waited for all of us to gather in the living room, then he got right to the point with no pussy-footin' around. "I've been dating Nancy for quite some time now."

You could have heard a pin drop. Mama and Daddy sat there, staring at him like he had two heads. Anna looked guilty—she knew what was coming—but Nancy was all goony and starry-eyed.

"The thing is, Mr. Gray, I'm being transferred to Biggs Airfield in El Paso next week. I want to marry Nancy and take her with me," Lewis continued.

Nancy just turned eighteen last week. She can get married if she wants to, and the old man knows it.

The old man looked at Nancy. "I'd like for you to wait. Finish school, then get married after graduation."

Nancy looked the old man right in the eye. "No sir. I appreciate all you've done for me, but I want to be with Lewis. I'm happy with him."

"What do you think your parents would have wanted for you?" Mama asked.

"They'd want me to be happy," Nancy answered without hesitation.

Lewis jumped in. "I have a good future. I'm moving up in the army, and I'm training to be a pilot." He paused. "For when the war starts," he added.

The old man's eyes were hard, he was suckin' his lip into his teeth like he does when he's pissed off and doesn't want to show it. "You mean the war we're not fightin'."

Lewis wasn't backing down. "The one we'll be fighting soon," he said. "That's why Nancy and I don't want to wait."

There's another reason they don't want to wait, but I don't think the old man's cottoned to it yet.

I overhear a lot of girl-talk when I'm in my bedroom, private stuff the girls wouldn't say if they knew I could hear. There was a lot of hushed talk between Anna and Nancy last week when they were huddled in the bedroom together.

"You have to tell him," I heard Anna say. "He'll do the right thing. He loves you."

Heh. I know what that means. Nancy's in trouble.

Love is one thing. Marrying somebody and having a kid is something else. Not all guys are keen to do the right thing, especially those older guys from Camp Gruber. Everybody knows they're only after one thing from girls. Their motto is love 'em and leave 'em.

Nancy's lucky. Lewis isn't like that.

"If your mind is made up, I won't stop you," The old man said. He had his poker face on.

"Thank you, sir. We'll go to the courthouse and get the license, then get married before I leave."

Lewis can't believe his good luck. The old man isn't saying no. The rest of us can't believe it, either.

"Thank you, Mr. Gray," Nancy stood up and went over to give the old man a quick hug.

The old man stood up. "You think about what I said. If you change your mind, you can still stay here until graduation. Now, if you'll excuse me, I have a meetin' to get to."

We heard the front door close and breathed a collective sigh of relief.

Mama smoothed her skirt. "I have a fresh baked apple pie in the kitchen. Will you stay for some coffee and dessert, Lewis?"

"Don't mind if I do."

I couldn't believe the old man didn't lose his temper. He'll be singin' a different tune when Anna wants to get married.

1942

May

I feel sick every day.

Oh, I get out of bed, get dressed like there's nothing wrong. It's all I can do to keep up the house and cook the meals. I depend on Henry to bring home the groceries, but he doesn't always get what I want if he thinks it costs too much.

"Your heart's giving out," Dr. Linda told me after my last examination. "You need to rest more. There isn't much else I can do for you."

I don't want to put a burden on Anna, and Henry's already too hard on Dwayne. I try to make it through the day on my feet unless I have one of my migraines. I want our kids to have what I didn't, some carefree time while they're young.

Anna started volunteering at the ration board after school her senior year. When she graduated, they hired her to be the head of the tire and gas ration office. She hands out ration books and helps people get stamps every month that they can turn in for gasoline and tires.

"All those soldiers from Camp Gruber are after a pretty young girl," Henry commented when she told him. "I don't want a daughter of mine working there. I won't allow it."

"It's okay, Daddy. I know how to handle them."

"I hope to hell you don't."

Anna didn't back down. "What difference does it make? I've taken the job, and that's that."

She doesn't talk back to her daddy very often. His face instantly flushed with anger. I stiffened, waiting for the worst.

"Just take it from me. On your head be it." To my surprise, he turned his back and left the room.

Dwayne seems to have settled down since his summer in Colorado. Henry says he's going to take him go out there next summer, too, if Letty says she can use him.

Dwayne's smart and getting good grades—in fact, his math teacher, Mr. Steinmetz, called us, suggesting that we come in to discuss Dwayne skipping two grades and entering college early.

"Do you know he has a photographic memory? Once he reads something, he has it memorized. That's a pretty rare ability," Mr. Steinmetz told us.

Henry wasn't impressed. "He's already one of the youngest in his class. If he graduates early, he'll just be sittin' around the house until he's eighteen. He'd enlist today if he could."

"He could enroll in college and apply for an exemption. Academically, he's brilliant. He'll do well. I'd be happy to write him a recommendation and help him apply."

"Nossir," Henry stood and held his hand out to me, my cue that we were leaving. "I appreciate you callin' us in, but the boy stays where he is and graduates with his class."

"We should consider what the teacher is recommending," I said as we walked to where Henry had parked the car. I hadn't wanted to say anything in front of Mr. Steinmetz. Henry would have been embarrassed. I'd never hear the end of it.

"I'm not paying' for Dwayne to go to college, and that's the end of it." Henry turned the key in the ignition. "He's rarin' to go fight in this war. He keeps on buggin' me to give him permission to enlist as soon as he's seventeen. That teacher, Steinmetz—he's a German Jew." Henry cleared his throat and spit out the open window.

I let it go. It's not what's best for Dwayne, but I don't have the energy to fight another losing battle.

Henry won't allow Anna or Dwayne to get a driver's license, even though he knows Dwayne's been drives the farm truck and tractor out in Colorado all summer long. He butts heads with Anna about having a respectable job just a few blocks away, but he'll sign for Dwayne to go overseas into God knows what kind of danger.

I have my own bone to pick with Henry these days. He's gone three or four nights a week. When I talk to my friends whose husbands attend the same meeting Henry does, they say their husbands are still only going once a week like always.

"Why do you have to go out again?" I asked him Thursday after supper when I saw he was putting his coat on to go out. Dwayne was in his room doing homework, and Anna was gone over to a girlfriend's house.

"You were out Monday, Tuesday, and again last night. What's so important?"

He looked annoyed. "I have things to do."

"What things?"

"If you must know, George and I are meetin' some of the other men for a drink down at the Big Fish Tavern."

"I'll come with you. I haven't been out of this house in ages. Just let me get ready."

"No, it's only George and me. None of the other wives are goin'."

"You said you're meeting some of the other men—like who?"

"None of your concern," he answered, slamming the door on his way out.

I know for a fact Henry isn't going out to meet George. Betsy was at card group yesterday, and she said they were leaving for Oklahoma City this morning to see her sister's new baby.

He's lying.

He's off to see his other woman.

Doreen

Some of the nurses who work on my floor talked me into going to a USO dance last month, and now I'm happy they did. I met my dream date while we were dancing to 'Moonlight Cocktail.'

His name is Jerry Carter. He's younger than I am, an army lieutenant who has an engineering degree.

"I want you to know I'm divorced," he told me after our third date.

I have to say I wasn't surprised. I'd half-expected him to tell me he was married. Guys lie about stuff like that all the time, and Jerry's the kind of guy a lot of girls would go for.

"Why the divorce?" I asked, curious to see what he'd tell me.

"I had to get married to a girl while I was still in high school. She got pregnant, and we separated not long after the baby came." He kissed me. "It was nothing like the feelings I have for you."

Daddy'll have a fit if he finds out Jerry's divorced, but I don't care. Jerry's tall and handsome, and a smooth dancer. He has a college degree, and before the war he had a good job as an engineer in a large firm in Dallas.

"I'll be going back to Dallas when the war's over," he told me.

"Why not stay in Tulsa? Daddy says the oil business'll boom again. There'll be plenty of jobs right here."

"Maybe—if you can make it worth my while." He twirled a piece of my hair around his finger.

Well, that just sent me over the moon. You'd think it was my first date ever, I was that giddy. I've never felt like this about anyone. He makes me tingle from the top of my head to you-know-where.

"I'm getting shipped out to San Diego next week," he told me last night. "Let's get married."

"Yes." I squealed. "Let's go tell my folks. They haven't even met you yet."

"Of course. How about tomorrow? We could go in the early afternoon after I wake up from night duty."

My face fell. "I'm working day shift tomorrow."

"Get someone to cover for you."

That's how we ended up driving to Okmulgee in George's 1938 Dodge and spendin' the afternoon with my folks. I called Grandma Ella, too, and she said she'd drive over from Bartlesville.

"I love Doreen," George told everyone after we finished with the introductions. "I know it seems sudden, but things are different now with the war on."

"I'm in love with him," I told them.

Della had the day off, so I helped Mama get lunch ready. We started making ham sandwiches in the kitchen. She spread the bread with mayonnaise and I put the ham and lettuce between the two slices.

"Have you told George about your troubles?" she asked.

My troubles. That's what she calls my breakdown.

"No, and I'm not telling him. I've been doing fine for a long time now."

"Well, he's bound to find out sooner or later. You should tell him before you get married. It's not good to start off with a lie."

"He won't care. I'll tell him after we've tied the knot."

Mama got stiff and quiet like she does when she doesn't approve of something I'm doing.

"Now, don't you say anything, Mama. And you might as well know that I've told him I was born in 1920. I don't want him knowing that I'm five years older than him."

"Another lie. Think about what you're getting into, Doreen. You don't know much about him. You haven't even met his family."

I cut the stack of sandwiches corner to corner the way I like them, placing them on a platter. "Can't you be happy for me just for once in your life? George doesn't have any family. He's an only child, and his parents passed on a few years ago."

Mama opened a bag of potato chips and put them in a bowl. "That's what he says. You only know what he's told you. He only knows what you're telling him, which isn't the truth."

"What he says is good enough for me," I snapped, grabbing the platter of sandwiches. "And don't go asking him if he's Catholic. I mean it. It doesn't matter to me."

Mama put a smile on her face before we left the kitchen, and so did I. We pretended to get along for the rest of the visit, which I cut short.

"We'd better get goin'." I was ready to leave as soon as we'd eaten. I took Jerry's hand. "I traded one of the other nurses for the late shift tonight."

Another lie.

Bill

This jungle in Burma is a tough place to be. It's even hotter and more humid than Oklahoma in August. We're in a bare dirt clearing chopped out of the trees and vines with machetes, living rough. We sleep two to a tent and store our personal supplies in empty wooden supply crates.

I check the tent morning and night for snakes, spiders, bugs, and any other pests. The ants here are big as my thumbnail, and their bite's hard to heal. I'm bothered by a red heat rash spreading on my neck and back, itchy and irritating. It's hard not to scratch at it, but even small cuts and scratches get infected, so I put up with the discomfort.

The water is nasty, brown and full of who knows what. We have to boil it before we drink it, so one of us is always on the wood detail to keep the fire going. One bout of dysentery is enough to stop us from getting impatient with the boiling routine.

"Find anything?" Sil, my roommate, peers in through the tent flap. He's a tall, lanky man from Jenks, the only other Oklahoman in camp.

"Just these two roaches. Man, I thought the roaches were big in Oklahoma, but these take the cake." I come out of the tent and throw the roaches on the fire.

"BeeBee said roaches can live for days even after you chop their heads off."

"Well, these rascals are good and dead. I can hear them sizzling," I go back inside the tent and start reading my book, the only one I have, *The Three Musketeers*. It's my eleventh time reading it, and I can practically recite it by heart, but I still love the story.

"Say, I heard some scratching noises on the outside of the tent last night," Sil comes into the tent and sits on his cot.

"Rats or mice. This place is full of critters. Maybe the monkeys'll run 'em off."

"Damn monkeys." Sil yawns, stretching himself out on his cot. He closes his eyes. "I'm gonna get some shuteye."

I'm envious of the way Sil can sleep anywhere, anytime, anyplace. Not me. Most nights I lay awake for hours, thinking about home, thinking about tomorrow's mission, praying I don't get malaria or tetanus. I toss and turn, trying to find a breath of air.

It reminds me of hot nights on the sleeping porch at the Okmulgee house up on the second story where the whole family slept in the summer. The porch had screened windows on all three sides to catch the breeze. Toward morning the air would cool down a little. That was the best sleeping time. Here it never cools off like that.

It's the dry season now. They say we'll get orders to leave before the monsoon comes, before the camp turns into a swamp and the roads turn to nothing but mud.

We're flying daily cargo missions, taking supplies to the Burma Road under the lend-lease program we have with China. The supplies we drop are taken by locals on foot over seven hundred miles to where the Chinese are fighting. We also fly in to take out wounded men, mostly from the British offensive forces. That can be tricky. There aren't many good places to land.

Our missions are relatively safe. There's some strafing, but it's largely ineffective. Occasionally an enemy fighter will engage one of us in an air fight, but the danger from enemy planes is nothing like our flyboys are experiencing in Europe. We try to avoid fighters whenever we can. Our cargo planes are good and steady in the air, but they aren't nimble, especially when they're loaded.

There's not a better bunch of men than the ones I'm with right now. A few of us trained together in Chicago, and more of us met when we trained in Miami, Oklahoma before we were sent over here. We keep each other's spirits up in spite of the primitive conditions.

Mail delivery is sporadic. It's a bright spot in our week when a mail bag makes it through to the camp.

A letter came from Doreen in the last mail drop.

Dear Bill,

It'll probably be Christmas by the time this reaches you, so I hope you have some kind of celebration over there. The blue star is in the window at the Muskogee house, and we pray for your safe return every day.

Gas rationing makes it hard to travel, even back and forth to Muskogee. I'm staying in Tulsa this Christmas and working a day shift for one of the nurses who has kids.

Big, big news—I've met the love of my life, a man named Jerry Carter. He's an engineer, and he's in the army. We met at a USO dance, and I was madly in love with him by the time the dance was over, if you can believe that.

Don't be stuffy about this—he's five years younger than I am, so I've told him I was born in 1920. When you come home, you have to remember to be my older brother. How's that for a promotion, big brother?

Joy's all wrapped up in high school. She went to her first school dance and had a good time, but she said the boy she went with was a drip. I told her that all boys that age are drips. Ha.

The folks are doing fine. I took Jerry to meet them. Mama didn't like Jerry. What a surprise! I didn't even tell her he's been married and divorced and has a son in Dallas. You're the only one who knows that, so keep it to yourself, big brother.

I don't care what Mama and Daddy think. When you come home, I'll be a married woman—maybe with a kid or two, like Kathy. No, I'm kidding. You'll be home long before that. I'm getting married for love, just so you know.   Love, Doreen

We don't even have a chaplain assigned to us to give a Christmas service. Some of the men decorated a palm tree with stars and crosses they cut out of scraps of cardboard from some of the packing. We stood around and sang a few Christmas carols, followed by a bountiful Christmas dinner of hash. How I'm learning to hate hash! Some days it's hash for breakfast, hash for lunch, and hash for dinner. Once I'm back home, I'm never eating hash again.

Each of us put a little gift, wrapped in brown packing paper or a palm leaf, into a basket and took turns pulling one out—a lighter, a pack of cigs, a picture of Dorothy Lamour, a pair of socks (slightly worn), a deck of cards, some lemon drops.

It's funny how those little gifts lifted our spirits and made us feel like it's Christmas even though we're in a jungle three thousand miles away from home.

Dwayne

I spent the summer with Aunt Letty again. I worked hard and I didn't cause any trouble for anyone. Except maybe for Linda Miller. I sure think she's cute. Aunt Letty let Robert take her car on a double date one Saturday night. We parked out in the boonies after the movie let out. Linda let me get to first base.

Robert and I rehashed the date after we got in bed. "I think she likes you. She would've let you go farther," Robert told me.

"Yeah, I like Linda, but not enough to get into trouble diddlin' around with her. I have plans."

I imagined the smirk that would be on Robert's face when he heard that. Maybe he'd gotten farther with Linda's sister. Probably he had. These farm kids marry early, but that's not what I'm aimin' for.

"Here's your wages." Aunt Letty handed me an envelope when I brought my suitcase downstairs. "It's sixty dollars."

I was embarrassed that she thought she needed to pay me on top of giving me room and board for the summer. "No, ma'am, I didn't come out here to get money from you."

"You did hard work. We'd have hired a man to do it if you hadn't come out. We think you earned it." She placed the envelope on top of my suitcase. "I won't take no for an answer."

I put the envelope in my pocket. "Thank you kindly. Hope the fall crops come in good."

She hugged me tight. "You take good care of yourself, now."

"Yes, ma'am, I will."

I went out to the car where the old man was waiting for me. This year the old man drove out to Colorado when he came to take me home. I knew why. He wanted to stop and see his other son, Joe.

"Stay here." He parked the car outside a white frame house in Aurora, a town right outside Denver.

"I could go in with you. I'd like to meet my half-brother."

"Not today. Wait here." The old man closed the car door.

He stayed inside about an hour, leaving me to wonder why he was so secretive about his first son, why he didn't want us to meet. The old man likes keeping people separated instead of bringing them together. I didn't see the point of it.

He came back out and started up the car. "We're on our way. We'll stop in Kansas City for the night at Uncle Bill's."

I looked over to see if anyone had come out to wave him goodbye. No one was there.

He was in a good mood for the rest of the trip. In the middle of Kansas he pulled over to the side of the road and stopped the car.

"Hardly any traffic here and the road's straight. Why don't you take the wheel while I take a nap?"

We changed places. I tried not to show how surprised I was. My friends were all driving already, but the old man hadn't let me get behind the wheel even one time.

He hadn't let Anna drive, either. I guess he thought she'd be dependent on a man like Mama was dependent on him. He sure missed the mark on that one. Some of her girlfriends let Anna practice driving on the sly, and she could drive as well as anyone.

"I'm gonna study for the written test," she'd told me. "I'm gonna have a car of my own someday."

I believed her. She has gumption.

We got home just in time for Labor Day weekend and the start of my sophomore year of high school. I used part of my money to get school clothes and a new pair of shoes, and saved the rest for what the old man calls incidentals—cigarettes, I'm partial to Camels—and beer. We hang out at the side of the liquor store waitin' until a soldier from the base comes along. He'll usually buy us a six-pack or two. We aren't goin' over to the Stateline very often 'cause of the gas ration, but we find places down at the river to get drunk.

Kee Raleigh's two years younger than me. He's the son of John Raleigh, an enrolled member of the Cherokee Nation and a lawyer in Muskogee who's recently been elected a judge. His real name was William, but we all called him Kee. His dad gave him that nickname after the chirping of the birds that were nesting in the house when he was born. The name just stuck. He lived most of the time out at his uncle's ranch, workin' cows.

Kee's nearly six feet tall, and scared of nothin'. Everybody thought he was older and he liked to run with us.

Every time he met a new girl, he'd tell her how he was related to Will Rogers. "My grandmother is the sister of Will Rogers' mother," he'd say. The girl'd bat her eyes at him, say "Really?" all gushy like he was famous, and he'd have her hooked.

"C'mon, Dwayne, take me with you guys the next time you go. I can get hold of some whisky. And some extra gas stamps." Kee was talkin' about goin' over to the Stateline with me and the boys on Saturday night and seein' if we could find some trouble there.

"Aw, hell, why not? Be ready."

"I'll be waitin' for you. I'm gonna tell my uncle I'm spendin' the night with you."

"Yeah, okay."

The four of us picked him up about nine o'clock. The night was pitch black, the kind of night when the stars don't show through the clouds and there's no moon. Kee brought an unopened bottle of whisky with him.

"Found this tucked back under the sink," he said, twisting off the cap. "Must've been a Christmas present or somethin', 'cause my uncle don't drink."

We had ourselves a good ole time until a fight started with a few Missouri yahoos, then we hightailed it outta there.

"Hey, Brenda Wallace is havin' a slumber party at her house tonight," Kee said. We were almost back to Muskogee. "All the cheerleaders're goin'. We should crash it, whaddya say?"

I was for it. "I'm in. Maybe we can get a peek of the girls in their undies."

"I'll drop you two off," Dave said. "I got to get up and go to church early."

He dropped us off at the corner. Kee and I hung around outside Brenda's house for a few minutes. All the drapes were drawn, so we couldn't see in, but we could hear music comin' from inside.

"Whaddya bet those girls're dancin' around with their chi-chi's bouncin'." Kee started laughing.

"Chi-chi's?"

"You know. These." Kee cupped both hands over his chest, and I started laughing, too. Before I could stop him, he ran up and knocked on the door.

Brenda's old man answered. He must've smelled the booze right away because he turned his head toward the living room and said, "Get upstairs, girls."

The girls ran past the front door to the stairway, clad in their shorty pajamas, chi-chi's bouncin', just like Kee said.

"Wait right here," her old man told us. "I'll be right back."

We were dumb enough to wait right there. He came back and had a shotgun pointed at us. "Don't you run off, now. The judge is on his way."

Next thing we know, a car drives up to the curb and we're gettin' collared by Kee's dad. "You boys get into the car." He started pushing us down the walk, one of us on each side of him.

"Dwayne, I'm takin' you home," he said as he started the car. "Don't be callin' Kee to go out with you any time soon."

The old man answered the door in his pajamas and robe.

"Your son's a menace to society," the judge told him.

The old man ignored the judge. He spoke directly to me. "Get some ice on that eye. Is everybody okay?"

"Yessir," I mumbled, staggerin' in the door and makin' for the kitchen.

"Then that's all right." The old man shut the door in the judge's face.

"I don't want to hear from Judge Raleigh again over you pullin' some kinda stupid shenanigans," he told me the next morning. "Don't need that kind of trouble. You can be friends with the boy. He's at least got the sense to spend most of his time workin' out at the ranch with his uncle." He gave me the eye. "Understood?"

"Understood."

When I came downstairs on Christmas mornin', there was a brand-new Winchester Model 12 shotgun and two boxes of shells sittin' under the Christmas tree. My name was written on a tag tied to the barrel.

The old man pointed to it. "We'll go out shootin' tomorrow. After that I'm gonna teach you how to take care of that gun."

"A shotgun for killing things isn't the kind of gift you're supposed to give at Christmas, Henry." Mama gave the old man a look that told me he hadn't consulted her about it.

"It's for killin'birds, not for killin' people." He gave me a wink.

Mama shook her head and looked away.

I held the gun up, admiring the burnished walnut stock, looking down the sight, barrel gleaming. "It's perfect."

I hugged the old man, and he seemed pleased.

"Maybe we'll take off after dinner today, and go do some shootin'. No need to wait 'til tomorrow."

Mama got up and left the room. He said it just to piss her off, ruin her day.

This Christmas wasn't a season of peace on earth, goodwill toward men. We were at war and the war effort was all the news. Roosevelt announced that manufacturing plants could close for this one day, Christmas. Otherwise, they ran twenty-four hours a day, seven days a week with no holidays.

I couldn't wait to go shootin' with the old man, but there's somethin' I want even more.

I want to fight.

1944

Doreen

Jerry is in California and I'm stuck here. He says there are so many G.I.'s that there aren't any apartments to rent. He's living in barracks on the base. There's no married housing open there, either, or so he says.

"C'mon, honey, don't be mad. I'm doing my best to find us a place," he tells me.

I have to take his word for it. I try not to believe that he's already tired of me.

I've been real lonely, so lonely I called and invited Joy to come and spend the weekend. I hate weekends when I'm not working. The empty time drags me down. I start feelin' depressed.

"I'll ask. I'd like to come for a visit." Joy lowered her voice. "Kathy's home again."

"Well, ask Daddy, not Mama." I took a puff of my cigarette, holding it out dramatically and pretending to be Betty Grable. "You know Mama. She'll say no. She's afraid I'll corrupt you with my wild ways."

I was surprised when Joy called back later and told me Daddy had given her permission to come.

"He'll drive me in Friday night and pick me up Sunday afternoon."

She sounded excited. I was relieved I wouldn't have to spend another weekend counting the minutes dragging by. Maybe I could use it for a song title—Counting the Minutes. I'll have to play around with it.

I fixed pimento cheese sandwiches for our lunch on Saturday. We went to see the movie *National Velvet* in the late afternoon. Joy's favorite, Kraft macaroni and cheese, was what I made for dinner. She likes hers with canned tomatoes on top. I like mine plain.

"Complete with a vegetable," she laughed, adding tomatoes to the mound of orange macaroni on her plate.

"At least the mac and cheese doesn't cost me any ration stamps." I poured a beer, and pointed to the bottle. "Want one? I have more in the fridge."

"No."

"Oh, c'mon. Go ahead. It's not every day you get away from the folks."

"Well, maybe just one. I don't really like the taste." She made a face.

"That's because you should have more than one. Every beer you drink makes the next one taste better." I opened another bottle of beer and set it on the table in front of her. "You don't want a glass, do you?"

She shook her head no and I handed her the bottle. She took a sip.

"Sales of boxed macaroni and cheese have skyrocketed these last two years," I commented as we continued eating. "Everybody's buying it. They've sold millions of boxes."

"We have it at least once a week. Mama hates all the cooking she has to do when Kathy's there and this is easy to make. Mama says if she never cooks another meal, it'll be too soon."

"Della did most of the cooking when we were growing up. I remember her pot roast—um, mm, mm. Mine never comes out that good."

"Well, we only have a woman who comes once a week now, and she just does the heavy cleaning. Now Kathy's gone off again and left the kids with us. She says she's going to look for work in Oklahoma City, but I think she just wants to get away."

"Sounds like Kathy."

"I don't like to complain, but it's like Grand Central Station in the bathroom in the mornings. When Kathy's there, Daddy's yelling at her to get out because she hogs all the hot water, then Walter Jr.'s combing his hair for an hour." Joy laughed and drew a square in the air with her finger. "Daddy made up a chart and taped it to the bathroom door that shows your bathroom time—ten minutes for each person. Nobody but him pays it any mind."

"Why don't you stay with Grandma Ella on the weekends?"

"Because that's when the country club needs her. She's gone from early in the morning until late, and Daddy doesn't like it when I'm there by myself."

Now, if it was one of the three of us, I could understand Daddy's concern, but Joy never gets into any trouble. Not like we all did at her age. I'd like for Joy to stay with me, but the folks tell me she doesn't want to change schools again. They're probably right. She's going to graduate this year, so maybe she'll come to Tulsa after she's out of high school.

My meal finished, I make my play. "Say, what're you going to do when you graduate? Why don't you sign up at St. Francis? I could help you get through the nursing program."

Joy's thin, not very strong, but she is smart. She'd make a good nurse if she could stomach it. I don't like nursing that much, but Joy's always cared about other people.

"No offense, but nursing's not for me. Too hard. Being around sick people all the time—it makes me nervous. That makes my asthma worse."

"What are you going to do? Teach? I can't see you in a factory, not with all that dust."

"I'd like to be a librarian, but you have to go to college. Daddy doesn't have enough money for that."

I got up and opened another beer for myself, leaning against the refrigerator. "I was just hoping you could keep me company while Jerry's away. I get awful lonesome without anyone here. It's hard being alone."

"I guess you figured Jerry'd be here with you after you got married."

"Well, I knew he was going to San Diego, but I thought I'd be able to go with him." I sat down across from her and lit a cigarette, blowing the smoke out so it went away from Joy's face. "There's somethin' I haven't told anyone else, and you have to promise not to tell."

Joy's eyes got big behind her thick glasses. She crossed her heart. "I swear."

She's still such a kid. It cracks me up.

"I'm only tellin' you this because you're my favorite sister. Kathy's such a bossy-pants she'd tell Mama and Daddy first chance she got. She always tries to get me in trouble."

"I won't tell. I promise."

"Well, here's the thing. We went away and told everybody we got married, but we really didn't. Jerry was married before I met him. They were real young, she was in trouble. He isn't divorced yet. He still has a wife who lives in Dallas, and a little boy."

"Oh, my God, Doreen. Mama and Daddy would have a fit if they knew that."

"They'd say I'm living in sin, but I don't believe in all that." I finished off my beer and went to the fridge to get another. "Jerry'll get around to getting a divorce once the war's over. After that, we'll get married, and no one will be the wiser."

"You're brave to live with him before he's divorced. I don't think I could be so brave."

"You could if you wanted someone bad enough. I got tired of having people look at me sideways like there was something wrong with me for not being married. I told Jerry I was younger than him, too. Men don't like women to be older than them." I wagged my finger at her, starting to feel a little tipsy. "You remember that when you find someone to marry."

Joy started clearing our plates and silverware, taking them to the sink. "I'll clear up."

She handed me her unfinished beer and said, "Want the rest? I can't finish it."

She's such a goody-goody, this little sister of mine. She was bothered by what I'd shared with her. She'll learn you can't get what you want playing by somebody else's rules. I found that out the hard way.

I drank the rest of her beer and sat at the table, keeping her company while she did the supper dishes.

"Let's get into our pajamas and play a game of Scrabble," Joy said, wiping her hands on a dishtowel.

I went over and gave her a hug. "See? This's what I'm missing. This's what I need, somebody here in the evenings to play Scrabble with me."

That's not all I'm missing. Jerry hasn't been writing to me like he did after he first left. Maybe he's noticed I'm too old for him. Maybe he's found out I lied to him about my age. Maybe he found someone else at a USO dance.

Am I just another conquest to him? Is he telling me the truth, that his marriage is over and done with, that I'm the only one?

I don't feel brave like Joy thinks I am. I don't think I'm going to Hell. I feel foolish, a woman who's waiting to get hurt again by a man who doesn't love her.

After Joy goes to bed, I look at myself in the long mirror on my bedroom door, turning this way and that. Jerry says he likes the way I look, says I have style, that I could pass for Joan Crawford. I've lost weight this past month, worried about whether I'm attractive enough to keep him.

Now maybe I'm too skinny. I pull at my face, looking closely for wrinkles. There are tiny crow's-feet already at the corners of my eyes that I dab with moisturizer.

People say I'm never satisfied, but it's because I don't know what other people really think. I'm forever trying to please who I'm with, or, like right now, whoever I imagine I'm with, whoever might be judging me in my imagination. It's like a bottomless sinkhole pulling me down.

My loneliness only gets worse as soon as I hear the door shut behind Joy when she leaves the next afternoon. I go to the cupboard above the fridge where I keep the liquor and break open a bottle of gin.

The last thing I remember is dancing around the living room to music on the radio. In the middle of the night I wake up laying on the rug in a pool of vomit with pills spilled out all over the coffee table. I must have taken too many.

I'm starting to scare myself. Too much alcohol on top of too many pills. I'm a nurse, for God's sake. I know better. But I don't stop. I can't stop. These bottles are my only friends, the only way I can keep going.

I pour myself another drink and toss it down. Hair of the dog. My next shift is on Tuesday, time enough to get over this hangover. That means I have to get through a whole day and night without boozing it up again.

I don't understand why it's so easy for some people. Take Joy, for instance. She has lots of friends, and everybody loves her.

I don't have friends. I have to invite my neighbors over for a drink to have some company. They don't really care anything about me. They only stay long enough to get whatever free booze I give them.

The other nurses at work don't invite me to do things with them, either. I'm not sure why.

Maybe I try too hard. Maybe I don't try hard enough. I don't know what's wrong, exactly, but other people seem to sense that there's something off about me.

I'm not a red-headed stepchild. I don't have shit on my shoes.

It's not fair. I just want to be loved.

Anna

"You must think I'm stupid or something." The tall, handsome soldier standing across the counter at the ration office looked surprised.

"I'm only askin' if you'd have lunch with me tomorrow." He spoke with a West Texas drawl.

"I'm having lunch with my daddy," I replied, kind of flip. "He'd have something not very nice to say to you about asking me out."

He laughed, showing his straight, white teeth. "Now don't go bringin' your daddy into it." He leaned across the counter. "Most of my girls' daddies like me once they've met me."

"Well, my daddy doesn't like anybody much, and he's picking me up here pretty quick, so I suggest you get yourself gone." I walked to the back of the room and sat down at my desk, telling him, "Cindy can finish up with what you need."

"What is it you need?" Cindy asked him, going up to the counter, not missing a beat. We've tag-teamed for each other before.

"Got what I came for." He tucked the ration book into his pocket. "I'll be back." He was smiling as he left.

Two other soldiers were waiting, watching and listening with interest.

"Say, what was all that about?" the first one asked Cindy.

She held up her left hand and pointed to her third finger. "Married. We aren't in the habit of dating married men."

The second one said, "He's not married. No ring."

"Oh, yeah? You think we haven't seen guys coming in here who take their rings off just so they can ask for a date? It happens all the time."

"You soldiers think we're stupid," I said, coming over to the counter to help the second soldier. I pointed to his ration book. "Look here, you guys come in getting coupons for these B books. The only way you qualify for the extra gas you get with a B book is if you live off base. Follow me so far?"

The first soldier said, "We got you. The only way we can live off base is—"

"If you're married. Ring or no ring, I'm not going out with anybody who has a B book."

"Okey-dokey," he said.

The second soldier chimed in. "I'll tell the other guy when I see him that he ain't got a chance."

"You'd be doing him and us a kindness. Tell the other boys, too. Get the word out."

"Yes, ma'am." The second soldier gave me a mock salute.

Daddy picked me up in his Buick a few minutes after five o'clock. "What's new?" he asked as I settled myself into the passenger seat.

"Nothing. Same as every day. Ration stamps and soldiers."

The handsome soldier was back again the next day, waiting for the office to open for business.

I was trying not to smile as I unlocked the office door. It tickled me that he'd come back again. "You might as well leave. It's another month before you can get more stamps."

"I'm not after ration stamps. One of the guys who was in here yesterday said y'all think I'm married." He followed me inside.

"Um hmm." I went around to the other side of the counter and looked him in the eye. "I don't go out with married men."

"Well, I applaud you for that, but I'm not married."

"Your B-rated ration book says otherwise. Now you have me thinking you're not only married and trying to cheat on your wife, you're lying to me as well." I tapped my fingers on the counter. "Maybe you're defrauding the government with a fake ration book? There's quite a penalty for that."

"I can explain." His eyes were twinkling.

"You must think I just fell off the turnip truck."

He smiled, and he had a smile that could light up a room. I felt a little quiver inside, deep down. It was a feeling I'd never had before. It felt dangerous. And good.

"Don't bother explaining," I added quickly. "My mind is made up. I know what you're up to."

He looked over at Cindy, who had arrived just in time to hear what I said.

She shrugged her shoulders. "You'd best leave before you get yourself in any deeper."

He started to leave, then turned back around. "I'm goin' to prove to you that I'm not married."

"Um hmm. I'll be here waiting. But I'm not holding my breath."

We watched him swing his lanky frame into a jeep and drive away.

"He's got it bad," Cindy remarked.

Three days later he was back.

"Look who's here," Cindy said, staring out the window. "And see who's with him."

Colonel Harry Bristol, the man who ran the camp, was getting out of a jeep. The handsome soldier was his driver. I'd met Colonel Bristol once when Daddy took all of us for dinner at the country club for my birthday.

They walked into the office together.

"Which one?" the colonel asked.

"The pretty one with the black hair."

"Miss, may I have a word with you? In private?" The colonel cocked his head toward the back of the office.

"Of course." I raised a hinged part of the countertop so he could come to the back. "Please come this way. We can go in the back room." He followed me as I led the way to a closed door at the back of the main room. "I'm sorry, our space is very limited."

The storeroom was stacked with boxes of ration books and stamps.

"That soldier out there is a good man," the colonel said. He sat down on top of a stack of boxes. "This is an awkward situation. I've been giving approval for the B ration books to all the guys at the base so they can get more gas."

"That's illegal," I told him.

"I know, but A rations leave them too short for the month. The base is quite a ways from town. I would've come sooner, but I couldn't afford taking time from the construction going on at the camp. Four barracks have to get finished to house German POW's. They'll be here next week." He waited for me to say something, but I didn't. He shifted uncomfortably on the boxes. "My lieutenant wants very badly to take you to dinner, but he says you think he's married. He's not married. You'd be doing me a favor if you'd agree to have dinner with him—and overlook my mistake about the B books."

"You'll need to change your approval policy."

"I'll do you one better. There's a lot of time lost when our men have to come into town to get their ration stamps. I have a lot of empty office space out at the camp. I can set up an office for you in the administrative building,and provide you with transportation there and back. Also, I can get you a raise in pay. Meanwhile, your coworker can keep the office here open for the townspeople."

"I can see how a ration office at the base would benefit you. And the people in town won't have to wait so long in line. It might work, if our supervisor approves it."

"He already has. I talked to him this morning." The colonel smiled, knowing he'd put one over on me. "I didn't tell him about the B book approvals, however. I hope that can stay between us." He stood up, dusting off his pants. "Now, what about my lieutenant?"

"I'll go to dinner with him on one condition." I held up my index finger. "One time only. Anything after that is up to me."

"It's a deal."

We walked out of the storeroom, the colonel first, me following behind. When we got to the counter, he introduced me to the soldier who was still waiting there. "Miss Anna, I'd like for you to meet Lieutenant Glen Delaney." He looked at Glen and nodded. "I'll be waiting in the jeep when you're finished."

"Are you convinced now that I'm not married?" Glen asked as the door closed behind the colonel.

"I am. I'll go to dinner with you once—only once. That's the deal."

"Let's make it soon. I've been waitin' awhile, and I'm not much of one for waitin'." He grinned wider. "Do I need to ask your daddy for permission first?"

I stayed cool. "Naturally, my folks'll want to meet you when you come to pick me up."

"How about tomorrow evenin' about seven?"

"Seven's fine."

"Address?"

I wrote my address on a slip of paper and handed it to him, saying, "Don't be late."

"Don't keep me waitin'." He stuck the paper in his shirt pocket, and started whistling as he went out the door.

"Oh boy, you better watch that one," Cindy said as we watched him get into the jeep.

"Yeah, you're right about that." I felt a shiver of anticipation.

When he arrived the next evening to pick me up, he was in uniform. It was neatly pressed, his shoes shined. I heard the doorbell ring and the door open.

"Glen Delaney."

"Henry Gray. C'mon in. I'll tell Anna you're here. Anna, your date's here," he called up the stairs.

Daddy isn't always polite to the boys I date, so I came down double-quick.

"Wow, you look great," Glen said.

"Thank you."

He looked around, trying to see into the living room. "I was hopin' to meet your mother before we left."

Daddy spoke up. "Not tonight. She's in bed with one of her sick headaches."

"Maybe next time?" Glen looked at me as he asked.

"Let's go," I said. He's out of luck if he's hoping to get a hint that there'll be a next time.

"I borrowed the car from the colonel." He opened the door of the black Ford coupe.

"He must feel really guilty if he let you take his car," I said, settling into the passenger seat.

Glen laughed. "He's a smart guy. He told me to tell you he thinks you're worth it."

He took me to Hanson's Steak House, the best restaurant in town. We were seated off to one side in a little nook, more private than most of the other booths.

"Did you arrange for us to be seated here in advance?" I asked, looking over the crowded room after the waiter showed us to our table.

"I aim to please since I only get one chance to make a good impression on you."

It was a good move on his part. I was impressed that he'd cared enough to arrange it. "What are you going to order?" I asked. Everything on the menu looked expensive.

"The steak is supposed to be the best in town. That sounds good to me. I'm sick of the food at the canteen. You go ahead and order whatever you want."

"I like steak. I'll have whatever you're having. Where are you from?" I was curious about his family.

"Altus, down by the border with Texas."

"It was hit hard there, wasn't it?"

"Yeah, my family's the real-life Grapes of Wrath story. Our farm just dried up and blew away, nothin' 'cept dust. You couldn't tell dust storms from tornadoes, it was that bad. The dirt came blowin' and got packed so tight against the house we couldn't even get the doors open."

"Did your folks make it through?"

"They tried their best, but nobody in that part of the country could stick it out. We loaded what we could in the pickup when I was twelve, another family of Okies headed for California—my mom and dad with me and my older sister, Bonnie, and my younger brother, Danny. I'm the middle one."

"Hard times," I said. Oklahoma and parts of Texas had been especially devastated by the drought years. "Our family's been lucky. The depression didn't hurt us like it did a lot of people."

Glen had a faraway look in his eyes as he told me the story of his family's migration. "Only jobs in California are pickin' crops, harvestin' grapes, potatoes, cotton. I picked ever' day after school. When I was sixteen, I left home to take the burden off my folks. Got a rented room that didn't cost much."

He paused to give our order to the waiter.

"Sounds like you have a lot of determination," I told him.

"Guess you could say that. I was determined to be the first one in my family to graduate high school. My best job was workin' for a mortuary. I drove the ambulance, went around pickin' up bodies. On my days off, I worked in the ice cream parlor down the street from where I roomed. I thought joinin' up was the best thing for me to do when we declared war."

"Seems like the colonel likes you." I smiled at him.

"I guess it's turned out all right. The army's been real good to me." He pointed to his blue eyes. "20/15 vision. They trained me to fly a P-38 for reconnaissance while I was in Oklahoma City. Now I'm here at the Muskogee Air Base trainin' other pilots, but not for long. I'll be gettin' shipped over to England soon. Prob'bly flyin' bombin' missions to Germany, maybe France."

The thought of him in danger made me feel uncomfortable. I changed the subject slightly, saying, "I'd like to travel. Not because of a war, obviously. I've been to Milwaukee and Colorado, but that's it. I'm just a Muskogee girl who wants to see the world."

"We might have more in common than you think, Muskogee girl."

"We might at that."

The waiter came with our food. The steaks were juicy and the vegetables were covered in a creamy butter sauce. It looked and smelled delicious.

He picked up his knife, then set it down again. "Would you like a cocktail or a glass of wine? I guess I should have asked you before. I don't eat out like this very often, to tell you the truth."

"No, thank you. That's all right, I'm a Baptist. I don't believe in drinking much. Not that I mind a beer or a cocktail if it's a special occasion."

"This here's a special occasion to me." He reached out and put his hand over mine.

"You're so sweet." I withdrew my hand. My skin tingled where he'd touched me, and I felt a warm flush on my cheeks as I picked up my fork.

We ate our meal, sharing small talk about ourselves and our work. It was a relaxed evening, and I realized as we left the restaurant that I'd had a thoroughly enjoyable time.

"Will you go out with me again?" he asked as we walked up to my front door.

The curtain moved slightly. Daddy was in there spying on us.

"I will. I didn't think I would have such a good time." I stood in front of him, tilting my head up. He was taller than I was by several inches. "It's been a very nice evening."

"I was tryin' to impress you."

"You don't have to take me to an expensive dinner, though. How about I fix a picnic?"

"I have to fly to Amarillo, but I'll be back next Saturday." He leaned forward and pulled me closer to him.

"Sunday after church? About noon?" I asked, my breathing quickening at his touch.

"Egg salad sandwiches are my favorite."

"Mama makes the best egg salad you ever tasted. Do you like buttermilk? I can get some fresh buttermilk delivered."

"Ummm, I do like buttermilk," he said. "So smooth on the lips."

I stretched up and kissed him. His lips were soft and warm, inviting. He wanted another kiss, but I pulled away from him, remembering Daddy at the curtain.

"I'll see you Sunday," I said.

"I'll be waitin'. I want your egg salad. Not your mother's."

I couldn't stop thinking about him when I went to bed, how handsome he is, how his mouth crinkles when he smiles, the way he kisses me, the way he's making his way in the world after his family had lost everything, the adventures he has ahead of him.

The way he kisses me.

He's strong, fearless, and smart. And he likes buttermilk.

I'm going to marry him.

Arthur

"How would you like to go back to Okmulgee for your senior year and graduate from St. Mary's?"

Joy squealed, jumping up and down. "Yes, yes, yes. When are we moving?"

"Well, here's the thing. You'll move back, but we're staying here. Grandma Ella is closing her boarding houses in Tulsa and Bartlesville. She's taken a job cooking for the Okmulgee Country Club. She bought herself a little house over on Sixth Street, and she's offered for you to stay with her until you graduate."

"I can't wait to tell Mary Alice. She'll be over the moon. Can I call her?" Joy was already halfway down the stairs on her way to the telephone.

"Make it short."

She looked back at me. "Can I go tomorrow? I'll get my clothes ready."

"Not tomorrow. We'll take you over Labor Day weekend before school starts up."

Gladys and I have been worried about Joy. She's never been very happy here. She misses her friends in Okmulgee, and I need to stay here for work. I hope to go back to Okmulgee someday and reopen my business, but it doesn't make sense to do that until the war's over.

What I didn't tell Joy is that Kathy is coming to live with us again—another reason why it would be better for Joy to be in Okmulgee with Ella. Kathy's pregnant with her third, and Walter, Jr. and Sally are a handful. The house will barely hold all of us even with Joy gone.

Gladys asked me about it when she came home from doing the weekly shopping. "Did you say anything to Joy about going to Mother's?"

"She was overjoyed." I couldn't help chuckling at my own joke. Gladys looked pained. She's heard it more than few times too often. "She already called Mary Alice to tell her the news."

"I'd better let Mother know right away. Before she hears it from somebody else."

We started putting groceries away. I felt my stomach starting to burn as I stretched to place cereal on an upper cabinet shelf.

It's hard to quit worrying when I want the best for everyone, and I said, "Joy might feel she's been pushed out when she finds out Kathy's coming."

Gladys didn't seem concerned. "She'll be gone by then. They aren't coming until the middle of September when Walter goes to his new job in Wichita. By then, Joy'll be happy being back in school with her friends."

We hugged. I was happy to hear the two of us are going have a week or two to ourselves with no children or grandchildren before Kathy gets here. That seems like the biggest luxury of all.

Bill

I'm flying missions nearly every day. The Japanese troops are in retreat in Burma. I hope that means I'll be deployed somewhere else soon.

What I'd really like is to be home again, sitting at the table and getting ready to eat a big pot roast with potatoes, carrots, and onions. I can smell it now.

We're restricted to rations most of the time, and those get old fast. All of us dream of food, real American food—hamburgers, steaks, pork chops with gravy, turkey and mashed potatoes, my grandmother's ice box cake layered with pineapple and whipped cream. We get some fresh fruit, jackfruit, papaya, and limes, but there's barely enough to feed the local people, much less us. At least the fruit keeps us from getting scurvy.

I also dream of freshly laundered shirts, clean socks, a thick mattress and fluffy pillow, my own bed in my own room, hot water from the tap, a flush toilet. And most of all, girls who smell like roses and wear freshly ironed shirtwaist dresses with high heels.

I wrote to Doreen last week and told her she better get her high heels on when Jerry comes home. Knowing her, she'll probably make some wisecrack about her wearing high heels and nothing else when she writes back.

One of the men shot a wild pig last week.

He came into camp carrying a pole on his shoulder, the pig strung up on it by its feet.

"Dig a hole," he yelled. "It's pit barbeque for the camp tonight, boys." He dropped the pole on a bare spot of ground.

"You shoot that?" one of the men asked, nudging the pig with the toe of his boot.

"Couldn't do nothin' else. Damn thing ran right for me."

We dug a pit while some of the boys who grew up on farms butchered the pig. We lined it with palm leaves to roast it. There was only enough to give us a few bites each, but, man, was it tasty. Like Thanksgiving.

We lost two planes last week along with seven good men. I think of Mama, saying that your death date is written up in heaven right beside your birth date. I wonder if this is the time my number's coming up whenever I fly another mission. Some of the boys keep count of how many missions they fly, but not me. I guess I got some of the Irish superstition from my daddy—keeping a tally is too much like tempting fate.

The girl who marries me better not want to travel because when I get back home I'm never leaving the country again. I've seen enough of the world to last me a lifetime. America's plenty good enough for me.

That's what I think about when I'm not in the air—home, food, girls.

Guess I'm feeling especially homesick. Today's my twenty-fifth birthday. I sure would like to see my folks. That'd be the best birthday present ever.

Anna

I'm running off to marry Glen. It isn't the kind of wedding I dreamed about, but no one's having big church weddings these days. I've never seen Daddy set foot in a church anyway.

The important thing is being with Glen. He says he'll find someone to marry us as soon as we get to the Army base in Harlingen, Texas.

And he says I can go to the dentist on the base as soon as we're married. He looked astounded when I told him about Daddy not letting us go to a dentist.

"I can't believe it. You should get your teeth checked and have any cavities taken care of before you lose a tooth. That's just money well spent."

Daddy's going to throw a fit when he finds out I'm gone, but Glen's going to be sent to England to fly bombing missions. We've talked about the fact that he may never come back. German pilots are well-trained, and a pilot who gets shot down in enemy territory doesn't have a chance. We want to grab happiness now. While we can.

Dwayne said, "Aw, he doesn't like anybody who takes you out. Nobody's good enough for his little girl." I threw a pillow at him, and he just laughed, saying, "You know it's true."

Daddy was waiting to confront me when I came home from a date with Glen last week. He stopped me as soon as I came through the door. "I don't know why you're going out with that man. What in the world do you have in common?"

"We both like buttermilk." I gave him a bright smile. There's no way I'd tell him how Glen makes me feel, or the fact that we agree Daddy has a screw loose about a lot of things.

Daddy smiled back, the kind of smile that let me know he didn't think my answer was funny. He's trying to find out if I'm serious about Glen. I don't trust what he'll say or do if he thinks I'm in love.

Mama might understand why I'm eloping, but she's too much under Daddy's thumb to help me. If I told her, she'd get scared, or take one too many of her headache pills. She'd let the cat out of the bag before I could get away.

I'm leaving tomorrow. Glen already bought my ticket for the bus. I took my old blue suitcase with the matching cosmetic bag off the closet shelf and hid it under my bed. I'll slip it out and pack it after everyone's gone to sleep.

The only one I've told is Dwayne, and I've sworn him to secrecy. He won't tell. He's good at keeping secrets, and he owes me. I've kept quiet plenty of times for him.

I'll be worried about Dwayne when I'm gone. He won't have me to take any of the heat. He tries too hard to impress Daddy, does some reckless things when he's out drinking with his buddies. I hear stories of how he starts fights over in the border town, how he goes looking for trouble.

He says he's going to join up as soon as he turns seventeen. I've tried to talk him out of it, but he seems determined.

"I'm goin' in the Navy. They'll take me if Daddy'll sign. He says he will."

I raise my eyebrows. "That's crazy. Why the Navy? You can't swim and you're afraid of the water."

"So what? They have life jackets." He stomps off to show me he isn't scared. Maybe he has to face his fears to prove something to himself.

Maybe the war will end before he's old enough to sign up. I'm afraid he'll get himself into something he can't get out of.

"I can't stay here just to watch over you," I tell him. "I have to think of myself."

"Don't worry about me," he says. "I'll be out of here soon enough."

I'm grabbing hold of my future with both hands and not letting go. I haven't ever thought of myself as a daring person, but I guess I'm finding out different. I only hope Mama and Daddy forgive me later when they see how happy I am. Maybe then they'll realize Glen's the right man for me.

Last week there was an evening when Daddy stayed at home after supper. He's gone to a meeting, or wherever it is he goes, nearly every time Glen comes to pick me up. "You act like you don't even like Glen," I told him. "What's your problem?"

Daddy looked at me and didn't answer for a minute. Finally, he said, "Glen comes from a family of Okies, that's what bothers me. He grew up poor, had nothin'. That's what I don't like."

"He's making something of himself."

"So you say. He's not good enough for you. Not by half."

"You never think anyone's good enough for me. Glen's going places, you know. He's smart, and he's a hard-worker. He loves me."

Daddy rolled his eyes at that. "If you say so. I don't have time to waste arguin' with you about it. I got to skedaddle." He went to the coat rack, put on a jacket, and left.

Daddy thinks nobody notices what he's up to, but Glen notices. Daddy's been leaving several times just as Glen comes by to pick me up.

"What's going on with your dad? He comes home, gets all cleaned up, then goes out again. That's not normal, Anna."

"I know it isn't," I told him.

I guess I've been like Mama. I know what he's up to, but I don't want to know. He's going to see other women. Margie Miller told me he's in and out of her next-door neighbor's house several times a week, usually at night. Her neighbor's a divorced woman whose name is Maybelle, but everyone calls her May. Imagine that.

It's amazing that Daddy has the gall to think Glen isn't good enough for me. It's no wonder Mama lays down on her bed with the curtains drawn, zonked out on those pills Dr. Linda gives her.

He's afraid I might run off, and he keeps a close eye on me. I happen to know he has a big meeting in Tulsa tomorrow. He's leaving early to pick up George, and they'll be gone until evening. The timing is perfect. I'll be too far away for him to come after me by the time he finds out I'm gone.

I'm a grown woman, making this decision on my own. I don't need him telling me what to do or who to love. Mama has lived in his shadow all her married life feeling heartsick and unhappy.

My marriage is going to be different. Glen and I will be partners.

We're going to be happy.

Dwayne

I've never seen the old man so mad. He didn't get home until late, so he didn't realize Anna was gone until this mornin'. He went to wake her up for work, found her bed empty and her gone.

He came stormin' into my room and dragged me out of bed.

"Where's Anna?" His tone cut like a knife through my confusion at findin' myself sprawled on the floor.

"Wha..?" I asked, still half asleep.

"Anna's gone. She must have told you somethin'" he growled, pacing in front of me.

"Didn't say nothin' to me."

He sat on my bed. I picked myself up off the floor and leaned against the wall, rubbin' my eyes 'cause they always itch somethin' terrible the first thing in the mornin'.

"Her clothes are gone. Her suitcase, too. She's pro'bly run off with that pilot, Glen, the stupid bitch."

There's no point in tryin' to reason with him when he's like this. I kept my mouth shut.

"She didn't tell you she was leavin'?" His fists were clenched at his side.

I was wakin' up to the situation now, knew I had to be cautious. "Nossir, she seemed just like normal." I sat down on the edge of the bed beside him.

He stretched out his fingers, seeming to shrink, his shoulders slumping. The rage was leavin' him, and he looked drained.

"Well, she better never come back here thinkin' she has a free place to stay."

I held my face blank. He stood up and faced me.

"She's made her bed. She can lie in it. Let it be a lesson to you, in case you get a wild hair about runnin' off."

"Yessir," I answered.

"If I find out you knew about this, I'll beat you silly." He pointed to his belt as he went out the door.

It was an empty threat. He's only beat me with the belt twice, once a long time ago when I was mean to Nancy, and once when I backtalked him in front of George. I'm big enough to take him. Not as mean, maybe, but more experienced at fightin', and with the advantage of youth.

He'll never beat me again, no matter what. That's already been decided whether he knows it or not.

I heard him down the hallway, waking Mama up, yellin' at her to get out of bed. She'll get the brunt of it now. It's goin' to be a bad, bad day at the Gray house. For once, I'm glad to be goin' to school.

I'm startin' to notice how mean the old man can be to Mama. I guess I've always known it, but it bothers me more now that I'm older and I'm datin' girls. I don't think a person should be that hateful to a woman, especially not to his wife. Mama's just tryin' her best to be lovin', to make things right.

Last weekend we were all in the livin' room listenin' to the radio. Just out of the blue, the old man looks straight at Mama and says, "You don't know how much I have. One of these days, I'll just up and leave you. You won't have nothin'."

Mama started cryin'. Anna and I looked at each other, then Anna spoke up. She knew he wouldn't rap her on the head like he does me for speakin' out.

"Go ahead and leave," she told him.

Daddy gave her a mean look, but he didn't say anythin' more. Mama left and went up to her room, still cryin'. The old man got his coat on and went out the front door like he usually does, goin' out to see whatever woman he's involved with these days.

And he wonders why Anna wanted out of here.

I can't wait to leave. Three more months. I'll be seventeen, and I can enlist in the Navy. I'm goin' to get the GI bill, go to college, and get a good job.

I'm gonna have a life away from this hellhole, get married to a nice girl and treat her right. I can tell you for sure it ain't gonna be nothin' like this.

May

My head is pounding. Henry's been in a state since Anna took off with Glen. I wish I had her courage. I think about leaving, but I can't. I can't imagine living on my own and trying to support myself. Dr. Linda says living with so much stress isn't good for me, but I feel my heart fluttering every time I think of leaving Henry. I live on the horns of a dilemma—I hate being here and I'm afraid to leave.

The phone rang yesterday, about an hour after Henry usually leaves for work. I'd just gotten dressed and was making myself some coffee and toast.

"Hello, Gray residence," I said as I answered the call.

"It's me, Mama. I'm in Texas, and I wanted to let you know I'm okay. I'm calling from a pay phone."

"Your daddy's in a right snit about you leaving like you did."

"I'm sure he is. Glen and I got married. I'm staying here in married housing at the base. Glen's leaving for England in just a few more days."

"Will you be all right there? Are you coming home when he leaves?"

"I'm fine. I already have a part-time job, filing papers for the army. It's boring, but it pays enough for me to have a little extra money. And no, I'm not coming home. I worry about you, though."

"Henry was mad the day after you left, but he's calmed down now. He won't like the idea of you living on the air base with all that riff-raff."

"Riff-raff? The people here are military personnel."

"You know what I mean—the Coloreds."

"Daddy's crazy for thinking that way."

The operator broke in. "It's twenty-five cents more."

I heard a coin drop.

"I'm out of change, Mama. You take care of yourself. I'll call next week."

"Okay, honey. I love you."

"I love you, too."

After we hung up, I started thinking about how mad Henry would be if he finds out Anna has called. He'll be mad regardless—if she doesn't call, he'll say she doesn't give a damn about us, but if he finds out she called while he's at work, he'll forbid me to answer the phone. Or worse, have it taken out.

He's always threatening to do something like cut off the phone service. Him—the man who doesn't believe in any kind of censorship—wants to take out the phone if somebody's saying something he doesn't like.

At least I have a little company as long as Dwayne's still here, but he'll be leaving soon. It's all he talks about these days, like he thinks going to the war is going to be so great. Once he leaves, I'll be alone all the time.

Henry's over at that divorcee's house every night, making excuses for why he has to go out. He thinks I don't know, thinks I'm totally stupid. That bleached blonde slut lives right next to the Millers, and Betsy Miller is the biggest gossip in Muskogee. I swear, she lives to rake up dirt on people. At least she tells me what he's really up to. The woman he's seeing is called May. Unbelievable.

Like I care. I used to care, but that was a lifetime ago. Before May, it was Helen Riley. He got tired of Helen pretty quick. Her four kids were always in the way. Before her it was DeeDee. After May, he'll be off servicing some other lonely divorcee or widow woman. Well, she's welcome to him.

I get so aggravated every time he goes out the door, I could just scream. I'd better go upstairs and take another pill to calm myself down. I'll have to call Dr. Linda later today and get another refill. She says I have to be careful because these pills are addictive, but I can't think about that.

I need them. I really, really do.

Joy

Grandma Ella bought me a white dress with daisy trim on the sleeves and collar to wear to graduation. I love it, even though it doesn't show under the gown. Mama and Daddy gave me a typewriter, and Doreen says she has a twenty-dollar bill with my name on it that she'll give me next time I see her.

Doreen didn't come to Okmulgee to see me get my diploma. She said she didn't have enough gas on her ration card to make the trip, but I think she'd been drinking when she called. It's hard to tell what's real and not real with her these days. She's my sister, and I love her anyway.

Kathy and Walter couldn't make it, either. I acted sorry and disappointed, but I was secretly relieved. I didn't want to get bossed around by Kathy or listen to her arguing with Walter. I especially didn't want to share our one tiny bathroom with five additional people.

Is that selfish? I guess it is. Oh, well.

The only person that I truly wish could have been here is Bill.

Mary Alice and I double-dated to the graduation dance. Freddy Frieze asked me to go with him, and she went with her steady, Benny Riggs, who was driving.

"Hey, Mary Alice, are you going to wait for Benny after he enlists?" Freddy asked, turning to look at Mary Alice and I sitting together on the back seat.

"Unless somebody better comes along," she answered.

"I'd ask her to marry me tomorrow," Benny said, not taking his eyes off the road, "but I'm going into the army next week. I want more than a few days with my bride."

Mary Alice giggled. "You know I'd marry you tomorrow if you asked me."

"I know. I wouldn't want nobody to be saddled with takin' care of me if I was shot up or crippled."

"I'd still love you."

She says that now because it's not real. We all know someone who's been faced with how they're going to cope with the death or disability of a soldier. Families are receiving notices every day that their sons, husbands, or brothers are dead, maybe missing in action. Or worse, that they're coming back to a shattered life—missing arms or legs, paralyzed, terribly burned, shell-shocked, brain-injured.

Do you still go on loving someone who isn't who they used to be? Someone who'll never be able to share the life you'd hoped for?

I've seen ambulances pulling up to the Veteran's hospital in Muskogee, and I've turned away so I didn't have to see. Our high school asked for volunteers to visit the soldiers who were hospitalized, but I didn't sign up. I feel guilty about it. It's too depressing to sit with that kind of pain and loss. I ask myself what I'd do if it was Bill who needed a visitor, and I tell myself I'd go if it was someone I loved. I hope I'm that kind of person. I don't think any of us really knows until it happens. For right now, I want to have happy thoughts.

Mary Alice and I start college in the fall. I can't believe I'm able to go, but Bill sent a letter with some money for me to use for school.

Dear Joy,

I'm so proud of you. EnJoy your graduation (ha, ha, get it?). I don't have any use for all the money I'm getting paid here in Burma—in the middle of the jungle there's no place to go and no one to go with—so I'm sending you this check for college. I may only be able to give you money until the war is over, but at least you can get a start. The folks don't have the extra, but you know I'm always here to help you out whenever I can.

Love, Bill

I feel guilty about taking Bill's money, but Mama says I shouldn't, that he wants to help me out. I've enrolled for one semester, and I'm going to study hard and make sure Bill knows I'm doing my best. Four of my other friends are going, too. We Okmulgee girls are all living in the same dorm together.

The college says they are only offering courses that teach us things to help with the war effort, but that's okay with me. I'm taking Shorthand, Intro to Accounting, and European History. I guess writing letters and keeping track of things could help with the war effort.

We girls will miss having the boys around. Most all of them are going into the service or working shifts at the munition plants.

"I'm not going to date. Ben and I are going to keep going steady while he's away," Mary Alice tells me.

"I'd like to date someone, but it has to be the right someone—good looking, not too tall and not too short, with a good sense of humor. Lasso the moon, right?" I tell her.

"You're beautiful," she says. "So thin."

I'm thin because of my asthma. I've never looked at it as a plus. I envied Mary Alice her curves, and wished I looked like a pinup girl, like Marjory Russell. Funny how I want more curves and Mary Alice wants less. Why can't we girls be satisfied with how we look?

The four of us went out to the quad on the first day of classes and took pictures of each other by the fountain. I wore my new dungarees and a blouse with the tails tied over my midriff. We all went to lunch in the cafeteria. The food is basic—I had a turkey sandwich with more mayonnaise than turkey, but who cares?

I'm supposed to be deciding what I want for my future while I'm here.

It's the opposite for me—I know more about what I don't want than about what I do want.

I don't want to end up like Doreen, living a lie. I don't want to end up like Kathy, married to a drunk with a bunch of kids and no home. I don't want to end up like Grandma Ella, cooking and cleaning for strangers, standing on my feet all day with bad knees.

The cautionary tale from the women in my family is to pick a man who doesn't drink too much. How do you tell? How much is too much?

When does having a beer or a cocktail change from harmless fun into something that's ruining your life?

Dwayne

I'm in the Navy. I made it through basic trainin' and they trained me to be a radio operator.

I got in a few prize fights as a welterweight boxer while I was still at the base. They set up a ring and recruited those of us who wanted to box. Man, was that fun. I won a few and lost a few, proved I could take a punch.

Some of the boys and I went out to the clubs in San Diego to have a little fun on weekends. I found out pretty quick they invited me to go along because they knew I liked to fight. We'd cruise the bars along the waterfront and look for queers to beat up. You'd be surprised how many we found.

Anna was shocked when I told her what I'd been up to. "Dwayne, I can't believe you're doing that." She'd flown to San Diego on an army plane to see me off.

"We were just havin' a bit of fun."

She stared me down. "That's not what I call fun. It's cruel. What in the world's the matter with you? Do you want to be mean like Daddy?"

"The old man's okay." I was sorry I'd told her what I'd been up to. I thought she'd understand, but I sure missed the mark on that one.

"Daddy's not okay, Dwayne, and you know it. The way he treats other people is disgraceful. Especially the way he treats Mama."

Yeah, I know it, but I don't like to think about it. When I do somethin' I know is wrong, I like to forget it.

Anna got over her mad when we were at the dock. She hugged me and kissed me before I went onto the ship. "I love you, brother. Take care of yourself and come home safe."

It's only a few weeks until I'm on a minesweeper in the Pacific. Let me tell you, that is no fun at all.

Being on the ocean wasn't too bad when I was stationed on the big destroyer, but the minesweeper is a different story altogether. We're sweeping along the coastal areas, and the ship is small.

Our job is to clear the way for destroyers. We use sweep wires to cut the wires on anchored mines. The mines float to the surface and are destroyed by gunfire. Underwater noisemakers deactivate the acoustic mines, and cable loops with electrical current neutralize the detonators on magnetically activated mines. The boys put out buoys to mark the left and right sides of the path we clear so the big ships can tell where the route is safe.

I wish I could be one of the guys who shoots the mines when they surface, but I'm stuck sitting at a desk down in the hull. To top it off, I'm also the youngest man on the ship. When the other men ask me about my age, I say, "I'm not a day over fifty."

A friend of mine, Lanny, leans against the bulkhead watching me work. My desk is nothin' but a tiny table, just big enough to hold the radio and a pad of paper. "You got it easy, Bucko. Just sitting down here on your keister, sending and receiving messages all day long."

"Brains over brawn," I tell him.

Lanny laughs, and says he's going topside.

Bein' the radio man isn't as easy as he thinks it is. I know everythin' that's happening out there—the good, the bad—and the really, really bad. Minesweepers sink all the time. A mine gets missed and explodes, the ship gets hit by enemy bombs or torpedos. The Swallow sunk just last week off Okinawa after a kamikaze pilot flew his plane right into it. It sank close to where we're sweepin' now, all hands lost.

I still can't swim more than a few strokes. I keep my lifejacket handy, but I don't think anybody's survivin' if the ship goes down. It'll sink in a matter of minutes. It doesn't take long. I try not to think about bein' in the water, fightin' to stay alive. Thinkin' about it's just invitin' trouble to come your way.

There's an old Navy superstition that no one onboard can wash a coffee mug or Neptune will claim your ship. I mean to tell you, it's a serious matter. A fellow was demoted just the other day for washin' his cup clean.

Lots of the men have superstitions they bring with them from home. Some keep a lucky charm in their pocket that they think'll protect them. Like that's gonna stop fate.

We're all scared of dyin' every minute of every day. That's the truth.

We've made a few stops at ports, but not many. Half of us get shore leave for a night, go out, get drunk on beer or whatever local swill we can find, come back to work with hangovers the next day. The other half goes the next time we stop. Same story.

"You got shore leave tonight?" Jamie Brown asks me.

We're moored in the China Sea in a little bay. The Captain says some of us can take an inflatable over to shore where there's a village.

"Yeah, but I'm not goin'."

"C'mon, Dwayne. We'll have a good ole time."

"No sir, not this time. Maybe if we ever get to Okinawa. There's a poker game tonight that I'm interested in, and it's happenin' right here." I can use the extra money. I'm savin' up what I win to buy a car when I get home.

These village ports are nothin' but muddy shitholes, I kid you not. The people are dirty, especially the ragpickers and the beggars. There's raw sewage runnin' down the streets. You can't drink the water. Pimps come around the bars tryin' to sell whores. Sometimes they bring out naked little girls and even little boys. It's disgustin', somethin' I never want my mama to even know exists.

The Navy tells us when we go ashore that we can eat any food that's been cooked, but you won't catch me eatin' it. There's been men who got so sick from parasites, they had to get sent home to the VA hospital.

I'm never leavin' home again. Never gettin' on another boat. Never eatin' another helping of jello.

1945

Bill

The war is over.

I'll be going home soon. I can't wait to get out of this tent, away from the jungle, the bugs, the relentless heat. I thought I knew what hot and humid was when I left Oklahoma, but the tropics have our summers beat all to hell.

I've made a list of everything I want to do when I'm home: hug my folks, eat a big steak dinner, go out dancing with a pretty girl, shower every day, sleep until noon, have a barbeque with ribs and potato salad and Grandma Ella's ice box cake. I want to buy a car as soon as they start rolling them off the assembly lines again.

My old job is waiting for me at Sinclair. I can't wait to dress in civies every day and go to work. Never thought I'd say that.

Doreen writes to me once a week. She's depressed in one letter and up in the clouds the next. She doesn't visit the folks much. She never did get along with Mama, and she's not going to let any of us forget it. She says it takes too much gas to go to Okmulgee, but that doesn't sound right. Probably it's because they won't let her drink at the house, and she likes to have to have a highball or two—or three—on her days off.

Jerry is back in Tulsa now with Doreen, and she says he came home all right. He had a cushy desk job in San Diego, never saw any action.

The three of us will have to tie one on when I get back.

Dwayne

We finally dropped the A-bombs that ended the war. About time, if you ask me. They say we might've got exposed to some of the radiation that carried on the wind, but I guess there's no way to tell. None of us are sick. Yet.

The damn war's over, but we sailors are still stuck here, sweepin' up mines like usual. The Japs just turned tail and ran, leavin' us to mop up whatever they didn't want to take with 'em.

We're dockin' at Okinawa later today. Our boat wasn't close to these waters during the Battle for Okinawa, but we all heard about it. We lost a lot of good men and a lot of good ships in that one. We're still findin' mines in some of the outer parts of the island that the other ships missed the first time around.

I'm takin' shore leave later today, and I'm gonna forget all about sweepin' mines. I'm gonna paint the town red with a few of my buddies. There's two destroyers docked here, too, hundreds of sailors ready to go out and have a good time.

David, Monty, and I found a little beer joint where they set up tables outdoors, and we got us a table and started pilin' up empty beer cans.

"This Jap beer tastes different than American beer." David made a face. "Yuck." He spit.

"Yeah, it's bitter, but after knockin' back two or three of 'em, you don't notice it so much," I told him. "Get a few more under your belt."

The stack of beer cans was higher than our heads by the time we left, and I was drunk as a skunk. David was sober. He said he couldn't stand the taste of the beer no matter how many he had, so he just stopped having 'em. We stopped at hole in the wall place and the two of them ate some kind of Jap fish with vegetables and rice. I told 'em I was stickin' to my rule about not eatin' nothin' when I'm off the ship.

"Wanta go get us some of them geisha girls?" Monty asked, wiping his mouth. "I'm fueled up and ready to go."

"Hell, no. All I need's is a case of the clap. Let's get on back and get some real food to eat." I wanted to put somethin' in my stomach to soak up the alcohol before I went to bed.

The three of us were singin' an off-key rendition of What Shall We Do With the Drunken Sailor on our way down the pier to get to our ship, when four men comin' off the Nestor stepped in front of us, blocking our way.

"Where were you sissy boys when all the fightin' was goin' on?" the big one asked, lookin' straight at me.

"Same as you. We're all sailors." I tried to push past him.

For once, I wasn't spoilin' for a fight. One of his buddies put out an arm and stopped me. The other two were stopping David and Monty.

"Some more than others," the big one says. "I'd guess from that accent you're either a Texan or an Okie. Prob'bly one of them Okie's trashing up California."

"I'm more than you can take on, that's who I am," I told him.

He came at me and he was a bruiser, six feet tall and probably two hundred pounds. I thought my buddies would back me up, but they were havin a time of it tryin' to keep his friends from joinin' in.

I was the one who got took.

When it was all said and done, some M.P.'s broke it up, but not before I got tore up pretty bad. A doctor from one of the ships had the emergency crew come and take me to the hospital.

I got put on a flight to a VA hospital stateside with a ruptured spleen and internal bleeding, plus a concussion, bruised kidneys, two broken ribs, and a broken clavicle.

I thought I was gonna die.

After a few weeks, I'd recovered enough to get transported to the VA hospital in Muskogee. I saw my folks for the first time in over a year. I was still bedridden, and I'd taken a turn for the worse the day they came to visit. I was kinda surprised the doctor let 'em in, and it gave me an uneasy feelin', like maybe the doc thought I wouldn't make it.

"Oh, Dwayne." Mama turned her head away, and I could tell she was cryin.'

"He's gonna be all right."

The old man always thinks I'm gonna be all right.

"It's my appendix." I had to force the words out between clenched teeth. "My white cells're too high. They're gonna take it out later." The pain was intense and I was so nauseous I couldn't lift my head off the pillow.

The old man went into lecture mode. "This's what comes of you gettin' drunk and fightin'. Hope you learned your lesson."

"Oh, shut up, Henry." Mama's irritation was stopping her tears. "He's sick, can't you see that?" She laid her hand on my forehead and bent down. "I'm gonna pray for you, honey. I love you, so you do your best to get well, y'hear?"

"I will, Mama." I was trying my best not to puke or cry in front of the old man.

She straightened up and walked toward the door. The old man stayed beside the bed, lookin' down on me.

"You'll be okay, son. We Gray boys have always been tougher than we look."

Anna

I fell in love with California when I was in San Diego to see Dwayne off. Since Glen's folks live there, we've decided that's where we'll live after Glen's discharged. The weather's good and the beaches are close.

I've found a cute little apartment in Santa Barbara. It's a one-bedroom in a complex with seven other units. It has a little balcony with space enough for two chairs where we sit and drink coffee every morning. If I stand up and stretch, I can get a tiny view of the ocean, and in the evening, we catch the cool ocean breeze.

Glen's enrolled in a photography class under the G.I. Bill. He wants to be a professional photographer. I didn't realize how artistic he is until after we were married. He has an artist's eye.

Right now we're living on love and what I bring home from my job at the insurance office. When Glen's finished with this course we'll have more money coming in. I'm not worried about money being tight. It'll get better. I have confidence in us being able to handle just about anything that comes our way.

There isn't hardly any work out there with so many G.I.'s coming home. People don't like to think about it, but the war created a lot of jobs. Lots of companies went into business supplying the troops with what they needed—munitions, airplanes, ships, uniforms, medical supplies. Now those companies have to lay people off.

"I hate the idea of you having to work," Glen tells me.

"I don't mind working, I'm lucky I landed this job before the war ended. All the women who were working in the plants are out of work now," I tell him. I pat my stomach. "Besides, you'll finish school in another six months and be able to support me when it counts."

By that, I mean when I get pregnant. We're already trying. Like so many others, the war years taught us to take the bird in the hand, not to wait to get two birds in the bush.

Who knows what tomorrow may bring?

Doreen

It was silly of me to be so worried about Jerry not coming back to me. He's home now, and he's divorced. At least that's what he tells me when I ask him about the divorce papers.

"I left them in Dallas. They're at my mother's," he says, lighting a cigarette.

That sounds fishy to me.

"Your mother could send them to you."

"I don't want to bother Mother with it. I'll pick them up the next time I'm there." His tone is sharp, but I can't let it rest.

I point to my ring finger where I'm wearing a fake wedding ring. "Which will be when? A year from now? Meanwhile, I'm stuck lying to my family."

He puts his cigarette in the ashtray and takes me in his arms. For that minute, I feel safe and loved.

"I'm not lying, I swear it," he whispers into my hair. "Why can't you just take my word for it?" He draws back and kisses me gently. "You know how much I missed you all the time I was gone."

I don't want to lose the warmth of feeling loved, so I give up. How it is that I always tell myself to give up and give in? It must be that I'm needy, scared of being alone again.

Jerry is one of the lucky few who's been able to get a job. Bill knew of an opening in the engineering department at Sinclair Oil, and he put in a good word for Jerry. He really likes it there, and we have enough money, even though he sends half his check to his ex-wife every month.

"I have to pay her alimony."

"For how long?" I ask.

"Three years. Let's wait a little while longer to have a baby," he tells me. "Just until I'm not saddled with this alimony."

Seems like all I do is wait. I'm tired of waiting.

A little while longer can be a lot longer when you're talkin' about fertility. I don't know how I can tell him that I've been lying about my age all this time. I can fake it on the outside, but on the inside those eggs are startin' to lose their luster.

Joy

I'm home from college for the summer. Bill's been home, working at Sinclair. He found an apartment and he's looking for a car.

"I'm taking a trip out to California as soon as I find one," he said. "My boss says the company might be opening offices in Los Angeles. I told him I want to look it over before I make a commitment, so he's given me ten days to go out there and see what I think. You come with me, Joy. It's no fun traveling alone, and you can help me drive."

"Freddy has a car for sale," I told him. "It was his mother's, but she died just a few days ago. I don't think he's advertised it yet. I'll give him a call. We can go over and take a look at it."

That's how Bill came to buy a car. He kicked the tires, did a test drive with Freddy, and made an offer. It was a black 1938 Ford with eleven thousand miles on it. After Bill washed and waxed it, it looked like new.

We left on a Saturday, driving through Oklahoma, then into Texas, and on through New Mexico and Arizona. We stayed at roadside motels. We'd stop for a big breakfast at a diner, then eat peanut butter and jelly sandwiches for lunch that we made ahead of time before we checked out of the motel room. We'd stop to look at the sights, or to buy cold Coca-Cola's or ice cream. Bill let me drive nearly half the time.

We spent a whole day at the Salton Sea, sunbathing in the desert air, hoping to see a movie star wander by. No such luck. Then we stopped near Oceanside to wet our toes in the cold saltwater of the Pacific. We sat on the beach until after the sun set, then had a fish dinner at a restaurant. We drove into Los Angeles and walked around Hollywood Boulevard. We looked at the stars set into the sidewalk at Grauman's Chinese Theatre.

Then we headed home.

Bill took the first two hours of driving. "California weather is okay, and the ocean is terrific. Los Angeles is too crowded for me," he said. "I'm gonna tell my boss I'll stick it out in Tulsa."

"I liked all of it, the desert, the ocean, the cities. I can't wait to get home. I'll tell everybody about all the fun we had, the places we went." I had my arm resting on the bottom of the open window, that side of my hair blowing wild in the breeze.

"I'm ready to stay home after being overseas."

"You'll be an old man if you don't find a girl and settle down pretty soon."

Bill laughed. "C'mon, now, I'm only twenty-seven. Daddy didn't marry Mama until he was twenty-seven."

"These days girls want somebody younger. You know—while they still have some gas in their tank."

"What would a virgin like you know about having gas in the tank? Girls want somebody who has money."

I smiled at him. "None ya beeswax is the answer to your question. But speaking of money, you don't have to keep sending me to college. School's okay, but I don't want to be a burden. I've already applied for a job at the school administration office in Tulsa, and I have a good chance of getting it. Mary Alice and I want to get an apartment together. She's quitting school and getting a job, too."

"Are you sure?" Bill asked. "You'll get a better job if you finish."

"I'm sure." I watched the Arizona landscape going by, dotted with Saguaro cactus and Joshua trees. "Maybe I'll go back later on my own, but I'm tired of school. I want to earn my own money and have some independence."

"Okay then." He thumped the steering wheel. "I'll start saving up to support a wife and family right away," he teased.

"You're going to meet the right girl one of these days. You're a catch—fun, good-looking, smart."

"Maybe. There's a lot of competition out there, so many guys coming back at once. Doreen's already on the lookout for someone pretty to hook up with me."

"Beware of Doreen and her friends. They all drink like fish," I told him.

"I stopped by to visit her and Jerry for a couple of hours before I left to pick you up," he said. "It looked to me like the two of them had been fighting. Jerry was obviously in a bad mood."

"That's Doreen's life for you, always some kind of drama."

"I worry about her. She's had it pretty rough."

"She's the one who makes it pretty rough." Bill has more sympathy toward Doreen than I have. I've about had it with her self-centeredness.

"Well, I don't know as she can help it," Bill said.

I let it go. He has a soft spot for her

All the same, this last year while I was in college, she didn't invite me over, not even once.

The other girls had relatives who invited them over for dinner occasionally, or came to take them out once in a while for a treat.

"What's with your sister?" Mary Alice asked. "I thought she'd be asking to see you."

"She's busy, I guess."

The one time I called Doreen and hinted that I'd like to come over, she said, "Jerry doesn't like company when he's home from work. Maybe we can get together on one of my days off. I'll call you when I know what my schedule is." She never did call.

Is it true that Jerry would object to me coming over? He isn't very friendly, but then he and Doreen don't come around us very often. Or is it just another one of her excuses because she's drinking too much again and doesn't want to feel guilty about it?

I told Mama my feelings were hurt that Doreen didn't take any interest in being with me while I was in Tulsa, and she said, "Don't feel bad. Bill's the only one she spends any time with."

There's a lot we don't talk about when it comes to Doreen. We don't talk about her mental problems. Or the difference in her when she stops taking her medication, or her lying, or her drinking.

Mama drilled it into all of us, "If you can't say something nice, don't say anything at all." I wonder why she thinks being nice is so important and who she learned it from—not from Grandma Ella, that's for sure. She speaks her mind.

That rule might work better if the world was a nicer place, but there are a lot of things that aren't nice at all. I guess that's what we're supposed to pretend isn't happening—reality.

Mama told me Dwayne Gray was sent home, and that he's in the VA hospital. Mrs. Gray asked Mama to tell me, and to let me know that he can have visitors.

"You should visit him when you come home next time. I told Mrs. Gray you'd be glad to."

"Maybe." I didn't like Dwayne from when we were kids, but we all were supposed to be visiting the men coming home from war, trying to raise their spirits and show our gratitude for the sacrifices they made. "Maybe Mary Alice would come with me."

"Bring her down with you next weekend," Mama said. "I'll get y'all some fried chicken, and you two girls can go to the VA together. Maybe he's grown up a little."

Maybe we all have.

1946

Dwayne

I think Mama might've put a bug in Miz Lannery's ear about me needin' to have visitors. Whatever the reason, I was sure glad to have some company of the female persuasion. I was the envy of the other boys in here for a few hours, I can tell you that, when Joy Lannery came to visit me.

She brought a friend of hers, Mary Alice, with her. I was sure surprised to see them. We were in the same class in high school, but we didn't run with the same crowd. I thought Joy was no fun, and she thought I was a thug. We were probably both right. I think she's real pretty now, and we had a good time talkin' together. She has a good sense of humor, and she made me laugh.

"How's your dog?" I asked her. "Wasn't his name Tuffy?"

"Oh, he died a few years ago. Lived to be ten years old."

"That's too bad. As I recall, he liked to play fetch." Also, as I recall, I was something of a little shit to Joy that day when I hopped the back fence to play fetch with Tuffy. I hope she's forgotten.

"Tuffy loved to fetch when he was younger. I remember the day you came over like it was yesterday."

Her eyes sparkled, and she gave a wry smile. Mary Alice also had a smirk on her face, like she'd been told all about it before they came to visit. I hate it when my misbehavior comes back to haunt me.

"Anyway, my folks didn't want to get another dog," she said.

"I want to get a huntin' dog when I get out school and get settled."

"I like all dogs, but the doctor says I can't have one in the house on account of my asthma."

"A good huntin' dog, like a coon hound or a pointer, lives outside all year round, so that'd be all right. You know, I have asthma, too. It's better now I'm grown."

"Are you going to use the G.I. bill?" Mary Alice asked.

"I'm going to Tulsa University. Probably get a business degree. I'm workin' on my application. Maybe one of you'd be willin' to look it over."

"Sure, I'll check it when you've finished with it," Joy volunteered. "My brother, Bill, graduated from T.U. in business, and he has a good job with Sinclair Oil."

"That's my dream, havin' a good job in the oil business. Can't go wrong there."

I felt more lonesome than I've ever been after those girls waved goodbye to me. Joy left a slip of paper with her address in Tulsa on it. I guess she wants me to write to her. Come to think of it, I think I'll get busy and do just that.

I wish I could get out of this wheelchair. It makes me look like a cripple, which I'm not, at least not permanently. I still have all my appendages in fine working order, but the doctor says he doesn't want me movin' around too soon with all the internal injuries I had.

I try to talk the old man into sayin' he'll let me drive his car when I'm discharged from here, but he's a tough old rooster. He's not givin' in. He doesn't feel sorry for me the way Mama does. He says it's my own damn fault I got beat up the way I did. Guess he's right, but I'd still like to drive his car when I'm able. I'm not exactly a kid anymore.

Sometimes Mama comes to visit me on her own. "Do not tell your father, but Anna calls me once in a while."

No one can hold a grudge like the old man. Anna leavin' like she did about broke his heart, though he'd never say so. He'd probably take the phone out if he knew Mama was talkin' to her.

"Anna likes California. Glen's going to school to learn how to be a photographer on the G.I. bill," Mama went on.

"What's the hell's he doin' that for? Seems like a sissy job. He's a trained pilot. He could fly commercial planes if he wanted to. Those guys make a lot of money."

"Now, Dwayne, that's not for you to say. Glen's artistic as well as smart. That's what Anna says anyway. She seems happy."

Okay, it's none of my business.

The term 'starving artist' was invented for a reason. Anna must've lost her mind along with her heart.

Joy

I'm completely surprised at what a good time I had while I was visiting Dwayne. Even though he's in a wheelchair, he's funny and amusing. It wasn't sad or smelly like I'd imagined. There's an atrium at the hospital where there were tables and chairs set up and we could sit outside. He met us in the lobby by the main entrance, so we were never back on the wards. We laughed a lot. After Mary Alice and I left, she told me she thought we'd make a cute couple.

Dwayne's really handsome. I remember him from high school, but we weren't friends. I hadn't liked him since the time he came over and all he did was play with my dog. He also ran with a pretty rough crowd back then.

I took some sandwiches and potato salad for the three of us to eat for lunch while we visited. I figured Dwayne would like to have something besides hospital food.

"What was it like to be in the Pacific?" Mary Alice asked, taking a bite of her sandwich.

"Mostly we were on the ship, but when we did get to shore, it was dirty. People there are poor. I didn't eat any of the food, and you couldn't drink the water unless you boiled it and treated it." Dwayne had eaten both of the sandwiches I brought for him.

"I'd like to travel one day." I said.

I put another helping of potato salad on his plate.

"I had my fill of it. Traveling—not potato salad—" He pointed to his plate and I gave him more. "I never want to go overseas again. That year on the minesweeper was enough adventure to last me a lifetime."

Lots of the men coming back from the war seem to feel like that. They're just so glad to be home and be alive. I'd like to see Europe once it's recovered from the war. I'd like to visit Ireland and England, see the country where my relatives used to live.

I told Dwayne I'd come back next weekend to visit him again, gave him my address, and he said he'd write. I hope he does. I might like spending more time with him.

Dwayne

Dear Joy,

The doctor says I can get out of the wheelchair this week, and if all goes well, I can go home next week. Full speed ahead!

Oh yeah, thanks for lookin' over that application. T.U. is full up, but I got all lined up at Stillwater come February 1. I had to turn down a two hundred and forty-seven dollar a month job to do it, tho. That hurt. What's money? I got loads. Heh, heh.

Better close now, Hon, it's about time for the fight and I've got a sneaky feeling anyone not tuned in for the first couple of rounds is just flat going to miss it.

As Ever, Dwayne

I just love you for you, Joy.

Dear Joy,

It's all peace and quiet around the Gray Hogan. Ma & Pa went to the show and young'un here is waiting for the Louis-Wolcott battle. Not that it promises much as battles go, but I'll get my enjoys hearing one nigger pound away on another.

Went to the show this afternoon and saw Brute Force—quite a show. For unrestricted mayhem and violence, it's a dandy. Sunday and Monday, Singapore is on, and from the preview, it promises just as much in excitement. I sure wish you were coming over. We could take some of this in together. There's a basketball game tonight, and some prize fights at the City Hall—Muskogee and it's many attractions.

I agree with you that this week has seemed long—damn long, come to think of it. I hope talking to you doesn't make things worse instead of better. I miss you enough as it is.

As Ever,
Dwayne

Dear Joy,

Boy, I've had some time trying to catch time to write. I've been running to Okmulgee to the hospital, and to the VA office off and on all week.

First, I go over to Okmulgee and get enrolled. Then the weather changes and I have to get up about midnight and go out to the vets for a couple of hypos, then the VA informs me that my records are among the missing and would I please come down and help them make up another record, etc., etc.

I finally nurtured my feeble mind to a decision and enrolled over at Okmulgee. I think I'll go over there until summer and then head for T.U. I'm carrying fifteen hours and guess I'll stay at the DeVoys.

I told you they'd appreciate you more over at that sweatshop if you didn't show up now and then. You should have told them not to be surprised if you didn't show more often—heh, heh.

We got a break in the neighbor situation today. Ray's sister and brother-in-law are moving in—which reminds me that the louse hasn't written since he went back to El Toro.

Well, Sugar, that's about all the news. Just because I didn't write don't think you weren't in my thoughts. Love you—how was the ice cream?

As Ever,
Dwayne

Joy

I invited Dwayne to come over and meet the folks since I've been seeing him so regularly. He's living at home now, but he'll be starting school in Okmulgee soon. Daddy and Mama moved back to Okmulgee, and they're living with Grandma Ella. Her knees are getting too bad for her to live alone.

Daddy started up his pipe supply business again, and I guess he's doing all right. He isn't making as much money as he did before, but he says business is starting to pick up.

I was in the back bedroom getting ready when I heard the doorbell ring. I heard Dwayne say, "I'm here to see Joy," then I heard Grandma Ella say, "You can go right back home again and change out of those overalls. You don't have any business showing up here to see Joy when you're dressed like that."

Oh, no. I hurried out and got to the front door just as Grandma Ella was shutting it in his face. I grabbed on to the doorknob and held the door halfway open.

"That young man's a disgrace, coming around here in his overalls," she told me. "What is he, ignorant? Doesn't he know any better?"

I could see Dwayne's face was red from embarrassment. I tried to rescue him. "It's okay, Grandma. Those aren't overalls, they're jeans. Everybody's wearing them."

"Work clothes is what they are," she fussed, "and not suitable for wearing on a date." She crooked her head and glared at Dwayne. "It's disrespectful."

"I invited him here to have coffee so I can introduce him to Mama and Daddy." I opened the door all the way.

Grandma Ella stepped aside to let Dwayne come in, but she wasn't finished giving him what for. "Next time you come over here, I expect to see you wearing a pair of good pants and a nice shirt."

"Yes ma'am, I will."

We sat down on the sofa in the living room while Grandma Ella went back to her room to show her displeasure. I didn't think she'd be coming back out to join us for coffee.

"She takes the cake," Dwayne said. "Not exactly the welcome I was going for."

"She's feisty, all right. I'm so embarrassed." My hands were shaking. I already felt nervous. Dwayne meant more to me than a casual date. We had a close connection, something that both of us felt was special.

He had a few strikes against him already with my family—he wasn't Catholic, he had a reputation for being wild in high school, and his father was rumored to be in KKK.

Dwayne put his arm around me. "Sugar, it'll be all right."

And it was. Mama and Daddy were cordial and Bill and Doreen dropped by. We ate lemon cake and drank coffee, joking around with one another. We had a good time.

"You let me know when you graduate," Bill told Dwayne as he was leaving. "I'll put in a good word for you at Sinclair."

"It'll be a while yet. I'm just startin' college, but I'll keep it in mind."

Bill added, "And just so you know, Joy is everybody's favorite sister. Treat her right."

"She's my favorite girl, so that'll be easy," Dwayne told him.

I went out on the porch to see Dwayne off, and he kissed me in a way I've never been kissed before.

"Don't go," I said. I kissed him back.

"I'll be back, Sugar. You can count on that."

I waved goodbye until he was out of sight.

I can't wait to see him again. I think I'm falling in love.

Dwayne

Dear Joy,

Boy! I have some time trying to get a letter off to you. I kinda pulled a 'quicky' on you and mailed that letter I wrote on Saturday.

You know I'm a pretty happy boy since that call I made last Sunday—we can talk that over this weekend. I can't express it in any damn letter.

Other than the little fervor of excitement you and I created Sunday, this place is as dead as ever. If things don't pick up, I think I'll go out and look up a couple more finders, heaven forbid.

I look for Ben to drop up this weekend. If he can get out of debt down in Spiro he may go to Okmulgee with me next semester. From what he says it'll take some scufflin' of loose dollars for him to get out of debt, though. And I imagine loose dollars are a little scarce in Spiro. Come to think of it, loose dollars are a little scarce, period.

It's late, darling, so better close for now.

As Ever,

Dwayne

I love you lots & lots

Hi to Doreen and Bill

Joy

Dear Dwayne,

Doreen got all crazy when she thought you saw her sunbathing in the back yard when you dropped by yesterday. I told her you probably didn't even look out back.

Anyway, I have to work all week, and maybe through part of the weekend. I miss seeing you, but I need the job. As soon as you can transfer to T.U., we can be together more. That'll be nice, won't it?

I keep thinking about Sunday. We need a few more times like that.

Love,

Joy

Dwayne

Dearest Joy,

You should see ole Dwayne now—swelled up like a poisoned pup—both sides. Heh. Oh well, best to get the mumps over with. I still manage to get a little food down, so it must not be too bad a case. I sure hope you don't get it, Hon.

It's so easy to stay in bed. Yes sir, beautiful weather, and Dad goin' to the fights every night. It's so easy. Oh, well, me and the radio get along pretty well. I can recite every commercial on KFMU.

How was the trip back? Okay, I hope. I sure hated to see you leave, darling. Damn, but I miss you. I need my nurse, ha.

No joke, the sooner I see you, the better. Selfish, I guess.

Better close for now. Remember I love you and think of you lots.

As Ever,

Dwayne

Hi to Bill. Tell Doreen I did not see her sunbathing yesterday. I did, really, but in my eyes, she doesn't hold a candle to you.

Dear Dwayne,

I'm going to be stuck in Tulsa for this weekend at least. Kathy and Walter are going to be in Okmulgee again, and there's no room at the inn for me. Sorry, darling, but Kathy came first and it seems like she still does. Does that sound selfish? I'm just put out that I won't be able to see you.

I hope your classes get more interesting soon. Study hard. I miss you lots.

Love,

Joy

Dear Joy,

How do you like my notebook stationery—such a fine texture and exquisite finish.

Lanny and I just got back from the show. It was some new picture called The Sea Wolf, remember it? I saw it about six or eight years ago.

Not much new around here or out at the school. Lessons are pretty well set by now, and it looks as though I may be a little busy.

I guess you're pretty well put out about having to be in Tulsa town while Walter and Kathy are at home. Too bad it didn't ice over this past weekend so they couldn't make it—heh.

Lanny just came up from the usual evening "schnapps" session here at the house—so better knock off the light and let the kid get some rest.

Oh yeah, I made my eight o'clock class this morning!!!!

I love you, shug, and miss you lots.

As Ever,

Dwayne

1947

Henry

"Hello and welcome." I held the door open so Dwayne and his girlfriend could enter.

"This is Joy." Dwayne introduced her as he ushered her into the living room.

May motioned to the sofa. "Nice to meet you, Joy. Sit right over here."

She's a pretty girl, reminds me of Joan Crawford. Too skinny for my taste, but Dwayne's not a big man. They look good sitting together, happy.

Watching them brings back memories of when May and I were first going out. We were never as young as them, never that happy. Both of us grew up like we were born old. I'd been married and divorced, had a kid by the time I met May. All that disappointment changes the way a man sees things later on.

"There's coffee here, and I set out some chocolate chip cookies." May was beamin'. She enjoys playin' hostess.

"I take my coffee black, thank you," Joy said.

She has good manners, seems a little shy.

"I'm glad your mama sent you to visit Dwayne when he was in the hospital. I sure do miss seeing her. We used to talk over the back fence and catch up with each other, but we've lost touch since y'all moved back to Okmulgee."

"Yes, ma'am. I'm glad I went to see Dwayne when he was at the VA, although after the way he treated me when he was a boy, I'd almost decided not to go."

"He could be rude back then, that's for sure." May put a cookie on a small plate and set it in front of Joy. "Here, I just baked these this morning."

"He was just bein' a boy," I remarked.

"When he first went in the Navy, he still had some wild in him, but I hope he's gonna settle down now." May smiled at me like she thought Dwayne had made up his mind to settle down with me.

Dwayne took his lighter out of his pocket and lit a cigarette. "I'm not settlin' down right yet, but once I get into T.U., I'm goin' to be ready. Right, Sugar?"

"We'll talk about it first, I hope." Joy looked at him sideways as she took a sip of coffee.

"Well, naturally, we will. But see, I've made up my mind, and you know when I make up my mind to do somethin', I generally get it done," Dwayne said.

"It's not how much you start it's how much you finish."

Joy laughed. "Mr. Gray, my mama tells me that all the time. I'm not sure it's helped me any. I have loads of unfinished projects stuffed into boxes."

"How're your folks doing?" I asked.

"Oh, they're fine. Daddy's business is up and running again. Mama's just the same as always, playing Mahjong with a new group of ladies." Joy took a sip of her coffee. "I'll be sure and tell them you asked after them."

I'd had about enough of coffee and cookie time. "Dwayne, come out back, and I'll show you the new gun I bought. We can let the ladies talk awhile."

As soon as we got outside, I said to him, "The Lannery's are Catholic."

"Yeah, I know. She goes to church every Sunday. What of it?"

Dwayne knows what I think about the Catholics. Secretive bastards, more loyal to the Pope than to the President. Separatists, too, out to destroy our democratic way of life, educating their children in private Catholic schools.

"You want to sign a paper saying you'll raise your kids to be Catholic? That's what the Lannery's will expect." I spit on the ground. "Hell, more than expect—it's a requirement if you want to marry that girl."

Dwayne looked me right in the eye. "That's for me to decide, if and when it comes to that. Best you let it go for now. There's nothin' you can say to change my mind about bein' with Joy."

We locked eyes, and I knew it was no use. He's stubborn, comes by it naturally.

He went back inside. I could hear all of them talkin' and laughin'.

May came out after a while and put her hand on my shoulder. "Dwayne and Joy are getting ready to leave. Are you going to come inside and say goodbye?"

I pointed to the whiskey bottle I'd gone and got out of the shed and took a swig. "Don't think I will. Tell 'em I'm busy."

May set her chin like she does when she's sure I'm bein' an asshole. "You're being pig-headed and rude, Henry. What's she going to think, you not coming to see her off? We know her folks."

Know her folks, yes. Respect them, no. Arthur Lannery's nothin' but a one-generation shanty Irish who lost his business. He took charity from the WPA while the rest of us supported him. Gladys Lannery's a stuck-up Yankee from Ohio. And they're Catholic to boot.

The Lannerys are damn lucky our men didn't burn 'em out while they were livin' in Muskogee. Arthur was smart to buy a house right in the middle of town.

I took another pull from the bottle just to piss May off a little more. "You say my good-byes for me. Like I said, I'm busy."

Doreen

I knew things weren't right. I found out Jerry isn't divorced, not even close. I finally got tired of being suspicious and got the number from Dallas information. I called the woman who says she's still his wife.

She didn't know anything about me. I should have known. Whenever I get close to being happy, it all turns to shit.

She was full of complaints about Jerry. "I'm filing for divorce. I got the name of a good lawyer from a friend of mine. Jerry sends me a little money, but he's never home. And now this? I'm just going to go ahead and call it quits."

I heard the strike of a match, then heard her inhale as she lit a cigarette.

"His son must miss him a lot," I said.

She started coughing, and I realized she'd swallowed some smoke when she started laughing at my remark. Once her throat cleared, she said, "Sister, he's been feeding you quite a line. We don't have any kids. Jerry doesn't like 'em, always said he didn't want any." She hung up.

I'm an idiot. People tried to tell me, but did I listen? No.

Am I going to leave him?

No, I'm not. I'm still in love with him. Not to mention the stack of lies on my own side of the ledger.

I don't want to admit to myself or anyone else that being with Jerry is a mistake. I tell myself all kinds of excuses instead. Maybe it isn't a mistake. Maybe he's really in love with me, and doesn't want to disappoint me. Maybe his wife will file for divorce, and we'll get married after all.

It isn't an ideal situation, but I can live with it. One thing I've learned is how to keep my mouth shut when something's bothering me. I've had lots and lots of practice at pretending to be someone I'm not.

Arthur

Coming back to Okmulgee is better than I thought it would be. People want to forget the war and the depression years and move on. The business is doing all right in spite of competition from a couple of bigger outfits, and the mineral leases are giving us a small, but steady, income. Our financial situation won't be what it was before, but it's good enough.

Bill came for lunch on Sunday last week. "What do you hear from Kathy?" he asked, taking a second helping of potatoes.

"Walter's working, and Kathy seems fine. Little Jimmy's healthy, the other kids are in school," Gladys told him.

"Have you seen Doreen?" I asked.

"We met for dinner at Antonio's, that Italian place around the corner from her apartment. She's working a lot. You two should drive up to Tulsa one Saturday. We'll go see her," Bill said.

That's a sore point with Gladys. Doreen has never invited us to stop by and see her apartment. Gladys thinks it's because Doreen wants to avoid us. I think Doreen has learned how to protect herself.

"Doreen could make the effort to come here. She knows we shouldn't be leaving Ella here alone. What if she was to fall?" Gladys asked.

It's a real concern. Ella can't be on her feet for more than a few minutes without one of her knees giving out. She mostly sits in her chair and crochets while she listens to the radio or reads. Gladys goes to the library every week to check out books for her and makes sure she has whatever she needs.

I don't worry about the older kids. Doreen and the rest of them can take care of themselves. What really worries me is Dwayne Gray, the young man Joy's dating now,. He's from Muskogee, and his father, Henry, is a member of the KKK, or so I've been told.

A few people have taken it on themselves to let me know he has problems. Dwayne had a reputation when he was in high school for being a hothead and getting drunk. It doesn't look like being in the Navy settled him down any.

After she came home from her third date with him, I asked her, "What is it about him that you like?"

"He's real sweet to me. He's smart." She took off her sweater and smiled. "He's also really good-looking."

Ella didn't like him from the first time she saw him. She made no bones about it, telling Joy, "He's old enough to know that he should respect you and dress nice when he comes to call."

"Oh, Grandma, he didn't mean anything by it."

"Baloney. Mark my words. It shows he wasn't raised right."

"Baloney yourself. You never think anybody is good enough for me."

"True enough. In spite of that, you'll rue the day when you find out who he really is. He's an angry man," Ella warned her.

"Now, that's not true. He's been nothing but sweet to me. He loves his mama—he's sweet to her, too."

"He keeps his anger hidden inside," Ella said. "It'll come out, though. I was married to an angry man for years. I can spot one a mile away."

"I don't know how you can think that." Joy's voice hardened. She was through trying to humor Ella. "He might not be perfect, but he's good to me."

Ella put her hands on her hips, determined to have the last word. "I know what I know."

I know Ella was trying to tell Joy something she isn't ready to hear. Personally, I don't like faulting a man for what he wears or what kind of family he comes from. My own father is no great shakes. It's what a man believes in that counts.

I don't know what to make of what Ella's warnings to Joy about Dwayne. Whenever he's around us, he's charming and funny. He's been in the service, is getting a college degree, seems willing to work hard. If he has the kind of dark side Ella says he does, I haven't seen it.

Our Joy's a sweet girl, good-natured, good-hearted. She thinks she's in love. Do I think Joy deserves someone better? Of course, I do. I suppose all fathers think that about their daughters.

We were sitting on the porch swing after sunset yesterday when she asked me whether or not I liked Dwayne.

"He's okay." I put my arm around her. "Let's make a Coke float and sit out on the porch awhile longer."

"I'll make them. You sit here." She jumped up and went into the house.

The fate of all fathers is to sit on the sidelines of their children's lives and hope for the best. My fingers are crossed that this budding romance between Joy and Dwayne runs its course. I hope it dies a natural death before any harm comes to her.

We named her Joy because we wanted her to be happy.

Anna

Glen and I have a beautiful baby daughter. Glen's first word after seeing us together was 'darling.' We looked at each other and knew her name would be Darlene.

I wasn't out of the hospital for almost a week, then I called Mama to tell her the news. She's excited for me. She said she's going to tell Daddy that he's a granddaddy. I hope he can be happy for us, but he hasn't shown any sign of forgiving me yet for marrying Glen.

It doesn't matter one way or the other. We're happy and healthy. Glen finished his photography program, and he's working for J.C. Penney doing portrait photography. He's good at it, able to get people to relax and look natural.

A lot of his work is scheduled on weekends when people are off of work and the kids are out of school. That gives him a couple of days off during the week when we can be together. I like to go with him when he wants to go out and take photos that interest him.

Tonight's one of the times we go over to the beach in the early evening, build a fire, roast hot dogs, and walk in the surf. Darlene was asleep, warm and snug in a sling against Glen's chest. One of the Phillipino women I met in the hospital had showed me how to make the wrapping.

"This's how we carry our babies," she told me. "They settle down as soon as they're next to you. They hear the heartbeat."

Glen takes in a deep breath, then says, "I want to live by the ocean for the rest of my life. The sea air is like a tonic."

"Fine by me." I don't care where I live as long as we're together.

He grabbed me and pulled me in to face him. "Let's build a boat together, a sailboat, a big one. One we can sail around the world if we want to."

"Uh, one problem—I'll have to learn to swim."

"That's nothin'. I'll have to learn to sail."

We crossed our pinkie fingers to seal the deal and walked on. When we got back to the apartment, we toasted our new dream with a glass of buttermilk.

Bill

Little sister's getting awfully serious about Dwayne. The folks seem kinda worried about it. Mama hinted that I might speak to her, but I'm not going to do it. Joy's old enough to make her own decisions. If there's one thing I've learned about love, it's like a steamroller on its own path, and God help whoever stands in the way of it.

I met a girl last weekend at the annual Sinclair picnic. Her name's Marjory Barrett, and she's the same age as Joy, pretty blue eyes and dark hair. She was wearing a white dress with a sailor collar with high heels. She looked like she'd just stepped out of a bandbox.

We were filling our plates at the buffet table when we met.

"That ambrosia sure looks good," I said. "May I serve some to you?"

"Thank you. I'm Marjory Barrett, by the way. Marjory with a 'j'." She looked over her shoulder. "My brother, Sam, is around here somewhere, but the food looked so good, I didn't wait for him."

I put a spoonful of ambrosia on her plate. "I like this kind with the little marshmallow bits. My mama makes it this way. I'm Bill Lannery."

We moved on down the line. There was a colored man standing at the end of the table serving the meat—smoked Virginia ham, pit barbequed ribs, and slow-cooked brisket.

"Ham, ribs, or brisket?" he asked.

"Ribs for me. I can't resist a good rack of barbequed ribs."

"Brisket, please," Marjory said.

"What do you say we sit together? I hate eating alone." I tilted my head toward the grouping of tables with place settings in front of empty chairs.

"That would be nice. I like to have company when I'm eating, too."

I led the way to one of the tables, setting my plate down. I pulled out a chair for her, asking, "Where are you from, Miss Marjory with a J?"

"Why, thank you," she said as she sat, scooting her chair toward the table. "I'm from Tulsa, born and bred. You?"

"Okmulgee boy until I joined the Army Air Corps, then I went to Burma."

"Are you a pilot?"

"Yes, ma'am." I sat down beside her. "Not a very exciting one. I flew cargo planes over the Hump. We dropped supplies to British and Allied troops who were supporting Chiang Kai-shek in China."

"Sounds exciting to me. What was Burma like?" she asked, taking a bite of brisket.

Most of us coming back don't talk about what it was really like in the war. I'm no exception. Folks at home don't need to know about the hardships, and I want to forget them. "Hot and humid, boring unless we were in the air. I'm happy to be back home. What do you do in Tulsa?" Usually, I pick ribs up to eat them and lick the sauce off my fingers, but something told me to use a fork. I began cutting off pieces of pork as I listened to her answer.

"I'm a Freshman at T.U. right now," she told me. "But I don't like it all that much. I still live with my folks, so my life it pretty much the same as it was when I was in high school." She made a wry face.

"I went to T.U., graduated in the class of '38. The joke about T.U. girls is. . ."

"We go to college to find a husband." She finished my sentence for me. She wagged her finger at me. "You'd better watch yourself, Bill. There's some truth to that for a lot of us."

Her brother came up to us and introduced himself. "Sam Barrett, Marji's brother," he said. "Mind if I join you?"

"Please do. I'll save the chair for you," I said.

He went to the buffet table to fill his plate, then came back to sit with us. I noticed he had helpings of all three meats. I was impressed by this bold move. I hadn't thought to ask for more than one.

"We Barretts fought in the American Revolution," Sam said, buttering a roll as he began sizing me up. "We came across the pond during the early 1600's." He looked at me expectantly.

"Lannerys are newcomers on the American scene. Irish and German Catholics fleeing religious persecution in the 1800's."

"Presbyterians here," Marjory said. "Who were probably Calvinists to begin with."

I raised my eyebrows.

She added, blushing, "History major."

We talked about the news of the day while we finished our meal, then went to look over the dessert table. I had chocolate cake and she had vanilla pudding. After dessert, Sam and I drank coffee and talked about the oil business until the party started to wind down.

Sam stood up and pulled Marjory's chair out for her. "It's about time I got you home," He looked me in the eye. "I like you, Bill. You should come by the house sometime, meet the folks." He shook my hand.

"I'd like that," I said.

Sam wrote Marjory's address and telephone number on the back of a dry-cleaning receipt he took out of his pocket.

I looked at Marjory as I took it from him. "I'll call you soon."

"I'll be waiting to hear from you." She blushed as she said it, her cheeks turning the color of ripe peaches.

I fell in love with her right in that very moment, fell in love with those blushing cheeks.

What people say is true. Falling in love actually feels like falling. It's like falling and floating all at once—a kind of crazy disorientation embedded in a flood of happiness.

It just knocked me for a loop.

Gladys

We're having a small engagement party for Joy and Dwayne this afternoon. I've hired Della and Cora to help with the food, and Clem's come over to help Arthur and Dwayne set things up in the back yard.

Henry Gray offered to have the party in Muskogee at the country club, but most of Joy and Dwayne's friends live either here or in Tulsa. We thought this would be best.

Joy asked Grandma Ella to make her ice box cake, and Della's making a red velvet cake.

Joy was very excited. "What about those little mints, Mama? I can get some of those at Turner's candy shop. We can put a little bowl on each table."

"Okay, Mama."

"If you're going to do that, stop in at the florist and see when Daddy can pick up the centerpieces."

I handed Joy the keys to the car. I handed a stack of white napkins to Cora to be ironed and folded. The good china was washed and stacked on the counter, ready to go out.

The doorbell rang before we were quite ready to begin receiving guests. May and Henry stood at the door when I opened it.

"C'mon in. We're still getting ready." I tried to sound hospitable, but I hadn't even put on my good dress yet. There were two rollers on the sides of my head where I wanted a wave in my hair.

"I'm sorry we're early. We didn't want to be late." May looked pale. "Maybe there's something I can do to help."

Henry very slightly shook his head no.

"Just sit here in the living room, and I'll have Della bring you something cool to drink. How have y'all been?"

Henry sat down beside May, and said, "We're doin' all right." He pulled at his collar. "I'm not used to wearin' a suit and tie. Usually this time on a Saturday, I'm playin' golf. I won the Muskogee golf tournament last weekend."

Golf. If there is a more useless game than golf, I'm hard pressed to think of what it might be.

"How nice," I said, putting on a smile.

May reached over to straighten Henry's tie. "You should see that trophy, Gladys. It's huge. I swear I can't decide where to put it."

"It's goin' to stay right where it belongs, on the mantle." Henry crossed his arms over his belly. He's still trim, not a man of substance around his middle like Arthur. "I'll be right back with some sweet tea. Make yourself comfortable while I finish getting ready." I went to the kitchen, where Della and Cora were busy getting pieces of cake plated.

"We got this under control," Cora said as I came in. "You go on and get ready for your guests."

"I'm going to do just that, but first I'm taking two glasses of tea to Dwayne's folks. They came early."

"No, ma'am. I'll take it to 'em." Della pointed to the hallway. "You go on."

I heard Joy come back as I was sitting at my dressing table putting on my lipstick.

"Look who I found," I heard her say to the Grays. "Dwayne was outside and I roped him into helping Daddy and me bring the flowers to the tables out back."

Joy came in a minute later to give me a hug from behind. "Thank you, Mama. Everything is great. It's going to be the nicest party."

"Go out and talk to Dwayne's folks while I finish putting on my face, I said, carefully blotting away my excess lipstick with a tissue.

People started arriving soon after that. Arthur and I were busy greeting them and showing them to their table. Joy's always been so popular. A lot of her friends came. Dwayne had buddies of his from the service come by, some with their wives, and a few of his friends from college showed up.

Walter and Kathy drove up for the afternoon, Doreen and Jerry came, and Bill brought his new girlfriend, Marjory. The only one missing from our two families was Dwayne's sister, Anna.

"Anna lives in California now, and that's too far to come with a new baby. We're hoping she can make it for the wedding," May told us.

People aren't staying close to home anymore. It's hard on families. We can't get together, even for weddings and funerals. I heard a man on the radio say that we're a society in motion since the war, which sounds about right. I don't mind it—out with the old, in with the new.

The serving table was set up buffet style, with Cora handing people their plates and pouring punch. I noticed Dwayne taking a pint bottle to a table where some of his friends from Muskogee were sitting. They weren't subtle about pouring it into their glasses of punch. Henry went over to stand beside their table so he could join in.

Joy and Dwayne were seated with Arthur and I, and May and Henry. The rest of our family was seated at a table near us.

Arthur stood to give the first toast, tapping his glass until everyone quieted enough to hear him speak. "It's my pleasure to announce the engagement of our beautiful daughter, Joy. Here's to you, my dear. May you have a lifetime of happiness, rich in love and laughter."

"Hear, hear," Walter shouted.

Bill stood up next. "Here's to Joy and Dwayne. It's a gift that you've found each other, and we wish you all the success life has to offer."

Henry stood up next. "To my son and his bride-to-be. Congratulations to both of you on this happy occasion."

There were some amusing anecdotes from Joy's friends, and some not-so-amusing ones about Dwayne from two of his Navy buddies. When most people were finished with their cake and punch, I signaled to Cora to begin pouring coffee and went to help her.

I filled a carafe with fresh coffee while Arthur went back to the party. As I handed a filled carafe to Cora and took an empty one from her, she said, "Della went home. She said to tell you she wasn't feeling too good, but she'll be all right. I'll stay after and help you clean up."

"Thank you, that's very kind." I took the empty carafe into the kitchen and stood at the counter thinking about Della. It wasn't like her to leave without saying something to me first.

Joy came in. "Mama, are you all right?"

I put my arm around her. "I'm fine, honey."

"The party's wonderful, Mama. I'm so happy." She twirled around. "Come on back. Don't be sad—I'm not leaving you and Daddy, just bringing Dwayne into our family."

I smiled at her, and we went back to the party. I couldn't shake my uncomfortable feelings. I'm not normally one to feel premonitions, but it felt like something was off. Something just wasn't right.

Della

I went into the livin' room to serve coffee to Mr. and Miz Gray, and as I leaned in to serve coffee to him, I saw it. A gold lapel pin that looked exactly like the one I'd bought for Elwyn. There was only one way to be sure. I wanted to yank it right off'n his jacket, but instead I straightened up and said, "I hope you don't think I'm speakin' out of turn, Mr. Gray, but that's a mighty handsome pin you're wearin.'"

"May made me put it on for show. She thought this old suit needed some sprucin' up."

Miz Gray reached out to touch it. "I say a little spot of gold always looks good."

"I hope you don' mind me askin', but where'd you get such a nice one? I'd like to get one like it for my brother, Elwyn."

They both looked surprised at my forwardness. I's been in service for years and they knows I been trained better than to make personal comments to guests.

It didn't stop me from askin'. I had to know.

He tried hidin' his irritation, smilin' a smile that didn't go past his lips. "I don't rightly 'member. Just somethin' I found left behind on one of the trains, prob'bly." He shifted in his chair. "You'd be surprised at what all things people lose when they're ridin' the trains."

Mr. Dwayne came in right then, Miss Joy followin' right behind.

"Hey, Mama. Hey, old man." Mr. Dwayne was grinnin' from ear to ear. "Isn't this somethin', your young'un gettin' engaged to the prettiest girl in town?"

Mr. Gray didn't answer him. He was still lookin' at me, holdin' my eyes with his. "I could use some strong, black coffee," he said. "You got any of that brewin' back there?"

"Yessir, I'll bring you some directly." I picked up the tray and started to leave.

Behind me, I heard Mr. Dwayne say, "That gold pin's just the thing, Daddy."

"Here, take it. It'll dress your suit up some, or so Mama says. She's the one made me wear it." I turned my head slightly so I could see what he was doin'. He took the pin off and handed it to Mr. Dwayne.

I went on into the kitchen and told Cora to make some fresh coffee. "I'm gonna see if Miss Joy or Miss Gladys needs some help." I left before Cora could fuss at me for not makin' the coffee.

Mr. Dwayne was in the back bedroom standin' by Mr. Arthur's desk, tryin' to put that pin on the lapel of his suit. He pricked his finger on its sharp point and put the end of his finger in his mouth, suckin' on it before the drop of blood got on the material.

"Damn it to Hell," he said.

"Can I help you with that, Mr. Dwayne?" I said, standin' in the doorway.

"I've never worn one of these things before. I'm all thumbs today."

He held out the pin. I entered the room and took it from him. Sure enough, the letters EJ were engraved on the back.

"Stand still now." I acted like I was pinning it through the fabric. "There's a little rough spot on the stick where it's catchin'. You don't want to be pullin' a thread in this nice suit. That rough place needs to be buffed out."

"Just put it on the desk, and I'll get to it later."

"You look mighty fine all the same." I placed the pin on top of the desk right in front of where he was standin'. He watched as I set it down.

He smiled, then smoothed his hair. "I'd better be gettin' outside and pourin' some special refreshment for my friends."

After he left, I picked the pin up and put it in the pocket of my uniform.

A coffee carafe with milk and sugar and four cups was on the tray when I got back to the kitchen.

"Mr. Gray wants that coffee pronto," I said, takin' my apron off.

"I got's to leave, Cora." I went up close to her and whispered in her ear, "That hateful ole man Gray had my brother Elwyn's pin. The one he was pro'bly wearin' the day he died." I opened my pocket enough to show it to her.

I couldn't help it. Tears started runnin' down my face, and I blinked my eyes to try and clear them. "That man's lyin' about where he got it from. He didn't find it on no train. Nossir. I see'd it in his eyes."

Cora stood frozen with shock at what I told her until I reached out and put my hand on her shoulder. "You stay and handle the party without me. I don't mean to be makin' no trouble on Miss Joy's special day."

"Oh, Mama, I'm sorry. Should I call Daddy to come and get you?" Cora asked.

"I'll walk home on my own. I needs some time to think." I glanced out at the back yard through the screened windows on the porch. "I'll just be goin' out the back 'n slip round the side yard. Not too many folk's come yet." I went through the door to the back porch, then stopped. "Sweet Miss Joy marryin' into that family—it ain't right."

Walkin' home did me some good. Gave me time to think 'bout what I'm gonna do now. I'm as sure as I can be that Mr. Gray killed Elwyn. He's a hater if ever I saw one. Hate stuffed all inside him, like one of them snakes from the jungle. He a cobra, lookin' nice and actin' cool until he strike out and squeeze you to death with his hate.

Clem was sittin' outside on the stoop when I got to the house. "I got my mama's garden spot all turned over. Whew, it was a job, too. What you doin' home so early?"

"You ain't never gonna guess what happened at the party." I sat myself down beside him.

Clem listened as I told him about the pin. "What you gonna do now, girl?"

"I swore I'd kill the man if ever I found out who done it. You heard me say it plenty of times."

"Yeah, I know's you said it." He picked a blade of grass and put it in his mouth to chew. "It was quite some time ago. Ain't your heart softened none since then?"

"I meant what I said. Don't matter none to me how much time gone by. I grieve for Elwyn ever' day."

"I know you do." He took my hand in his.

I took the pin out of my pocket to show him, turning it over in my hand to show him the engraving on the back. "I ain't never took a single thing wasn't mine before today."

"That's stealin', baby. It only takes once."

"It ain't stealin'. It was mine to give away, so it's mine to take back."

"You best put it somewhere safe if'n you're gonna keep it. Somewhere it can't get found."

I stood up to go into the house. "I know just the place."

"While you in there, call my sister, Becca, and ask what Rollie knows 'bout Henry Gray," he called after me. Clem's sister lives in Muskogee, and her husband works at the railroad yard.

Sittin' on my dresser is a leathette jewelry box my Auntie Tina give me for my nineth birthday. It's lined with pink satin. It still plays a little tune when you open it. I loosened one side of the satin lining in the lid and slipped the pin inside. After I tucked the lining back in no one could tell the pin was there.

I dialed Becca, even though it's long distance and told her why I was callin'.

"Hey, Rollie, it's Della," I heard Becca say. "She wants to know what you hear 'bout a white man name of Henry Gray."

Rollie took the phone. "Hey, Della. What you askin' 'bout Henry for?"

"I saw him today is why. He was wearin' a pin I gave to my brother, Elwyn. The one who got killed up there in Tulsa. I'm thinkin' he mighta been the one killed him."

There was silence for a minute, then Rollie said, "Gray's nobody you should be messin' with. He's KKK, and he lets it be known that he's high up. And what I mean is, he's in with the sheriff and the police, plays golf with every muckety-muck in town. If he puts the word out, you're gone. Ain't nobody gonna come lookin' for you, neither."

"Okay, then," I said, my heart sinkin'.

"I'm tellin' you true." His voice lowered so I had to strain to hear him. "Gray killed Aloysius Poole quite awhile back, run him down in the road like a dog. Couldn't nobody never prove it, though." He paused. "You gots to be careful, woman."

"Appreciate you tellin' me."

Clem and I sat outside on the stoop in the twilight, watching a red sun set behind the high clouds on the western horizon.

"What you gonna do?" Clem asked when the light faded and the June bugs started flyin' past our heads, latchin' onto the screen door.

"I don't know."

"I got an idea might work, but it's Old Testament."

"Eye for an eye sounds good to me. What you thinkin'?"

"I could fix up his car, make it look like an accident. Cut the brakes so's they look worn, so's nobody could tell."

I thought about it. "Might hurt his wife and not get him."

"If he's Klan, he'll be drivin' to those Wednesday night meetin's ever' week. Could make it so's he has the car trouble when he's goin' back home."

"How'd you get it done?"

"Sneak into his garage through the back yard, or if that don't work, do it while the car's parked at the meetin' place."

I took a deep breath and blew it out. "I'll go over with you."

"No, ma'am, you surely will not. This here's a one-man job."

I didn't say anything.

He said, "We'll wait awhile. Let summer come and go, put some time between today and when it gets done. Then I'll drive over to Muskogee one night, do the deed."

"His blood's on nobody's hands but mine. You wouldn't be doin' it if'n it wasn't for me."

"Then we got ourselves a plan." He stood up and brushed dirt off his overalls. "Leave it be for now. I'll let you know when it's time. Until then, let's talk no more about it."

We went in the house and turned on the lights, listened to some blues music on the radio before bed.

Talk or no talk, it'll be on my mind ever' day 'til it's over and done.

1948

May

I sit alone here night after night while Henry goes out with his new amour. She's twice divorced already. This time it was Selma Lee who phoned to tell me.

"I worried about whether or not to come out and tell you, but I'd want to know if it was Jim messing around," she said. I could hear her shush one of the dogs. "Her name's Priscilla, if you can imagine that."

"What's she look like?"

"A floozy with bottle-blonde hair who tries to look like a movie star, all permed and waved."

"Red lipstick?" I guessed.

"Always," Selma Lee answered.

"How old?" I took a puff on my Kool menthol cigarette.

"Younger than us by a long shot," She snorted as she laughed. "I'd say thirty-five or so, but she's plump—not fat, I don't mean to say that—but plump enough that her wrinkles aren't showing. She could be older."

I was closer to fifty than I wanted to admit. Henry didn't like women who were more than ten years younger than him. Probably too independent to interest him.

"It's a damn shame he doesn't appreciate all you do for him," Selma went on. "That's just the way of the world. Men are always lusting after something new and shiny. You should get yourself a honey bunny. Show Henry that two can tango."

I hung up shortly after that, knowing that Selma Lee would keep me posted on what Henry and Priscilla were up to. She'd keep everyone else in our circle apprised as well. It was embarrassing, but I tried to ignore it as best I could and take the high road. At least Henry wasn't bothering me.

Getting myself a man is not even on my list of things I want to do. God in heaven. I can't stand the one I'm with, and I sure don't want to have to put up with another one. Besides, if Henry ever found out, he'd shoot us both, gaining his freedom and a whole lot of sympathy at the same time.

Too bad it doesn't work like that for a woman. If I was to shoot him and Priscilla, I'd be in the State pen before you could snap your fingers twice. That's Oklahoma justice for you.

Anna knows what Henry's up to. She says Dwayne does, too, but he acts like he doesn't notice. He's more like his daddy than I care to admit.

I made the mistake of complaining about Priscilla the last time Anna called.

"Why don't you divorce him?" she asked.

"What would I do? How would I support myself? I haven't worked in nearly thirty years, and I have these headaches nearly every day." I knew I couldn't function in a job and take the pills I need. I can't make it a day without my pills.

"He'd have to pay you alimony, that's how. You deserve it, all these years you cleaned house and cooked meals for him while he's running around with other women."

"I'd be disgraced, a divorced woman."

"Divorce isn't the stigma it used to be."

"It is at my age."

"Well, I hate it that you're so unhappy, Mama."

"I've been unhappy this long, I guess I can stand it awhile longer."

"You think on it. You could always come out here to Santa Barbara and stay with us."

That is exactly what I'd have to do. I'd have to become a burden to Anna and Glen, or foist myself on the newlyweds. I've never lived on my own. The thought of depending on my children and living in a place where I don't have any friends isn't appealing.

My life with Henry isn't so bad. I'm used to him and his meanness. I can tune him out or escape to my bed. He gives me money for food and some extras. In return, I don't say much when he's only comes around to eat supper and change his clothes.

I have moments of enjoyment. *My Friend Irma*'s on the radio tonight, my favorite show. Between listening to my radio shows and baseball games, plus the books I get from the library, I'm pretty well entertained.

People might say my life is full of disappointment, but I never expected anything different. Aunt Irma had one thing right—this life is nothin' but a vale of tears.

Arthur

I was laying on the ground in the back yard, unconscious, when Gladys found me.

She went in and called for an ambulance, then came back out to stay with me until the ambulance arrived.

"I was scared to death," she told me later. "I thought you were gone."

It wasn't my time, I guess. When I opened my eyes, I was in the hospital with a doctor and several nurses standing around me.

"Mr.Lannery, are you with us?" the doctor asked, shining a bright light into my eyes.

"I'm here." My voice came out in a raspy whisper.

"You've had a heart attack. We're giving you some medicine to help your heart, and we're keeping you here in the hospital for a few days."

I closed my eyes. A long rest sounded like just the ticket.

Joy

"Oh, my God, Daddy's had a heart attack."

Grandma Ella phoned Bill to say Daddy was at the Okmulgee hospital and Mama was there with him. Bill said he'd tell Doreen, then he phoned me, and I phoned Dwayne.

"I'm sorry, Sugar, is he gonna be okay?" Dwayne asked.

"I don't know. Bill's going to pick me up after work, and we'll go down there. I just wanted you to know."

"Pick me up on the way and I'll go with you and Bill."

I started to cry. "I don't know if they're even letting him have visitors."

"Okay. Well, don't worry about comin' to get me, Sugar. Call me later. Let me know how he's doin'."

"Okay. Bye." I cried for several minutes after we hung up, so scared that Daddy would die. Finally, the tears stopped coming. I washed my face and put a cold washrag over my red, swollen eyes.

Bill came right on time to get me, and we talked about the good times we'd had with Daddy on the drive down to Okmulgee. Bill kept me laughing with stories about how irritated Daddy used to get with the practical jokes he and my sisters pulled when they were growing up.

Mama met us at the hospital. She told us that Daddy could only have one visitor at a time, and only for a minute. I couldn't believe how small Daddy looked when I saw him lying in that hospital bed. He always seemed like a such big man to me with his deep, bass voice and his outgoing personality.

All of us knew of Daddy's deep-seated fear of hospitals. "It's where people go to die," he'd say.

Bill and I decided to go back to Tulsa later that night. I called Dwayne as soon as I got back home. "We have to get married as soon as Daddy's well enough to walk me down the aisle. It's really important to me."

"That's all right with me, Baby, anything you want. Your daddy's aces." I heard the sound of a lighter and the crackle of the cigarette as he lighted it. "He's the only one who'd let me drive his car when I first got home from the Navy."

I could hear him rustling papers around in the background. He had a final exam tomorrow, and I'd interrupted him while he was studying.

"I've got to go now. You just set the date, honey, and I'll be there."

"I love you," I told him.

"Love you more."

Doreen

Everybody's fussing over Mama when they should be paying attention to Daddy. He's the one who had the heart attack.

"How do you think he's doing?" Mama asked me. I picked up the chart and started reading it after the doctor left the room.

"He's doing fine," I said, looking at the page of lab results. "He'll have to take it easy, like the doctor said, but it looks like he'll recover."

I'm getting some respect for my nursing skills now that Daddy's sick. Mama and I are getting along better this past year. I'm still on the lookout for criticism, but she seems to have mellowed. Kathy, on the other hand, is as bossy as ever, and she's about to drive me nuts.

I'm going back home tonight. Daddy's out of the woods, and I've had all I can stomach of the nurse/dutiful daughter/little sister routine. Time to get back to Jerry and my own life.

Jerry and I got married three months ago after his divorce was final. He kept telling me it was over, but I wouldn't believe him until he finally showed me the papers. The next weekend we went over to Missouri and found a Justice of the Peace to tie the knot. Of course, we didn't tell my folks. They think we're already married.

I asked Joy and Dwayne to come over and have a drink with us to celebrate. Jerry and I asked them to go to Missouri with us to be our witnesses.

"Now, if you don't want to, just say so," I said after we'd had a couple of drinks.

"We'll do it. We got nothin' else goin' on. Right, Joy?" Dwayne said.

"Okay, but if you ever tell Mama and Daddy the whole story, leave out the part about me and Dwayne going with you." She took a sip of her drink. "I don't want the folks thinking I'm hiding things from them."

Even though you are? I wanted to roll my eyes, but I didn't.

"Deal," I said.

Jerry's happier than I've ever seen him. We have a nice apartment, a new car, and good clothes. I quit working at the hospital. Instead, I went to work at a medical clinic with four doctors. Now I have regular daytime hours and weekends off.

Jerry and I spend time together going to movies or for drives out in the country. We'll stop at some little Mom and Pop place we pass and try out the homemade pie. We have fun just being together.

He doesn't know about the Lithium I'm supposed to be taking. I don't like the way it makes me feel so flat, and I've been taking Valium instead. I tell Jerry that the Valium helps me sleep, but if I'm really having trouble sleeping, I have another prescription for Seconol that I hide in the back of a drawer in my nightstand. What he doesn't know can't hurt him, right?

I hope our marriage stays like this forever.

I keep thinking about what Jerry's ex-wife told me, that Jerry doesn't want to have kids. He doesn't pay much attention to Kathy's kids if they're around when we visit the folks. He never brings it up, never asks me if I'm ready to get pregnant.

I always thought I'd want babies, but I'm not so sure now. Could I handle the stress, the lack of sleep, the mess, the noise? Could he?

He's a perfectionist, fussy about things being clean and in order. Yesterday he was going around the living room making sure the ashtrays were perfectly aligned on the side tables. He bought a silent butler, his way of telling me to empty the ashtrays more often.

Family life might not suit him at all. Kids are messy, unpredictable, and far from perfect.

I've decided not to push it. If he's happy and I'm happy, why rock the boat?

Henry

I'm about ready to write Anna a letter to thank her for runnin' away to get married. That's how disgusted I am that Dwayne's goin' right ahead and getting' married to a Papist. They're getting' married in the Catholic church, and he's signin' away his right to raise whatever kids they have to the damn Catholics.

"I told you so. They're gonna make you do everythin' their way," I told him. "It's a crock."

"C'mon, Dad, it's my wedding. So what if it's in the Catholic church? You said you'd go."

I was experiencing a rare moment of sentimentality when I told Dwayne I'd go to a church for his wedding. Now I was stuck eating my own words. "And I will go. Because I love you, and I like Joy, and because I won't go back on my word. That don't mean I approve of it. This'll be the first time I've been in a church since I left Colorado."

All the talk at the house is about colors and flowers and cake, and all the rest of the damn folderol that goes along with havin' a church wedding, even though Joy says it isn't goin' to be formal.

"It's going to be small, just a few friends and our families."

And the damn priest, I thought inwardly. I smiled a thin smile and tried not to grit my teeth. "That sounds fine."

"Is Anna gonna be able to make it?" I asked May. I know she sneaks around and talks to Anna on the phone when I'm not here.

"She says it's too far to come with the baby. She's sending Dwayne a nice card with some money."

May doesn't share Anna's news with me very often. Occasionally, she asks if I want to read a letter she's received from Anna, but I always tell her I'm not interested. She'll tell me what it says anyway if I just keep my mouth shut. That's the only way I get any news about what's goin' on with Anna.

"It's about time you got yourself a new suit," May said. She was watching me try on the one suit I've had hangin' in the closet for the past fifteen years. I've worn it to funerals and the country club on occasion. "That one's getting a little tight. Unless you want to wear a truss."

Damn it, she's right. I've gotten thicker around the middle and the chest. The fabric of this jacket barely meets in the middle. Even when I suck my stomach in, I can't button it. "Maybe I'll go down to the haberdashery tomorrow and get fitted for a new one. Do you think black or navy?"

She didn't miss a beat. "Black, so you can be buried in it."

We both laughed like she was making a joke. I'm not so sure.

I'm not the best husband in the world. Certainly not the worst, but definitely not the best. I'm a good provider, but I have a number of faults that I don't care to correct.

I shrugged my way out of the old suit jacket. "I'm goin' out for a while tonight. You can put this in the Goodwill box."

She smiled as she picked it up. "You could wear it over to Priscilla's and impress the hell out of her."

Della

Miss Joy's gettin' married today. We been waitin' for this day to carry out our plan. I took a big platter of my special fried chicken over to the Lannery house yesterday.

Miss Gladys opened the door. "Why, thank you, Della. You didn't have to do that."

"You know how much I loves Miss Joy. Clem and me, we wish her all   the   best."

"Joy isn't here, but I'll be sure to tell her you came by."

When I got home, I told Clem, "I'm havin' second thoughts about this. I don' want Miss Joy to have any grief on her weddin' day, even though I hate to see her marryin' the son of that murderin' so-and-so."

I was the one came up with the idea of doin' the deed while everybody was at the weddin', but my intuition was tellin' me now that somethin' about it wasn't right.

"Don't go gettin' cold feet and makin' excuses. There ain't never a good time to do somebody harm." He took his hat off to scratch his head. "Let me check it out. Mebbe there's a chance while everyone's in the church to slip under Gray's car quick-like, get the job done."

"In case you get seen you can say you were passin' by and saw a leak, was checkin' it out 'fore anybody got hurt," I said.

"Yep," he grinned. "Just another nigger helpin' out the white man." He shuffled a few steps, hummin' an old tune.

Miss Gladys asked me to help out with the weddin' festivities even after I left the engagement party without tellin' her.

"No, Miss Gladys, I'm gettin' too old," I told her when she called. "Ask Cora. She needs the work more'n I do." Since then, Cora was the one workin' for Miss Gladys. Cora told me what all they were doin'.

Clem drove our old pick-up truck into town and parked it two blocks away from the church. He had on his work overalls, a screwdriver and knife in one of the pockets.

"Be careful," I told him.

"You know I will," he said, closing the door.

When he came back a few minutes later, he slid into the driver's seat and said, "I couldn't do it. The Gray's car is all decked out with old shoes hangin from the bumper and 'just married' written on the back window in red paint."

I snorted. "That old coot won't let his son drive all this time, and now he lets them take his car for their honeymoon? Who'd have thunk it."

Clem started the truck. "Well, I'll be checkin' out the Klan meetin' place once Miss Joy comes back. This's only a delay. Nothin' for you to get upset over."

"I'm not upset." All in good time—this wasn't the time.

Clem knows that when I make up my mind to do somethin', I'm like a dog who dug up a nasty ole bone.

There has to be justice for the wrong done to Elwyn. I ain't givin' up on that. No way, no how.

Arthur

The house seems empty with just the three of us here. Joy and Dwayne are living in housing for married students at Tulsa University. The university converted barracks that were built during the war for troops into small apartments for students. The barracks were thrown up hastily after the war started, and they were made of cheap materials.

We gave them an old sofa we had on the back porch and a coffee table for their living room. They bought a used dinette set and bed.

Grandma Ella hadn't been impressed when we took her to visit Joy for the first time. "Living on love, I see," she said, casting a critical eye over the bare living room. She doesn't like Dwayne much, never has.

We didn't bring Ella with us when we came to visit them today. Gladys hired Cora to be at the house for a few hours while we were gone.

Joy ran outside as soon as we pulled up. "I have a job," she announced.

Gladys put her arm around Joy. "Let's go in and you can tell us all about it."

We went inside and sat on our old couch. Dwayne brought two chairs from the dinette for him and Joy to sit on.

Joy was excited. "I'm going to work for the school district. They offered the position to me yesterday. I'll be handling the desk in the office, doing attendance rosters, stuff like that."

"Which school?" Gladys asked, running her finger over the top of the coffee table. "East High School. Stop checking for dust, Mama." Gladys drew her hand back.

"When do you start?" I asked.

"Next Monday. I'll take the bus there and back. The bus stop is only a block away."

It was close to noon. Joy brought out a tray with small plates and glasses. She served u tuna sandwiches cut in fourths without the crusts, potato chips, deviled eggs, and a pitcher of sweet tea.

"How's business?" Dwayne asked me, reaching for a sandwich and a napkin.

"We're doing well. Oil's come roaring back since the auto plants are manufacturing cars again. Everybody wants a new car."

"We'd settle for a used one, wouldn't we, Dwayne?" Joy asked.

Gladys had already told her what we had in mind.

"All in good time, Sugar." Dwayne reached for another sandwich. "These sandwiches are good, Baby." He ate it in two bites and reached for another one.

I decided it was time to get to the point now that Dwayne had some food in his belly. "Mama and I bought one of those new Pontiacs. Drove it up here today. Since we won't be needing it anymore, we thought you and Joy might take the old Ford off our hands."

Dwayne swallowed the bite he was chewing before he spoke. "I don't know what to say. That's very generous of you." He looked over at Joy. "It's too much, though."

"Say yes, Dwayne. Our own new used car. We can go for drives, and with me working, it'll make things easier."

Dwayne's eyes narrowed. "Give us a minute," he said, grabbing Joy by the wrist. "Let's talk about it in the bedroom." He kept hold of her arm as he led her into the bed room.

The walls were thin. We heard every word.

"Did you know about this and not tell me?"

"I thought you'd be happy. Don't be mad. I wanted it to be a surprise."

"It's charity." Dwayne's voice had a hard, angry tone to it.

"It's not charity when it comes from family. It's a gift from Mama and Daddy. If we don't take the Ford, they'll just sell it, and they can't get what it's worth."

We could hear Dwayne pacing back and forth. "We can't afford it, Joy."

"I'll be working, so we can afford it. My job'll pay for the gasoline and insurance. C'mon, Dwayne, don't get all stiff-necked about this. They want to help us."

There was a minute of silence, then we heard him say, "Okay, then. If it'll make you happy."

"It does make me happy."

When the two of them came back into the living room, I rose and started for the door. "Let's go outside. You can see our new car and take a look at the Ford. I drove the Ford up, and Mama drove the new car."

We went outside and looked at the new Pontiac. It was a shiny cream color with tan upholstery. We all got in, and I took everyone for a spin.

As soon as we came back, I signed the Ford over to Dwayne for a dollar, handing him the handwritten bill of sale and the keys. "It's eight years old, but it runs good. Make sure you keep the oil changed regular, and it should last you a good while."

"Thank you. We'll take good care of it." His expression was hard to read.

Gladys and I talked about Dwayne's reaction on the way home.

"He didn't seem that happy about taking the car," Gladys said. "I hope we didn't make trouble for Joy."

"We caught him off guard is all. He's not used to being given things. He didn't even want to take that ratty, old sofa, remember?"

"It's not charity if you're family," Gladys declared.

"That's how we see it, but that's not how Henry would see it. The Grays gave the kids a toaster for a wedding present. Other than that, what have they done? Not so much as a spoon."

"I worry about Joy. Listening to the way Dwayne was talking to her today, I can't help but wonder if Mother wasn't right about him. He seemed so angry."

I took a deep breath. I've had the same concerns about Dwayne's temper.

"He has a lot to overcome," I told her. "Maybe Joy can help him. All we can do is wait and see."

Joy

The phone rang.

"I'll get it," Dwayne said. "Okay," I heard him say. "Where?" He paused. "Okay, we'll wait to hear from you later on."

Something had happened by the way he was talking. As soon as he hung up, he came in and said, "My folks were in a car accident. The old man's okay, just a little banged up, but Mama had a heart attack. She's in the hospital in Muskogee."

I put my arms around Dwayne and held him close, feeling him tremble. "Oh my God, Dwayne. I'm so sorry."

He pulled away. "I need a smoke." We went into the living room and sat down.

"How'd that happen? Henry's such a careful driver."

"Said the brakes failed and he lost control on a curve. The car's gettin' towed in. Where's the damn ashtray?" He didn't say it in a nice way.

I got up to get it. "Sorry, I washed it out today and it's still in the drainer."

Dwayne didn't say anything until I came back and set it on the table.

"The old man said for us not to come down tonight. He'll call us tomorrow mornin' about Mama after he sees how she's doin'."

"We should get down on our knees and pray for her," I said, taking his hand. He let me lead him into the bedroom when he finished his cigarette, and that's what we did. We prayed for God to intercede for May, kneeling on the floor by our bed like we did when we were kids.

Henry

My mechanic, Mike Miller, told me the brakes had been tampered with.

"Are you sure?" I asked.

He held up the cable. "It's the damn'dest thing. Lookee here," he pointed and ran his finger over one end, "You can see they tried to make it look worn, but these lines are still too smooth. They don't look right." He put the cable down. "Have any enemies?"

"No more'n the usual." I picked up the cable to examine it. "I'll be damned. Well, fix the brakes and I'll be back later on to pick up the car."

I called the sheriff and asked him to meet me at the country club bar.

Once we had our drinks in front of us and the waitress was out of earshot, I took the broken pieces of brake cable out of my pocket and put them on the table. "Take a look at this."

"Looks like it's been cut. Here and here. What do you make of it?"

"Miller says it's what caused our accident."

"I'll do some askin' around. Got any ideas about where I should start lookin'?"

"Not really. Things've been pretty quiet lately. Don't know anybody who'd have it in for me."

"Could be from somethin' happened a while ago. You never can tell. People hold grudges." He finished his drink. "Well, you give it some thought. If anything comes to you, give me a call."

"I don't want to worry May. She's still in the hospital. Let's keep this between us."

"Will do."

I pointed to his glass. "How 'bout another round? One for the road?"

He looked at his watch. "Not tonight. Molly's girl, Gina, is havin' a birthday to-do in 'bout an hour." He grinned. "Takes after her dad. That girl's six years old, and, I mean to tell you, she's a pistol. Gonna be hell on wheels by the time she's a teenager."

He left, and I signaled to the waitress to bring me another drink.

Della

Cora overheard Miss Gladys talkin' to Mr. Arthur 'bout the Grays havin' a car accident.

"Henry came out of it with hardly a scratch on him. May had a heart attack, though. She's in the hospital."

Oh, Lord, this is terrible news. I finished out the rest of my day's housework half in a daze.

I told Clem what had happened as soon as he got home.

He took his hat off and wiped his forehead with his bandanna. "That's too bad 'bout Miz Gray. She musta been with him. Hadn't counted on that bein' the case."

"We got to have a better plan, one where he's by hisself."

"Could just stop him on the road 'n shoot his ass. No better'n what he done to Elwyn."

I couldn't believe Clem was talkin' 'bout usin' a gun. I said, "You okay with that? You only have the huntin' rifle."

"I can get a pistol, don' you worry none 'bout that. Or just shoot 'im with the rifle, like he got hit by a stray bullet from some fool who was out huntin'." He filled a glass with water from the tap and turned around to face me, leanin' against the sink. "We'd have to know when he's comin' to Okmulgee next, or when he's out of town. He'd have to be alone."

"Let me think on how to go about findin' that out," I said. "Cora don't hear everythin' that's goin' on."

Dwayne

Joy and I drove down to Muskogee to visit Mama, then went on to Okmulgee for Arthur's birthday. Bill managed to put in an appearance, but Doreen gave Joy some excuse for why she and Jerry couldn't make it. Walter and Kathy were back living in Kansas City, too far away to come.

We gathered around the dinin' room table and sang Happy Birthday, then Gladys served up cake and ice cream. Arthur's lookin' like his old self now, all recovered from his heart attack. He opened his presents: a new diary book from Gladys, a new set of braces from Bill, and a new tie from us, navy blue with tiny green stripes.

I excused myself to use the facilities after the gifts were opened. As I passed the back bedroom, I remembered the lapel pin I'd borrowed from the old mand and left on Arthur's desk the day of our engagement party.

"Say, is it okay if I look again for that gold pin I left in the back bedroom?" I called from the hallway.

The others were already out on the porch, but Gladys was still in the dinin' room, clearin' the table. She called back, "I haven't found it, but you can look."

Arthur had papers stacked up neatly on the desktop. I moved them around, careful not to get them mixed up. I didn't find it. I pulled out the drawers and rummaged around thru pencils, pens, rubber bands, paper clips. Nothing. I got down on my hands and knees to look underneath.

"I couldn't find it," I said when I joined them on the front porch. I sat down and Joy reached over to brush a piece of lint off my pants.

"I'll ask Cora when she comes," Gladys said. "Maybe she put stuck it somewhere when she was cleaning. She's usually careful to tell me if she finds things like that."

"Don't bother. It wasn't mine to begin with."

I didn't want the pin for myself. It struck me as curious when we were at the party that the old man even had it on until Mama said she thought it looked nice. The initials engraved on the back didn't match anyone I knew. I figured maybe it was a keepsake from one of his relatives. I thought I'd better return it before he asked me for it. But it's been quite some time since the party. He hasn't missed it.

I'll tell him it got lost in the shuffle if he gets around to askin' me to give it back.

I didn't think any more about it.

May

It took me having a heart attack for Henry to wake up to what all I do every day. Having the house all to himself with nobody to see to the cleaning and the supper hasn't been easy for him. He hasn't been able to flit around like he usually does. To keep up appearances, he's had to spend his evenings visiting me in the hospital for the past ten days.

"I don't like doin' all this woman's work. I'll call Anna and see if I can't make amends. She could bring the girls out here for a bit and take care of you like a daughter should.". This is what he told me the day before the doctor discharged me from the hospital.

"Get some help in, Henry," I said, trying to mask my irritation. "Anna might come and she might not, but she isn't a solution for the long term." Having a baby to deal with plus a little girl running around the house would just make things harder for me. I already knew Anna was pregnant again and having some problems with the pregnancy.

She wouldn't be coming, regardless of whether or not Henry got around to making amends.

Which, as it turned out, he never did. Never even made the effort to call her. But, at the time, he said, "I'll ask around. See who I can find."

"Better make it quick. I'm coming home tomorrow."

"I'll have things ready," he promised.

The house was clean when I got home. Fresh sheets were on the bed, and the lamp sat where I could reach it on the bedside table, along with my pills and a glass of water.

"Thank you, Henry. This's real nice," I told him as I settled into the bed.

"I'm goin' out tonight," he said. "I'll put your bed jacket here. You get some rest."

I guess he couldn't wait one more night.

He's managed to find a young white girl to come in two half-days a week to do the laundry and the heavy cleaning. Her name's Molly. She's nice enough, comes on time and does what I ask of her. She cooks us a hot meal before she leaves for the day.

On the days she's not here, Henry comes in from work, makes us a simple meal like sandwiches, or eggs and toast. When he's finished eating, he changes his clothes, and leaves again.

He stands in the doorway of the bedroom before he goes out and says, "Don't wait up."

As if I could. As if I'd want to.

Della

Auntie Bertie's like a second mother to me. She was my mama's best friend who's know'd me since I was born. She's also a conjurer of sorts, into the voodoo arts she learned from her Jamaican mama. She runs a little side business makin' up charms and potions for folks. Some of 'em are love charms, some have a darker purpose.

I was after one of her darker potions.

She got up from where she was sittin' on her porch when she saw me comin' down the dirt lane toward the old shanty house where she lives. It was painted white at one time. Now it's mostly gray where the paint has worn off.

"I was born here," she told me once. "I ain't never leavin', not unless it's feet first."

She hugged me as soon as I got up on the porch. Auntie B.'s a big woman. Gettin' hugged by her is like bein' squashed between two fluffy pillows.

"I missed you, girl." She started pullin' back and motionin' to the other chair on the porch.

"I missed you, too, Auntie."

"Sit yourself down and tell me all about it. I reckon you're here for a reason."

No sense beatin' round the bush. Auntie B. has the second sight.

"I need a forgettin' potion."

"Want to tell me why you in need of such a thing?"

"It's got to do with my brother, Elwyn," I told her. "You remember him, don't you?"

She started rockin' back and forth, the rhythm of her movement oddly soothin'. "I do. Yes, I do. He's been in the spirit world now for many years, ain't he?"

"He's gone a long while, yes, ma'am. He's the reason why I'm comin' here to you."

"A spirit don't be needin' no forgettin' potion." She gave me a sideways look.

"It's not for Elwyn. I'm after the man who killed him." I need Mr. Gray to forget what I'm about to do to him, but I didn't want to tell that last part to Auntie B.

"Um hmm." She reached out and put her hands on both sides of my face, holding me so I couldn't look away. We locked eyes, and she held on lookin' at me like that for a long time.

Finally, she let go and settled back in her chair.

"You be full of anger, but it's the righteous kind. I'm not sayin' I agree with the path you're choosin', but I'll give you somethin' for 'im. He won't remember nothin' you done once you put the drops in his mouth." She raised her eyebrows. "Pay attention now, girl—it won't kill 'im. I don't do no killin'."

"No, ma'am, I know you don't."

"And you best be comin' round more often to see me," she added. "I miss your mama somethin' awful."

She got to her feet. "Come back in a week. Bring me a nice package of that cut up chicken from the Crescent Market when you come. I'm cravin' fried chicken lately. And make me up a jar of your lemonade."

She hugged me when I left, and that hug felt just like it did when it was my mama huggin' me, even though my mama was a skinny woman all her life. I swear, I don't know how Auntie B. does that.

"It'll be all right, girl" she whispered.

I went back a week later after making a stop at the Crescent Market for a package of chicken. A jar of my lemonade in a quart-sized mason jar sat on the floor next to the back seat.

She was sittin' out, right where she'd been when I'd left her.

"Hey, Auntie B," I greeted her.

"Hey, girl. I see you got the chicken."

"From Crescent Market, just like you said. Here's the lemonade." I held the jar up for her to see.

"Take those inside. I'm gonna fry that chicken up, shake it in a paper bag with some flour and seasonin', and listen to it sizzle. I do love the smell of fried chicken."

I went inside where it was dark and still cool from the early morning air. It smelled of herbs, lavender, mint, chamomile, other smells I couldn't identify. There was an old refrigerator in the kitchen. When I opened it, one shelf was filled with tinctures. The chicken fit on the other shelf where there was only half a loaf of bread.

I went to the shelf above the sink, and got two glasses, recognizing the floral pattern stamped on the outside of them in blue and pink. The Piggly Wiggly stores gave them away in a promotion they ran several years ago. For every twenty dollars you spent, the store gave you one of these glasses. Every house in the county had a cupboard full of them.

I went back outside and handed a glass filled with lemonade to Auntie B.

She took a sip. "I've missed your lemonade, girl, yes, I have." She reached into her pocket and took out a small glass vial. "Two drops and two drops only. Won't stay in him long, mebbe thirty minutes, but he'll be forgettin' what happened. He won't never remember what all happened to him that day."

I took the vial. The liquid inside was a deep purple color. "What's in it?"

She gave me a sideways look and took another sip of lemonade. She didn't answer, and I didn't ask again.

We sat together, sharing the kind of silence enjoyed by old friends where words aren't necessary. As I took the last sip of my lemonade, Auntie B. said, "Leave the glass. I'll get it in a minute. You take care now, girl."

"Yes'm, I will." I left the empty glass on the porch, putting the vial into my pants pocket as I started walking.

Henry

It happened on a dark night that smelled of sulphur and rain. There was a heavily overcast sky with no moon behind it. I was drivin' home from Tenkiller, listenin' to *Little White Lies* playin' on the radio, after having a few drinks with George. He'd been glad to see me.

"Where you been hidin'?" he asked me. "It's been too long since you been out here."

"I'm between women," I answered. "Too damn much trouble for an ornery ole cuss like me."

I didn't see the log across the road until it was too late.

The car bucked hard, turned onto the driver's side and slid a ways like that, then rolled into a ditch before it came to rest. I must have hit my head, gone out for a minute or two. When I came to, my left leg was pinned by crumpled metal.

I felt something wet in my left shoe. *Must be bleedin',* I thought. Someone will come along. Sooner or later. Probably later. It wasn't a road many people traveled after dark.

Then I heard a scrapin' sound, wood on asphalt. Someone was pullin' the log off the road.

I tried shoutin', but my mouth was dry, and my voice came out in a hoarse whisper. I tried again, swallowin' a few times to wet my tongue and get my voice to workin'.

"Hey." This time my voice came out louder. Someone would be able to hear me if they came close to the car. I heard steps. I called again, louder. "Hey. Over here. Help."

A shadowy figure looked down at me through the passenger window. I couldn't see the face.

Why can't I see the face? Oh, Christ. That's because it's a Colored. Wouldn't you know.

"Help me. My leg—it's pinned over here."

The face disappeared.

I felt fear, and it sickened me. "Don't go." My voice sounded small. I knew there was no one to hear.

I smelled gas. Must be leakin' from the line.

A figure reappeared. It looked smaller, different from the first one, but still dark.

"I'm gonna give you some help." It was a woman's voice. I couldn't place it, but it sounded vaguely familiar.

"I'm in real trouble here."

"Yessir, you are."

There was something odd about the way she said it, something off in her tone. I felt myself drawin' back, my instincts tellin' me that this was no rescue.

"I'm bleedin'." A wave of pain hit me. The words came out pitiful, almost a whimperin' cry, and I felt embarrassed by my helplessness.

She opened the passenger side door, and a flashlight flicked on. I could see it was a woman, a Colored woman. She pointed the light in my face. I put my hand up to cover my eyes.

"Help's comin'. I'm gonna hand down a jar of lemonade to you. Take a drink. The sugar'll make you feel better." She stuck her arm down, a pint mason jar in her hand.

I reached my right hand up toward hers, and I took hold of the jar, pain shootin' through my leg as I stretched. I had to turn my head up to take a drink. A lot of it spilled down my neck and onto my shirt.

The lemonade tasted like elixir of the gods, sweet and tangy. After the first sip, I gulped it down without a second thought.

"That's good. Hand that jar back to me now," she said.

I held the empty jar up toward her, and she took it from me.

She disappeared, taking the light with her.

Don't leave me, I thought. *Don't leave me.*

I started to feel woozy, struggling to stay conscious.

She came back a few minutes later and leaned through the door. I could see her shadowy figure looking down on me. She flicked the flashlight on again, the light full in my face.

"You're not gonna remember this later." She paused. "Be that as it may, I want you to know why this's happenin' to you."

"Whaa…?" I groaned. This wasn't makin' any sense.

"You killed my brother. Elwyn Johnson? E. J. Those were his initials on the back of that pin you took off him in Tulsa."

My stomach turned over and my bowels clenched as the image of a street and the man I shot in Greenwood flashed through my mind. I saw myself removing the gold lapel pin from his suit. It had been forgotten, stuck at the bottom of a drawer for over twenty years, until May made me wear it to Dwayne's engagement party. In a flash, I made the connection.

Fear fueled a burst of energy. My voice came out clearer, stronger, like my life depended on what I said next. "Don't know nobody by the name of Johnson. You got the wrong man."

The chillin' sound of her laughter cut like a razor through the warm night air.

"You think I don't know who you are? What you did?"

"You got it wrong," I whispered.

"Nossir. You been foolin' yourself all this time, thinkin' you can hide the hate in your heart, thinkin' you can bury the evil you done like it never happened. Well, no more." She paused.

I had nothin' left to say.

Our conversation ended with her speaking in a voice as soft and gentle as my mother's. "This here, Mr. Gray—this here's Elwyn's justice."

Thank you for reading this second book in the three-book series, <u>The Laurel Wreath.</u> If you enjoyed this book, you might want to try the prequel, <u>The Laurel Wreath: Second Chances.</u> Keep a lookout in 2021 for the third and last book in this series, <u>The Laurel Wreath: Revolution.</u>

I'd like to ask you for a favor. If you enjoyed the book, please take a minute to write a one or two-sentence review on Amazon. It would be of great help to me.

**First Section in The Laurel Wreath Series: Revolution
Look for it in 2021.**

"You cannot buy the revolution. You cannot make the revolution.
You can only be the revolution. It is in your spirit, or it is nowhere."
Ursula K. Le Guin

1949

Joy

I wish I could take back what happened like it never did, write a different ending to the day.

Now I feel afraid—afraid of what the future holds, afraid of eternal damnation, afraid of what my family will say, afraid of losing my self-respect. Afraid more than anything of giving in to what I know is wrong just to please Dwayne.

I felt elated on my way home yesterday, nearly giddy with delight. The Piggly Wiggly was on the way, so I stopped to pick up something special for our dinner, something to remember years from now when I imagined us telling our children how happy they made us.

I pushed the shopping cart to the meat aisle and picked out two T-bone steaks we couldn't afford, then got lettuce and tomatoes for a salad. I had potatoes at home.

"The way to a man's heart is through his stomach. Always feed him first. Don't ask for anything until after he finishes eating," Grandma Ella told me. She was free with her advice in the days before I got married.

A wonderful meal for a wonderful evening. I had something to tell Dwayne, not something to ask, but what Grandma Ella said had turned out to be true. He was always in a better mood once he'd eaten.

"What's the occasion?" Dwayne asked, coming in and looking at the steaks sitting on the counter. His tone was grumpy. He works part-time at the campus bookstore three days a week. Yesterday was one of his workdays.

He frowned. "We can't afford to be buyin' steaks."

My stomach turned over, and I gave a nervous laugh. I hate it when he's like this. He's always in a bad mood when he comes home from his job.

"What's the deal with you and this job? You're in such a bad mood."

He swung his book satchel on one of the kitchen chairs. "I just hate waitin' on those rich kids. They come in wavin' their money around, buyin' crap, pennants and pom-poms." He waved his hands in the air, imitating the swoosh of a pom-pom. "The G.I.'s like me,who fought for this country, are strugglin' to make ends meet."

I hugged him, stroking his wavy black hair. "I know it's hard now, but it's going to get better," I whispered in his ear. "You have me to come home to."

"I know it, baby. I love you," he said. He pulled away. "I'm gonna have a beer while you're gettin' supper ready."

He went into the living room to relax, sitting down with his beer. The potatoes were nearly done. I made a salad and put it in the fridge to chill while I cooked the steaks the way Dwayne likes them, medium-rare.

"This looks real good, honey," he said, sitting down at the kitchen table. "Bring me another beer, will you?"

"Thank you, kind sir. I aim to please," I teased, opening a beer and putting it on the table in front of him.

"David let it slip there's gonna be a pop quiz in my business class tomorrow. I'm gonna have to study a bit."

When Dwayne says he has to study, it means he has to read the material. He doesn't have to spend hours and hours learning it. He says he can recall anything he's read.

"I see it in my head all typed out," he said. "Pretty good trick, I guess."

I guess. That's not how my mind works. I'm not dumb, but I can't recall something by reading it one time.

"All fueled up and ready to go," he remarked, patting his stomach as he pushed his chair away from the table. "I'd like another one of these," he said, pointing to the empty beer bottle.

"Go study while I clear up." I pushed my chair back and stood up. "I have a surprise for you later."

He smiled a lascivious smile, patting my ass as he went by.

I washed and dried the dishes, putting them away before I wiped down the stove.

He closed his book as soon as I came into the living room. He was laying stretched out on the sofa. "The excitement's killin' me, darlin'. What's the big surprise? Dessert?"

"Not dessert," I said. He moved his legs off the sofa so I could sit beside him.

"I went to the doctor today," I said, unable to contain my excitement. "We're having a baby."

He pushed me away.

"We've only been married three months. How'd that happen?" He looked angry. This was not the reaction I'd been hoping for.

"I thought you'd be happy," I said, tears filling my eyes. "I don't understand."

He got to his feet and started pacing. "You don't understand? You were supposed to be using birth control."

I was using the rhythm method, sanctioned by the church, combined with douching. My sister, Kathy, had assured me it was the best way not to get pregnant unless I wanted to use a diaphragm. That was a mortal sin in the eyes of the church.

"What's wrong with you? Why aren't you happy?"

"How do I even know it's mine?" he asked.

My heart felt like it was breaking. "You know I was a virgin when we got married," I said, tears streaming down my face. I wiped them away with my hand.

"We can't afford a baby. You have to do something."

"Do something? What do you mean?"

"Doreen probably knows who can get rid of it."

I couldn't believe my ears. I stood in front of him to stop him from pacing. "I'm not getting rid of it, Dwayne. That's murder."

"Then I'll call Doreen for you. We're not havin' baby. That's all there is to it." He stomped out to the kitchen. I heard the refrigerator door opening, the pop of another beer being opened

I went into the bathroom and turned the water on in the sink, splashing my face with cold water over and over until I stopped crying. I didn't see the face of a mother looking back at me from my reflection in the mirror. I saw the sad face of a young woman who has to decide between having a husband or having a baby.

I cried myself to sleep.

Chapter One

She grew up with a killer.

Growing up with a predator, she'd developed a sixth sense, a radar that other people didn't have. She felt it in her quickening heartbeat, the involuntary hormonal release and resulting hypervigilance that occurred when she met someone who had predatory inclinations. But her thoughts were elsewhere as she walked along the familiar sidewalk, immersed in ideas for the article she was writing. She pushed away the feeling she was being followed.

First mistake.

Rule Number One: Stay alert and trust your gut. Always.

It wasn't dark yet when she'd folded up her laptop and left the cozy warmth of her usual table in the coffee shop located inside the library. When she got outside, she saw the storm clouds gathering on the western horizon, deepening the twilight so quickly the halogen lights hadn't come on yet.

A cargo van was parked in front of Chrissie's Bagels with its side door open, like someone was making a delivery. A heavy blow to the side of her head came before she could think 'Men in White Vans'. She was pushed into the empty space in the middle of the van where she sprawled on the floor. The prick of a syringe in her arm happened before she could resist. The last thing she heard was the sound of the van door sliding shut and closing.

Then nothing.

Until now. She struggled her way to consciousness as her senses started waking up. The smell of damp concrete, slightly sandy, acrid. It felt cold against her cheek, rough-textured and hard. She was lying on her right side. When she opened her eyes, it was dark. No light coming in. Either it's night or there aren't any windows. She listened, didn't hear a sound.

Her memory started taking her back to the last thing she remembered. *I was walking home. It was nearly dark. Maybe it's still night.* She started wiggling her fingers and toes.

Her hands were tied behind her back with something thin. She could feel it with the tips of her fingers. It felt like plastic. Electric cords or zip ties. Not flat, rounded. Cord.

She tried moving her legs. Her feet were bound together at the ankle. She tested the binding. It felt thin, tight. Cord, not a rope.

She bent her knees and lifted her head. Maybe she could maneuver herself into a sitting position if she rolled onto her back.

If only I'd done more sit-ups in my work out routine. She hated sit ups, but a stronger core would come in handy now.

She rocked herself, balancing on her right buttock until she was in a half-sitting position with her weight full on her hip. It hurt.

I'll have a pressure bruise there.

She saw more shapes as her eyes adjusted to the dark. She felt like laughing. *Stress response. Don't panic.*

What do I know? I'm probably in a basement, maybe a warehouse.

There weren't many basements in Medford. The water table is too high. Probably up on a mountain or a hillside, not in the valley.

She started to scoot, trying to find a wall she could use for leverage to pull herself up. Or maybe find a light switch. Legs out, heels on the floor, flex knees, lift bottoms, brace with heels. It was painfully slow. She felt the burn through her clothes from the abrasive floor.

It's good I still have my tennis shoes on.

She made out the vague outline of a cinder block wall. She tried to stand by pushing her back up against the wall, getting her feet under her as far as she could, and trying to inch up the wall. It took several tries before she inched herself up the wall far enough to stand. Her finger tips were raw from where she'd tried to use the mortar lines to support her. She was sweating, panting with exertion by the time she was on her feet.

I've let my fitness go to shit. Must work harder when I'm out of here.

She worked her way along the wall. She came to a shelving unit, stepped out a foot and continued to feel her way along the edge of a shelf. There was the sound of glass jars rattling against the metal shelf as her weight shifted it. Then she came to another wall.

She felt as high as she could with her hands. She didn't feel anything. She rubbed the back of her head up and down as far as she could, trying to feel a light switch. Nothing.

She peered into the dark interior. Something white was hanging down. Sliding her feet a few inches at a time away from the wall, she made her way across the floor to it. It was a white string tied to a light bulb in the ceiling.

It's too high. I can't reach it.

Could she jump high enough to grab it with her teeth? She didn't think so.

She heard a door open. Wooden stairs appeared in the dim light, the steps descending into the basement behind the far wall. She heard heavy footsteps before she saw hiking boots and denim-clad legs come into view.

Then she saw his face.

"Oh, my God," she said. "It can't be you."

About the Authors

Diane resides in Beloit, Wisconsin, with her husband of fifty-two years, and their three dogs. She's an active member of a weekly critique group, Stateline Night Writers, and is also a member of the Chicago Writer's Association and the Wisconsin Writer's Association.

She has done extensive research into her family background. She began writing memoirs and family stories in 2010. The Laurel Wreath is a three-volume work of fiction based on familial historical events and relationships.